Unlucky in Love

Dana Gricken

UNLUCKY IN LOVE

ISBN: 979-8-88653-475-7

Published by Satin Romance
An Imprint of Melange Books, LLC
White Bear Lake, MN 55110
www.satinromance.com

Published in the United States of America.

Cover Design by Caroline Andrus

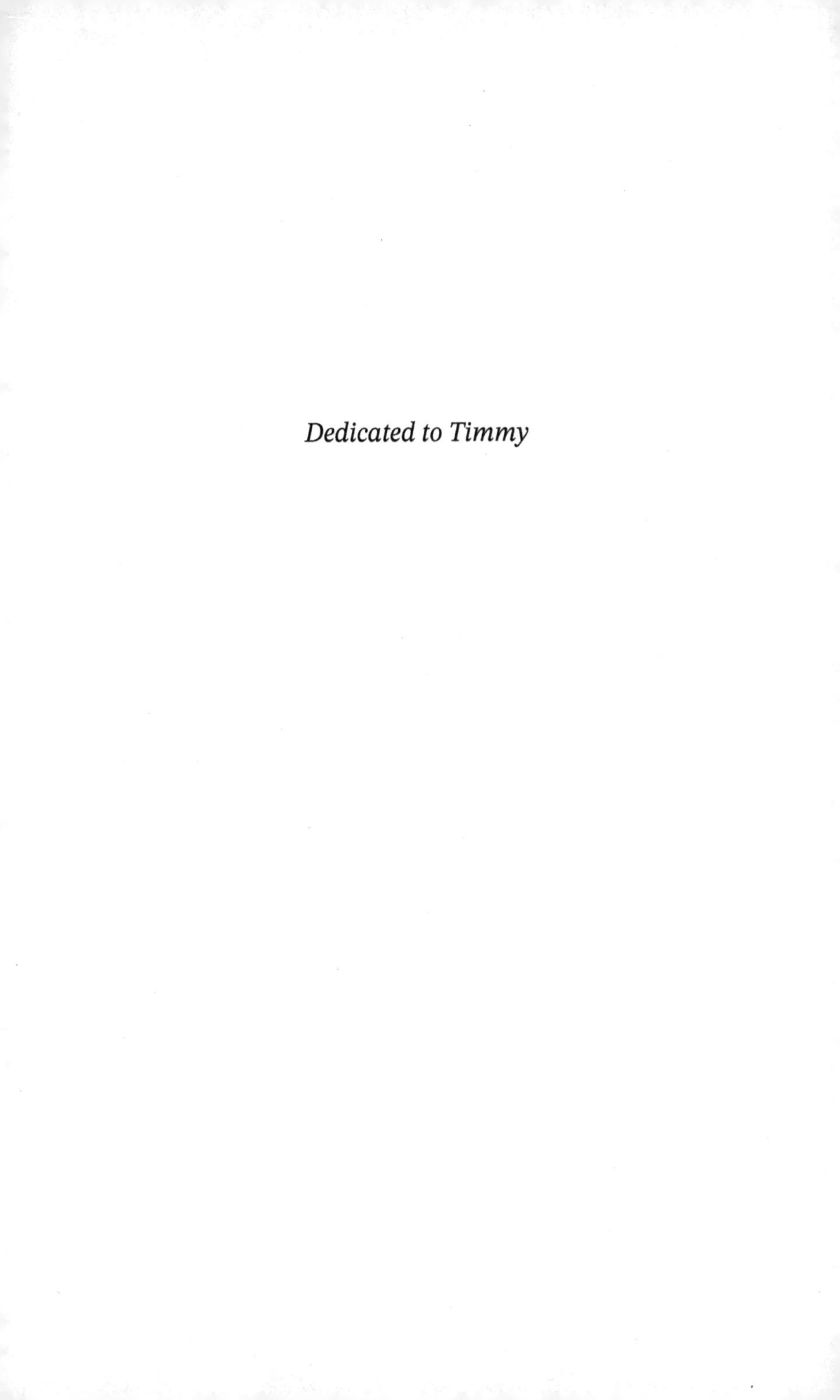

Dedicated to Timmy

Chapter One

"I don't think this is working out."

I looked up from my meal, glancing at my date across the table. "What, the lemon pepper salmon? I think it's amazing."

He sighed. "You know that's not what I'm talking about, Ang. I meant us. *We* aren't working out."

Oh no. This wasn't the romantic three-month anniversary dinner I had planned. No, Adrian had brought me here to break up with me. He could've told me that *before* I shaved my legs, curled my hair, and put on my sexiest black dress. What a waste.

"Oh," I said, setting down my fork. "That…that sucks."

That was all I could think to say. Sadness tugged at my heart, my lip trembling. Adrian continued staring at me from across the red cloth-covered table.

Some of the diners eating around us glanced over, hearing the end of our conversation. I sank in my seat as my cheeks blazed hot. *Estelle's* was the fanciest restaurant in the small town of New Harbor, Massachusetts, and I knew news of our break-up would make its way around town soon. Gossip here spread like wildfire.

"Yeah," Adrian said, reaching for my hand. I tried not to recoil. "I'm really sorry, Ang. It's just…things are busy with work, and I'm not really in the right space to be in a committed relationship right now. But it's been fun. I really enjoyed our time together."

Now that he's had his fun, he wants out. Typical.

I cleared my throat. "Yeah, yeah—I agree. Well, thanks for not breaking up with me over text, at least."

"Of course. I figured you deserved the news in person." He rose to his feet, removing his wallet from the pocket of his blue dress pants, the color a perfect match for his eyes. Then he placed a wad of cash on the table. "Here—dinner's on me. It's the least I can do. Stay as long as you'd like and enjoy your meal. Seriously, try to have a good night, Angie. See you around."

I nodded as he gave me one final smile, then reached for his jacket off his chair and headed for the door. As I sat at the table alone, eating my romantic dinner for one in front of candles and a bottle of wine, I didn't even cry. I was so used to getting my heart broken that it didn't sting anymore.

And if I had to be honest, there was a part of me that was glad Adrian had broken up with me first. Deep down, I knew we weren't right together, even if I couldn't explain why. Maybe it was a good thing.

I raised my arm to flag down our waitress. "Excuse me? I'd like another glass of wine."

"Coming right up," the young woman, whose name tag read Sarah, said, scurrying toward my table. She noticed the empty seat. "So sorry to pry, but…was that man your date?"

"He was," I said, handing her the empty wine bottle. "Why?"

"Well, before you arrived, he was totally staring at me. Then he asked for my number on the way out. I thought he was single. Sorry—didn't realize he was in a relationship."

I almost laughed. But I guess I didn't have a right to be jealous or angry—not anymore.

"And, just between us," Sarah continued, "he comes in here a lot. He had some blonde woman with him last week. It looked pretty romantic. He even ordered a bottle of our most expensive champagne for her."

"Huh," I said, clutching the tablecloth in anger. Adrian had never done that for me. "I...I didn't know that. Thanks for telling me."

"Of course. Not to get involved, but you totally deserve better. Give me a sec and I'll be back with your wine."

I nodded, watching Sarah walk off to the kitchen as I thought about her words. *Did* I deserve better? And if I did, where was my Mr. Right?

I sighed, then blew out the candle in front of me. It just didn't seem like true love was something I would ever have.

Sarah returned a few minutes later, filling up my wine glass. I stayed for a while and finished my meal and the bottle. Feeling tipsy, I got up to pay, realizing Adrian hadn't left any money for a tip. Not surprising.

Scoffing, I left Sarah twenty percent—figuring she earned it after telling me that little tidbit—and walked out of the restaurant with my to-go bag. I walked down the street through the darkness, stumbling. I shouldn't have worn my best heels and drank all that wine. That was a bad combination.

As I walked down the street, cars passing me, my anger at Adrian and this whole situation grew stronger. Who did

Adrian think he was, with his stupid perfect hair and stunning blue eyes? Leading me on and then breaking up with me when things were getting serious? Douchebag.

I cut through the residential street, noticing Adrian's house down the block. The curtains were closed in his living room, but I saw a light on. He was inside, and so was someone else. A curvy silhouette that looked a lot like a woman.

"That two-timing son of a..." I stopped on the sidewalk, staring down at my takeout bag with a mischievous idea. "Oh, I'll show him."

I had been to Adrian's house a few times and knew he didn't have any security cameras. He was far too cheap for that. So I snuck over to the bush in front of his house, then opened my takeout bag and reached in. I pulled out a scoop of my leftover salmon and mushed it in my hands.

"This is for being a cheating scumbag," I grumbled. "And for making me shave for nothing!"

I flung the leftover salmon at the front door, watching as it smeared across the wood. Some of the smaller pieces of salmon flung off and sprayed across my dress. It made a loud thump, and I saw the silhouettes in the living room turn around. Not wanting to get caught, I spun on my heels and ran off as quickly as I could.

With my heart pounding as I raced away through the dark, I started to laugh. Somehow, throwing food at his house was a lot more exciting than any date Adrian had taken me on. And we were finally even. I cut through a few back alleys, heading to my house in the distance. I walked up our brick pathway, kicking my heels off my aching feet. I removed my keys from my pocket, then unlocked the door and entered the foyer. A light was still on in the living room as I carried my heels in and locked the door behind me.

When I turned around, entering the living room, I spotted Grandma sitting in her rocking chair. She was watching some old black and white movie on the television while doing a crossword puzzle in her blue satin pajamas. She looked up from her book, smiling and lowering her glasses onto the bridge of her nose. Her hair was as white as snow, her wrinkled, blue eyes shimmering. Despite nearly being eighty, she still had a youthful playfulness.

"There you are, dear. I didn't want to go to bed until I knew you were back home, safe and sound," she began, setting the crossword puzzle on the coffee table in front of her. "So? How did the three-month anniversary dinner go?"

"Just great," I grumbled, putting the takeout bag down on the dining room table. "Adrian broke up with me."

Her face fell. "Oh, sweetie...I'm so sorry. But it's his loss, you know. Not yours."

"Yeah," I said, breathing out. "At least I've had practice before. Getting dumped is a pastime of mine."

"Hey, we've all been there," she said, slowly rising to her feet. "Your grandpa wasn't the first man I dated. I had to kiss a lot of frogs to find him."

When my parents divorced when I was ten years old, I decided to live with my grandparents. I had lived with them until my grandpa died last year. I always got a little choked up when thinking about him. Now, it was just me and my grandmother, and I dreaded the day I'd lose her too. She was my best and longest-lasting relationship.

I snorted. "I think Adrian was more of a snake than a frog. Found out he was flirting with and seeing other women."

Grandma shook her head. "See? You're much better off. It seems he did you a favor."

"Maybe," I said, unzipping my dress in the back. "Or

maybe...this is a sign I should stop dating. I haven't had much luck."

"Oh, you can't give up," Grandma urged as she stepped forward. "So, you've met a few bad apples. But there's still a whole orchard out there! Trust me, a beautiful young woman like yourself will find her dream man. I believe that."

"I'm glad someone does," I murmured. "I'm going to go change. Get out of this uncomfortable dress. It's got pieces of salmon all over it."

Grandma raised an eyebrow. "And why is that?"

"Oh. I...kinda threw it at Adrian's house on the way home. Smeared it all over his front door. Some of it got on me too. An unfortunate blowback incident."

I expected Grandma to get angry at that—to chastise me. But then she started laughing. And I had to admit, it made me crack a smile too.

"Well, that's one way to show a cheater," she began. "Good for you."

"You aren't mad?"

"No, of course not. And...maybe one day I'll tell you what I did to my best friend's husband for cheating on her while she was pregnant. Let's just say...his truck never started properly again."

I shook my head, walking toward the stairs. "Good to know what you're capable of, Grandma."

"Hell hath no fury like a woman scorned!" she called out.

I laughed, heading up the stairs to my bedroom. Grandma's very old orange cat, Nutmeg, meowed at me as I passed. She was sleeping on Grandma's bed and was half-blind and half-deaf. Nearly twenty years old, that cat was determined to get the most out of her nine lives. Grandma joked Nutmeg would outlive us all.

I took a small detour to pet Nutmeg before entering my room, flicking on the light. I stripped out of my dress and threw it across the room into the hamper. I quickly put on my pajamas—baggy shorts and a tank top, the least sexy thing I owned. As I put my purse away, I heard a knock on my door.

"Sweetie?" Grandma poked her head inside the door. "I wanted to show you something. When you're ready, meet me in my room."

I turned around, nodding before she walked away. I wondered what she was up to.

After slipping my feet into my fuzzy slippers, I headed down the hall to her bedroom. Grandma was on her knees, pulling an old shoebox out from under her bed. She placed it on the bed beside Nutmeg. The old cat didn't stir.

"What's that?" I asked.

"Everything your grandpa ever gave me," she said, opening the box. "I kept everything from our first date to our wedding to our fiftieth anniversary a few years ago. Couldn't bear to throw anything away."

As Grandma started taking things out of the box, setting them on the bed, I took a seat beside Nutmeg and watched. Grandma was right—she really *had* kept everything from old movie tickets to jewelry and handmade cards.

"This one is my favorite," Grandma said, handing me a giant card. "Your grandpa made that himself out of construction paper. Go on, open it."

When I opened the heart-shaped card, it read: "To Esther: you'll always have my heart, no matter where you are. I'll love you forever, near and far. Love, Lou."

"Wow," I said, still staring down at the card. "He really, really loved you."

When I looked up, Grandma's eyes were glistening with tears. "Yes, he did. We had a lovely fifty-two years together. And I hope you have the same thing one day."

I sighed, handing her back the card. "Grandma...I'm just not sure that kind of love exists anymore. What you and Grandpa had was beautiful, but I don't think it's in the cards for me. It wasn't in the cards for Mom and Dad."

Grandma winced, putting the heart-shaped card back in the box. "I know, dear. But you know why? They stopped communicating. They forgot that they were friends first and lovers second. That's why your grandpa and I lasted so long. We always maintained respect, friendship, and believed in each other. Through everything, all our ups and downs."

I stroked Nutmeg, hearing the old cat purr beneath my hand. "That's lovely, but I've never found anyone willing to do that with me. Seems all the guys I've dated are only after a free trial before they want out."

Grandma sat with me on the bed. "Not all, I assure you. You want to know what your grandpa told me a few months before he died?"

"What?"

"That he wanted you to find love. Someone to accept you for all that you are, cherish you, and make you feel wanted. If you give up, you'll never find that. And both your grandfather and I will be sad."

Grandpa really wanted that for me? I tried not to choke up. He and Grandma had both been such big comforts after Mom and Dad's divorce. My immovable center.

I rose to my feet, pointing at the ceiling. "Well, then tell him to send someone good my way. I've had enough cheaters and losers to last a lifetime."

"If only there was a direct phone line to Heaven," Grandma joked, drying her eyes. "Anyway, I just wanted to show you all that to help you believe in love. Good men are out there, wanting something that lasts. And I hope you find someone great. But you must promise me you'll never give up."

I sighed, knowing I couldn't resist my grandmother. "All right, all right—I won't quit. But I'm going to be a lot more selective."

"Good for you. Nothing wrong with having standards." Grandma checked the clock. "Now, it's terribly late and I need to get my rest. I'll see you at the bakery bright and early tomorrow."

"Sounds like a plan," I said, heading to the door. "Goodnight, Grandma. And thanks for trying to cheer me up."

She smiled. "What are grandmothers for? Goodnight, dear."

I nodded and headed down the hallway, shutting my door. I brushed my teeth and washed my face before getting into bed. Just as I laid down, my phone started to ring. I noticed it was my mother's Caller ID.

"Hello? Mom?" I answered, sitting up in bed. "Do you know how late it is?"

"Sorry, hun. But I had to vent to someone." She paused, taking a drag of her cigarette. "Did you know your father's new girlfriend is only a few years older than you? I saw the pictures on Instagram. He took her on some trip to the Caribbean last week. He's never even taken me there, for crying out loud!"

I sighed. "That sucks. Anyway, Mom, I have to get up early tomorrow—"

But she cut me off, just like always. I never could get a word in edgewise with her.

As Mom ranted about Dad, using me as her shoulder to cry on again, I checked the clock. I knew I wouldn't be getting much sleep tonight. And as she rambled, all I could think about was Adrian's betrayal and how lucky Grandma was to find a good man like Grandpa.

It was luck I was sure I would never have—in this lifetime *or* the next.

Chapter Two

Mom continued to complain about Dad and his younger girlfriend for another hour, though I had stopped listening a while ago. I let my mind wander to the bakery I ran with my grandmother and all the tasks I needed to complete tomorrow. As the clock ticked later and later, I knew I'd have to do something to get off the phone.

"...and his new fling is young enough to be your sister!" Mom shrieked. "It's disgusting, that's what it is. But maybe I should follow in your father's footsteps and look for a younger man. I'm in my sexual prime, you know."

Gross.

"Um, Mom, sorry to interrupt," I began, clearing my throat. "But I really do have to get to bed. I've got work early in the morning and Grandma needs me."

"Oh, I'm sorry. I didn't realize how late it had gotten," Mom replied, taking another drag of her cigarette. "I haven't spoken to her in a while, not since your grandpa died. How is my darling mother doing?"

I eyed the hallway, listening for Grandma's snores. She was finally sleeping. After Grandpa had passed, sleep became tougher for her. I was glad she was getting better rest.

"She's doing okay, I think," I replied, sighing. "I know she misses Grandpa a lot. I do too. Running the bakery just isn't the same without him. But Mom...can I ask you something?"

"Of course, Angie. What is it?"

I cleared my throat. "Do you...do you believe in love?"

Mom scoffed. "Love? I did, once. When I was young. But after everything I've been through with your father...I just don't know. I think it's a lie that movies make us believe. In truth, love is hard and doesn't often work out. I think it's a sham, if you ask me. Why?"

"Just...just wondering. Grandma really believes in it."

"Oh, I know. Did she give you the same spiel she gave me growing up? That true love is out there, and I just need to find it?"

I sat up straighter. "Yeah, she did. Earlier tonight when this guy I was seeing broke up with me."

"See what I mean? Love is a lie," Mom sneered. "Your grandmother's from an older generation where that was expected of them. To get married, to have children. I say you should just be happy and live life for yourself. Forget about love. After your father and I divorced, I did. And I don't regret a thing."

But Mom wasn't exactly what I would call happy. Was it possible she was making a mistake by giving up on love? Was I?

"Right," I said. "Well, thanks for the advice. I'll keep it in mind."

"Good. And I'm sorry about the break-up. But as I said, it's probably for the best. Now, get some rest, hun. I'll talk to you again soon. Love you!"

"Okay, Mom. Love you too."

After we hung up, I turned my phone on silent, leaving it on the nightstand. Then I rolled over and closed my eyes, my mind flitting back and forth between what Mom and Grandma had said.

To love or not to love. That was the *real* question.

When morning came, bringing sunlight through my curtains, I stretched and yawned before rising to my feet. I put on a pair of jeans and a simple white t-shirt, then grabbed my apron for the bakery. The colors of our shop, Lucky's Baked Goods, were red and white, matching all our décor.

After I brushed my teeth, washed my face, and combed my hair, I walked downstairs, finding Grandma sitting at the kitchen table in her lemon-themed apron. She was eating oatmeal and drinking while writing in her journal. Nutmeg had staggered over to her food bowl and was loudly crunching on some kibble. Grandma looked up at me with a smile as she wiped crumbs off her apron.

"Good morning, dear," she began. "Tea and oatmeal are over there for you. Both are piping hot—I just made it a few minutes ago."

"Thanks, Grandma," I said with a smile, grabbing a bowl of oatmeal and pouring myself a cup of tea before joining her at the table. "What are you up to?"

"Oh, just thinking up new desserts," Grandma said, staring down at her journal. She tapped her pen against the paper. "Your grandfather was much better at this than me. The bakery was his—he was the talented baker, not me. I feel like I can't do it justice."

I placed a hand over hers. "You're doing great, Grandma. I'm sure Grandpa would be very proud of you."

"Thank you, dear, that's kind of you to say. It's really all

I have left of him now, besides the memories and photographs. And I want to keep his beloved shop going." She slid her journal away, taking a long sip of tea. "Say, I heard you talking on the phone late last night. Have you found a new flame already?"

I snorted, taking a bite of my oatmeal. "Ha, I don't think so. It was Mom—she called to complain about Dad. For an hour! I had to get off the phone before I fell asleep. We had an...interesting conversation about love."

Grandma sighed. "Oh, your mother. Let me guess—she doesn't believe love is real? That it's just a Hollywood illusion?"

"Yep, that pretty much sums it up."

"You know, I have no idea why. She grew up seeing a very healthy relationship between your grandfather and me. We never fought—never had a reason to. Always settled our disagreements calmly and made sure the other knew they were loved. I thought we set a good example."

"I'm sure you did, Grandma. You did for me. But I guess Mom's perspective on love changed after the divorce."

"One bad marriage is not love's fault, my dear. Love is the greatest thing in the world when you get it right. It's a shame your mother doesn't see that," Grandma said sadly, looking down at her journal. "Anyway, it's nearly Autumn. What do you think about pumpkin spice cupcakes...but with a twist? A sprinkling of bacon on top?"

"I think I want one right now," I joked. "I love that idea. What else have you written down?"

Grandma skimmed her journal. "Hmm, let me see. I'm saving my white chocolate peppermint mousse for Christmas..."

After going over new culinary creations for the next half hour, we finished our breakfast and tea and headed out to our cars. Grandma had her old, creamy-white sedan while I had just bought a beat-up red pickup truck. If I ever found a man I could love as much as my truck, I knew it would last forever.

We pulled out of the driveway, then I followed Grandma down the street. New Harbor was busy for a Monday morning—everyone was heading off to work and school. I waved at our neighbors as I drove downtown. Big cities were overrated. Small, friendly little towns were where it was at.

I followed Grandma into the parking lot behind Lucky's Baked Goods, my favorite place on Earth. I practically grew up there while helping Grandma and Grandpa run the bakery. It was a safe place for me, especially when my parents were going through their messy divorce. I locked my truck and followed Grandma to the back door.

"Oh, I have something to ask you, dear," Grandma said as she got out of her car, walking next to me. "About how tall would you say you are?"

"Uh, five-four, I think? Haven't checked in a while."

"Good, good. How about your hobbies? When you aren't working here, what are you doing?"

I paused near the back door. "This is starting to sound like an interrogation. What are you up to, Grandma?"

"Nothing, dear. Just wanted to know my granddaughter a little better. In her own words."

"Well, all right. I like reading, hiking, going out to restaurants. You know, normal stuff."

"As I expected. One last question, sweetie. What would your dream date be?"

I sighed. "Dream date? Hmm...I don't know. I don't think I have one. I think any place can be a dream date if you're with someone special."

Grandma smiled. "A lovely answer. Thank you."

"Of course. But...why did you want to know?"

"As I said, just curious," Grandma said, reaching into her pocket for her key. She unlocked the back door. "Come on, let's get this shop open for another day."

Confused, I followed Grandma inside through the back door, wondering what was going on. The back door led into the kitchen where we kept all our baking supplies, both dried and fresh, and a few ovens that we owned. A list of orders hung on the wall.

"Can you be a dear and open the front door and prepare the tables?" she asked, hanging up her purse on the wall. "I need to get a few things ready back here."

"Sure thing. Be right back."

As I turned, pushing through the kitchen door, I noticed Grandma reaching into her pocket for her phone. Then she started typing something. What was that woman up to?

Shaking my head, I walked out of the kitchen, heading to the front of the bakery. We had about a dozen tables with white cloth and red chairs set up. I usually spent my days at the cash register, taking orders and selling customers whatever Grandma baked. This had been her job while Grandpa baked before he passed away. It was a good thing he had left us all his delicious recipes in his recipe book, but it just wasn't the same running the shop without him. He had the special touch that made everything taste perfect.

I took the chairs off the table, setting up for another day. Then I quickly swept some dust off the floor and threw it into the small garbage can. When everything looked decent—including the baked goods we'd made yesterday—I walked to the door, unlocking it and putting the OPEN sign on the window. I had just started wiping down the counter when I heard the door open with a chime.

I spun around, noticing a handsome man walking into the bakery. He was six-three with a chiseled jawline and some light stubble, wearing jeans, a plaid shirt, and dress shoes. I knew mostly everyone in our small town, and he wasn't familiar. He looked lost as he wandered inside and glanced around.

"Hi," I began, setting down my rag. "Welcome to Lucky's Baked Goods. Can I help you?"

"Nah, no need," he said, staring at the pictures on the wall. "Just checking things out."

"Well, all right. Let me know if you need anything. We just opened for the morning so my grandmother's in the kitchen, whipping up some treats."

"Thanks. Looks like a nice place," he said, turning to me. His green eyes sparkled in the light. "Is business good?"

"Decent for a small town like this. My grandpa used to run this place for thirty years before he passed away. Baking was always his true love and Grandma helped him save enough money to buy this place in town. Now, me and my grandmother are keeping his legacy alive. He was pretty famous for his desserts in New Harbor."

"Ah, I see. Sorry about your grandpa. Losing a grandparent is never easy."

I nodded. "Thanks, that's for sure. You know, I don't think I've ever seen you around. Are you new here?"

"Yep," he said, removing a badge from his pocket. It read FIRE DEPT with symbols of a fire hydrant and an axe. "Name's Henry Brant. Was just hired at the fire station a few days ago. Arrived in town this morning and decided to look around before checking in with Chief Teller."

"Nice to meet you. I'm Angela Linden," I said, shaking his hand before he put his badge away. "How are you liking the town so far?"

"From what I've seen, it looks like a nice place. Smaller than my hometown of Boston but I can get onboard with that."

"Funny coincidence! My grandpa was born in Boston. My parents still live there. I've been there on vacation—it's lovely," I said with a smile. "Since you're new in town, I'd like to give you a sample on the house. You like cupcakes, right? Do you have any food allergies?"

"None—and yes, I love dessert. I'll pretty much eat anything. And thanks, that's kind of you."

"Of course. Wait here, I'll see if my grandma has something delicious in the back for you."

He nodded, playing with his phone while he waited. I felt myself blushing. He was handsome—probably the cutest guy I'd ever seen, even more attractive than Adrian. Maybe this Henry guy was the new start I had been hoping for.

And maybe Grandma had been right all along.

I pushed into the kitchen, my eyes landing on Grandma who was rolling dough. She had turned on the radio to the old station—*Don't Be Cruel* by Elvis Presley was playing—as her phone sat beside her. And it was dinging over and over again.

"Wow, you seem busy," I said. "What's with all the notifications?"

"Oh, nothing, dear," Grandma said. "I heard the door chime. A customer already?"

"Yep. He's new in town—checking things out. Henry Brant. He just got a job at the fire station."

Grandma's eyebrows lifted. "A firefighter, hmm? I bet he's quite handsome. And muscular."

"Grandma, please," I said with a blush. "Since he's new around here, I wanted to give him a sample of something fresh. Got anything ready yet?"

"What do you take me for? Of course I do," she said with a wink, turning toward the oven. She pulled out a large tray of cupcakes. "These are fresh. I'll bring them out —I want to meet this new firefighter for myself."

I shook my head, waiting by the door as Grandma put on her oven mitts and carried the tray of cupcakes. When we entered the dining area, Henry was still there, looking at our menu on the wall. He nodded politely when he saw us.

"Ah, this must be your grandmother," he began. "I'm Henry Brant, a new firefighter in town. Nice to meet you."

"A pleasure," Grandma said, putting the cupcakes down and shaking his hand. "I'm Esther Linden. I used to run this place with my husband before he passed away."

"Yes, Angela told me that. I'm so sorry."

"Thank you, that's kind. Well, help yourself to a cupcake. On the house for firefighters. That's a selfless job."

"Thank you. It's not easy, that's for sure," he said, grabbing a chocolate cupcake. He bit into it and nodded. "Man, that's amazing. You're very talented."

Grandma beamed. "Thank you, Henry. When you get to the bottom of the cupcake, you'll find a little message. A good fortune. My husband, Lou, got his nickname Lucky because of it. Angie, why don't you tell Mr. Brant about it? My muffins need me."

Grandma winked at me, then backed up into the kitchen. I cleared my throat and turned to Henry who was finishing his cupcake. "It's just like my grandma said—my grandpa put messages in his desserts. Edible paper and ink. He wanted to open a bakery but wanted it to be a bit different."

"That's a cool idea. Kind of like fortune cookies."

"Yes, exactly! It's been a big hit with customers and tourists. Something else that's really popular is our custom desserts," I said, gesturing at the menu board. "The specials change every week. Until I can think of more. Grandma lets me be in charge of them myself. Right now, we've got the Homer Simpson donut—yellow icing and pink sprinkles. We have a Spock cupcake, drawn in the design of the Vulcan hand sign, and a Star Wars cookie. Basically, I make it green and small like Yoda."

Henry snorted. "That is adorable."

"Thanks. So, what does your fortune say?"

Henry opened the small cupcake up, reaching for the piece of edible paper inside. "Hmm, that's interesting..."

"What is it?" I asked, leaning in curiously.

"You will find love," Henry said, showing me the strip of paper.

Grandma. She must've planned that on purpose.

"Oh," I stammered. "That's a good omen. Maybe it'll come true."

He winced. "It's a nice sentiment, but I don't think so. But thanks for the free cupcake. It was amazing."

When he chucked the cupcake wrapper and fortune into the garbage, I wondered why he was such a cynic. Then I saw the glint of a wedding ring on his left hand. Of course—a man that handsome had to have been married. My hopes for a fresh start were dashed.

And when I spotted Adrian approaching the bakery, opening the glass door with a blonde woman behind him, I realized my day was going to get even worse.

Chapter Three

I couldn't run or hide with Adrian so close. I had no choice but to stand there and face him—face the guy who dumped me last night and whose house I had thrown food at. Not my proudest moment.

"Hey, you okay?" Henry asked, studying my face.

Before I could respond, the door opened with a chime, then Adrian entered the bakery with a pretty blonde woman. Probably the same woman he was with at his house last night after leaving our date. My blood boiled like hot soup, but I took a deep breath, trying to keep my cool. Adrian wore his usual suit while the woman was dressed in a black skirt, red blouse, heels, and a briefcase. She looked around the bakery as he approached the counter.

"Angie, nice to see you," Adrian began, leaning on the counter. "I don't mean to accuse you of anything, but I have to ask. Someone threw food at my door last night. Was that you?"

Henry's eyes were on me as I shook my head, busying myself with the stack of order forms sitting on the counter.

"Sorry, but no. I mean, come on—I'm twenty-four, not twelve. Why would I throw food at anyone's house?"

When I glanced at Henry, he seemed almost amused. His eyes danced with delight. Did he find this funny?

"Okay, just making sure," Adrian said, moving away from the counter. He seemed to buy my story. "It was probably my damn neighbor's kids again. They're always causing trouble."

"Well, good luck with that," I said, finally looking up at Adrian again. "So, was there something you needed?"

"No, not really. Just wanted to ask you about that and check on you. You know, after last night. How are you?"

"I'm fine," I said, a little too quickly. "More than fine. I'm great."

Adrian nodded. "That's good, I'm glad to hear that. I hope there's no bad blood between us. I'd really like us to stay friendly."

I gritted my teeth. "None whatsoever. Now, I don't mean to be rude, but I do have to get back to work."

"Oh, of course—I won't keep you. I'm heading to the office as well," Adrian said, then noticed his companion staring at us. He cleared his throat. "Alison, this is my... friend, Angie. Angie, uh..."

"Linden," I corrected, rolling my eyes. "It's Angela Linden, Angie for short. After all this time, you still don't know my last name?"

He blushed crimson. "Sorry. Uh, anyway, Angie, this is my associate, Alison Sharpe. She just started working at my law firm a few weeks ago."

A few weeks ago? Maybe that was when he decided he was done with me. And the mystery woman that the waitress told me Adrian had been with. Figures.

"Nice to meet you," I lied, nodding at Alison. "Can I interest you in our desserts?"

"No, thanks," she replied. "I'm not a fan of dessert. Too rich."

"Really?" Henry asked, raising an eyebrow. "That's... strange. Everyone loves desserts."

"We all have our preferences," Adrian said, looking Henry up and down. "Who are you? I don't think we've met before."

"Henry Brant," Henry said, shaking Adrian's hand. "Just moved to town. I'm a new firefighter at Chief Teller's station."

"Ah, I see. I'm Adrian Dowell," Adrian said, glancing down at their joined hands while wincing in pain. "That's a strong grip you have there. You must work out a lot."

"Yeah, it's part of my job. Sorry," Henry said as he let go. "Sometimes I don't know my own strength."

Adrian flexed his hand. "No kidding. Anyway, it was nice meeting you. I'm sure I'll see you around. And I hope you have a great day, Angie. Say, I'm in the mood for something sweet before work. Got any cupcakes ready?"

"Sorry," I said with a shrug. "They aren't ready yet."

Adrian glanced at the tray of cupcakes sitting there. "Oh, uh, right. Well...see you around. Come on, Alison."

The blonde woman nodded, glancing back at me for a moment. She chased after Adrian as he walked toward the door. Once they had vanished outside, the chime of the bell following them, I groaned and laid my head down on the counter.

"You alright?" Henry asked. "That looked tense."

I lifted my head. "Yeah, I'm fine. That's my ex. Well, sort of. We'd been seeing each other for a few months.

Anyway, he broke up with me at dinner last night. The waitress said he was a lying cheater. A total scumbag."

Okay, I ad-libbed a bit there, but it was true.

"Ouch," Henry said. "I can't stand cheaters. I...have some experience with them. Unfortunately."

"I'm sorry to hear that. It kinda feels like he led me on," I said, placing the cupcakes in the glass window. "Anyway, no point wasting time on it. I need to move on. Adrian clearly has."

"Yeah, I could see that. If you ask me, it's his loss. I wouldn't lose too much sleep over it."

I smiled. "Thanks, Henry."

"No problem—just calling it like I see it. But...I *am* curious about something."

I shut the glass window to the tray of cupcakes, wiping sugar off my hands. "Shoot."

"Did you really throw food at his house?"

I looked up at Henry. "Will you think I'm crazy if I say yes?"

"No," he said with a laugh. "I think cheaters deserve that. And food fights are hilarious."

"Then yes, I totally did. And you know what? I had the time of my life. Very therapeutic."

Henry laughed again, a beautiful sound to my ears. "Well, I'm glad he got what was coming to him. I don't know, I just got this vibe from him that he's..."

"Kind of a douchebag?" I filled in. "Super pretentious?"

"My thoughts exactly," Henry replied. "What did you see in him in the first place?"

I sighed. "I don't know. I liked that he was confident and pursued me. And he was fun—we had a lot of great dates. But I guess he wasn't ready for a serious relationship. And he clearly had no concept of loyalty."

Henry shook his head. "So, like I said—you're better off."

Grandma came out of the kitchen, carrying a tray of blueberry muffins. She set them down on the counter.

"Ah, Henry—you're still here," she began with a smile. "You know, I can probably handle things. I don't think we'll get too many customers this early. Why don't you two get to know each other? Angie, you can teach him all about New Harbor over coffee. There's a lovely coffee shop down the block."

When I looked at Henry, he seemed visibly uncomfortable, backing up. "Uh, that's a nice offer, but I really do need to get going. I should check in with Chief Teller and get settled. Anyway, it was nice meeting you two. Have a great day."

"You too," I said softly, watching as Henry rushed outside.

As he was leaving, our only employee, Mackenzie Teller, was entering the bakery. She and Henry nodded politely at each other before she stepped inside and put her schoolbag down. Henry got into an SUV parked on the street and sped off. Mackenzie was nineteen, the daughter of our town's fire chief, and studying to become a pastry chef at a local college. She had fiery red hair with freckles, wore overalls with sneakers, and was usually a bit shy and awkward. But weren't we all at that age?

"Hey, Mackenzie," I began. "Glad you could make it."

"Thanks! And so sorry I'm late," she said, stepping closer. I noticed she was carrying a plastic coffee cup. "My alarm didn't go off this morning, and I was up all night trying out a new recipe—"

She tripped over her untied shoelaces, falling to the floor. Grandma and I both ran around the counter to help her up. Fortunately, her coffee hadn't spilled. Now *that* would've been a tragedy. Mackenzie's face was as red as her hair when she rose to her feet again.

"Oops," she said. "Sometimes I can be a total klutz. Or, like, all the time."

"It's all right, dear. As long as you're okay," Grandma said, wiping dust off her overalls. "No classes today?"

"None," she said, lifting her coffee. "So I can work all day. Even stopped to get coffee before coming in so I wouldn't be as tired."

I smirked. "Or did you just stop by the coffee shop because you think the barista is cute? Melissa something?"

Mackenzie blushed even harder. "I...okay, you caught me. I'm crushing hard. But I really *did* need the coffee."

Grandma laughed. "A crush—how adorable. Have you asked her out yet?"

"No," Mackenzie said sadly, looking down. "I don't think she'd go for a girl like me. I'm a giant nerd."

"We're all nerdy about things we like," I replied. "You should talk to her. Give her your number."

Oh, great—now I was sounding like Grandma with all her love advice. She was really rubbing off on me.

"I agree," Grandma said, glancing at me with a wink. "Love is always worth taking a chance for. You know, I had to work up the courage to tell Angie's grandfather I liked him. And we had the best fifty-two years together. I'd do it all over again if I could—no matter how scary it was to admit my feelings."

She was giving Mackenzie advice, but somehow, it felt like she was talking to me. But my history with love wasn't going so well lately. First Adrian, now Henry. I was striking out hard.

"I'll think about it," Mackenzie said, sipping her coffee. "Anyway, where do you need me?"

"Head into the kitchen, dear. I need you to bake some cupcakes while I work on English muffins," Grandma said. "I'll be there in a second."

Mackenzie nodded, grabbing an apron off the nearby table and tying it around her waist. She left her coffee on the counter before scurrying into the kitchen. When we heard a crash, both our heads shot toward the door.

"Mackenzie, you okay in there?" I called out.

"I'm fine!" she yelled back. "Just tripped. Again. Don't worry!"

Grandma shook her head. "That girl is so clumsy. So, what did you think about that new man in town?"

"He was nice," I said, dusting a nearby table. "I think he'll fit in around here."

Grandma smiled. "He was very handsome, wasn't he?"

I sighed. "Is that why you tried to get us to go out for coffee?"

"Of course—I figured it couldn't hurt. I think you two would make a lovely couple."

"For one, he got tense when you said that. I think you made him uncomfortable," I said, turning to Grandma and putting the duster down. "And two, he had a wedding ring on his left hand. So, he's married, which is probably why he was weirded out."

"Oh," Grandma said, her face falling. "I had no idea—I didn't even notice the ring. How disappointing. I'm sorry, Angie."

"Eh, it's all right. Probably wouldn't have worked out anyway. And did you slip that fortune into his cupcake on purpose? That he'd find love soon?"

Grandma laughed. "Guilty as charged. I was trying to play matchmaker."

"Well, it didn't work out. Turns out he already found love. Which is pretty on par with the way my love life is going."

Grandma looked sad, reaching for my arm. "Angie, please. Don't give up—"

"It's all right. I'm not upset or anything." I cleared my throat, not wanting to talk about Henry. It stung a bit that he was taken—even more than Adrian breaking up with me. "Now, what else do you need me to do?"

Grandma dropped the subject and handed me a list of tasks from sweeping the floors to baking an apple pie. The whole time, I thought about Henry—and how lucky his partner was. Luck that I didn't have.

As I worked side-by-side with Mackenzie, chopping up walnuts for a dessert, she nudged me. "I see you finally met that Henry dude. He's the new guy in town, right?"

"Yeah, he is. A firefighter," I said, glancing at Mackenzie. "How'd you know?"

"My dad's the fire chief. Duh." Mackenzie rolled up some dough to make croissants. "Sometimes I listen when he talks about work. *Sometimes.* And he's been mentioning some new Henry guy all week. That he was super desperate to get a job in town."

"Really?" I asked, pausing. "Why?"

Mackenzie shrugged, continuing to roll croissants on a baking sheet. "No idea—Dad didn't say why. Just that Henry had a lot of experience, probably too much for a small town like this, and kept begging for a job. Even took a huge pay cut. He was making more money back in Boston, apparently."

"Hmm. Interesting..."

As I baked more desserts with Mackenzie, slipping nice, edible messages inside the flour, Grandma came back into the kitchen. She was holding her smartphone with a mischievous grin.

"Uh oh," I began, wiping flour off my hands with a towel. "I know that look. You're up to something—again. What are you doing now?"

There had been so many schemes Grandma had been involved in—and all in the name of finding love for me. To name a few, she once chased a hot volleyball guy a mile down the beach to get me his number.

He was gay, so nothing happened. Then there was the time she had a sign on the back of her car saying 'MY GRANDDAUGHTER NEEDS TO FIND HER SOULMATE! CALL HER IF YOU THINK YOU'RE THE ONE."

Naturally, no one called.

So, yeah, I was a little skeptical of her up-to-no-good face. I hoped whatever she was doing wasn't crazier than the last.

"Oh, nothing, nothing," she said, but I could tell she was lying. "Ang, could you be a dear and run to the grocery store for me? We need flour and eggs."

I frowned. "But I just checked our stock. We have more than enough—"

"Well, I'd like to keep it that way," Grandma interrupted. "Please?"

I nodded, removing my apron. "All right, no problem. I'll be back soon."

She grinned. "Oh, take your time. And thank you."

I still didn't know what Grandma was so giddy about. Shaking my head, I said goodbye to Mackenzie as she put her croissants in the oven and walked out of the kitchen. I grabbed my jacket from the closet and left the bakery. Then

I got into my truck, pulling away from the street and heading toward the grocery store only a few blocks away from our shop.

When I parked around the back and entered the store, it was mostly empty. I grabbed a basket near the front door and headed toward the flour aisle. Just as I approached the bag of flour, another man had walked up, reaching for the same one. I glanced up at him.

"Oh, sorry," I said. "You go ahead—take it."

"No, it's all right," the man replied, grinning at me. "Two things I don't believe in—taking candy from a baby and taking flour from a beautiful woman. It's all yours."

I blushed, putting the bag of flour into my basket. "Thank you. My grandma will be happy. She owns the local bakery."

The man studied me. "Oh, right—you're Angie Linden, aren't you?"

"Yeah, I am. How did you know that?"

"It's a small town. People talk a lot—especially about your grandmother and her awesome desserts. I'm really sorry to hear about your grandpa."

"Thank you. We miss him a lot."

I paused, taking in the man. He was handsome as well—blonde hair, blue eyes, and a hint of stubble. He had toned arms underneath his leather jacket. He wore jeans, boots, and had an expensive watch on his arm.

"I bet," the man said. "Anyway, where are my manners? I'm Jack. Jack Hawkins."

"Nice to meet you. I think I've seen you in passing before."

He nodded. "Yeah, I've lived here for a few years now. Moved here to open a business. Unfortunately, it didn't work out. We shut down a few months ago."

"I'm so sorry," I said with a frown. "Owning a business is tough. Especially after COVID."

"Yeah, you're telling me. I've gone back to marketing now. I work from home and don't get out much," he said, making me wonder why he was telling me all these things. "Anyway, I've got some time right now. I'd love to try some of your famous desserts. Mind if I visit your shop?"

I smiled. "Of course—let me just get some eggs and you can follow me to the bakery."

He nodded, smiling back. "Perfect. Here, let me carry that for you."

What a gentleman. Swoon.

He took my basket, following me around as I grabbed eggs and headed to the cash register. As I left the store with Jack, chatting and laughing, I wondered if love had found me—finally—and if it would break my heart or be the happy ever after I was dreaming of.

Hopefully, for my sake, it was the latter.

Chapter Four

I pulled away from the grocery store in my pickup truck as Jack got into his sedan and followed me. I headed around the block to our bakery and parked in the back. As I stepped out, Jack walked over, looking up at the bakery.

"Nice place," he said. "How long have you been here?"

"Oh, over thirty years," I said, getting my groceries out of the back of the truck. "My grandma and grandpa own it. It was always my grandpa's dream to own a bakery, and Grandma helped make it happen. She's the sole owner now that he's passed on."

"What an amazing woman," Jack said with a smile. "I'd love to meet her."

"Then you're in luck," I said, smiling back at him. "She's just inside. Come on—I'll show you around."

Jack nodded, following me around the side of the shop to the front doors. We entered, the chime echoing above our heads. Mackenzie was selling a customer a cupcake while Grandma was humming to herself in the kitchen. I could hear her through the open door.

The bakery had its usual customers—retirees, kids skipping school, and those on their day off, looking for a treat. Grandma came out with a rack of chocolate chip cookies that were still steaming.

"Chocolate chip cookies, fresh and hot!" she called out. "Come and get 'em."

A boy around twelve walked up to the cash register, his eyes wide. "I'd like one of those cookies."

Grandma paused, eyeing him as we watched. "Shouldn't you be in school, young man?"

The boy hesitated. "Well...yeah. But I don't really like school. It's lame."

"Why do you think that?" Grandma asked, displaying the cookies behind the glass.

The boy shrugged. "I don't really have many friends. And my teacher's super strict."

"I'm sorry to hear that," Grandma said, grabbing a cookie and placing it into a bag. "Here—a cookie on the house. It isn't much but I hope it'll make you smile."

The boy grinned, taking the bag from her. "Thanks, Mrs. Linden—you're the best!"

As the boy left, his schoolbag in tow, I smiled. Grandma was always helping people. And I knew she wanted to help me, but love was proving to be the most difficult venture of my life so far.

"That was nice of your grandma," Jack whispered. "I'm sure that kid will remember that."

"For sure," I said. "Come on—let's introduce you two. Grandma, are you busy?"

"Not at all, dear," Grandma said, taking off her gloves. "What can I help you with? Who is this?"

"This is Jack. Jack Hawkins," I introduced, gesturing at

him. "I met him at the grocery store. He really wanted to meet you."

"Is that so?" Grandma asked, her eyes twinkling. "Well, it's nice to meet you, Jack. Welcome to our bakery."

"Thank you. It's a nice place."

"It's my favorite," Grandma said, taking the bag of supplies from me. "Thank you, dear. You know I'd hate to run out of supplies. Now, Jack, would you like a free sample?"

"That would be great, yeah."

"Perfect. My granddaughter can find you something," Grandma said with a wink, gesturing at Mackenzie. "Come, dear—I need some help in the kitchen. I'm interested in that new recipe you were talking about."

"Oh, of course!" Mackenzie said, turning toward the kitchen with her eyes wide. "I've been practicing in class and at home, but it still needs a little fine tuning. It's got chocolate fondue, sprinkles, and strawberries..."

As they entered the kitchen, chatting about desserts, I walked around the desk. "All right, so what's your favorite? Muffins, cookies, cupcakes?"

"I like them all," Jack said with a smile, leaning on the counter. "Surprise me."

"You got it," I said, reaching into the glass counter and pulling out a cupcake. "Here—a red velvet cupcake, made by myself earlier. Totally free for first-time customers."

"Why, thank you," he said, taking the cupcake. He bit into it and nodded. "Delicious. You're really talented."

"Thanks, but I can't take all the credit. My grandparents taught me everything I know. My grandpa's soufflé is still my favorite."

"Well, you'll have to show me some recipes sometime,"

Jack said as he finished his cupcake. "Maybe—if this isn't too forward—we could grab coffee? I can give you my number."

I hadn't expected to find another date so soon. It took me off-guard. "Oh, um..."

"Hey, if you're not interested, no worries," Jack said, wiping crumbs off his jacket. "No pressure at all."

"I am. Interested, that is," I said with a nervous laugh. "I'd love your number, that'd be great."

He smiled, reaching into his pocket. He pulled out a business card and handed it to me. "Perfect—here you are. Call me anytime, I'll be around. I work from home so my hours are flexible."

"Great, thank you," I said, placing the card in my apron. "I'll do that."

"Looking forward to it. Now, I have to get home to start working, but it was lovely meeting you, Angie," he said, heading to the door. "I hope to hear from you soon."

He left the bakery, the door chiming behind him. I removed his business card from my pocket and stared at it for a few seconds. Could I really do it? Move on so fast, and with a total stranger? Even Adrian and I had known each other for a little while. He had been a customer for a month before I worked up the courage to ask him out.

Of course, if I'd known what I know now, I never would've talked to him in the first place. I stood there in the silence and wondered if I should take Grandma's advice. To start putting myself out there more. What did I have to lose?

The door to the kitchen opened behind me, then Grandma walked out. I shoved the business card deep in my pocket as she turned to me. "Mackenzie's a fast learner

—I have no doubt she'll graduate with honors in her baking class. Oh, where did Jack go?"

"He had to head home to work. But he said the red velvet cupcake I gave him was delicious."

Grandma smiled. "That's good. And he was cute, wasn't he?"

I rolled my eyes. "Not this again, Grandma."

"Oh, come on—just admit it. He had very nice features. And biceps."

"All right, okay. He did," I said, turning to her and wiping the counter down. "He even gave me his card to call him sometime. For a date."

Grandma's eyes lit up. "That's wonderful! See, you thought you wouldn't meet anyone after Adrian. You were wrong, darling. There are many, many wonderful men out there."

"I'll believe it when I see it," I grumbled. "I might go out with him but I'm going to be cautious. No more rushing into things—Adrian proved why that's a bad idea. So, anything else you need me to do?"

Grandma was just about to respond when her phone buzzed. She pulled it out of her apron pocket, looking at the screen. "Ah, yes. I need you to take the garbage out back to the dumpster, please and thank you."

"All right," I said, eyeing her phone as she quickly put it back in her pocket. "You sure everything's okay?"

"Everything's a-okay," she said with a smile. "I'll be in the kitchen, making a lemon tart if you need me."

I nodded, letting Grandma enter the kitchen first. I made sure all our customers had what they needed before heading into the kitchen and walking toward our garbage can. I lifted the heavy garbage bag, then dragged it to the back door with a groan. I lugged it over my shoulder as I opened the door and threw it into the dumpster.

As I wiped my hands off, I heard footsteps behind me. A man was approaching—looking dapper in suede shoes, brown slacks, and a striped sweater. He wore glasses and carried a black bag with him. His chocolate brown eyes glimmered in the sunlight, his beard thick and dark.

"Excuse me?" he asked. "I'm looking for directions. Do you think you can help?"

"Sure, of course. Where are you trying to get to?"

"Lucky's Baked Goods," the man replied. "I've heard it's the best bakery in town. And I've got a massive sugar craving this morning."

I laughed. "Then you're in the right place. Lou—nicknamed Lucky—was my grandpa. My grandma and I run this shop. The bakery's right here. Come on, I'll show you to the door."

"Great, thank you. I can't wait to try a dessert," the man said, following me around the side of the bakery. "I've heard lots of good things online."

"I'm glad the reviews are so positive," I said, opening the front door. "After you."

He nodded, entering the bakery as the bell chimed above our heads. "Thank you...um, what's your name?"

"Angela. Angela Linden," I said, shaking his hand. "But everyone calls me Angie. My grandma is Esther, and Mackenzie's in the kitchen somewhere. She's our employee."

"Nice to meet you," the man said, pulling his hand away. "I'm Ty Wilson. I'm a teacher in the town over. Grade five."

"Ah, that's lovely. Well, come on in. Let's get you a treat

before school starts," I said, walking toward the counter. "We give away a free sample to every new customer."

"Generous," he said, peering in at the glass counter. "I'd like a cookie, please. That double chocolate one."

"Good choice," I said, grabbing a paper bag and the tongs. I placed the cookie inside the bag and handed it over. "Here you are—on the house."

He took it from me, opening the bag. Once he removed the cookie, he bit off a piece, nodding. "Fantastic. Really, it's amazing."

"Thank you. We work very hard to make our desserts taste the best," I replied. "I'm sure my grandma will be happy when I tell her."

"Oh, please do," he said, taking another bite. "So, are you into baking too?"

"Yeah, it's pretty much ingrained into who I am. I grew up baking with my grandparents a lot."

He swallowed another bite. "And your parents? Do they bake too?"

"Oh, no—they don't. My mom grew up around it too but never cared much for cooking or baking. My parents divorced when I was ten, then I chose to live with my grandparents. I've been living and baking with them ever since. Well, just my grandma now since my grandpa passed."

His face fell. "Oh, I'm so sorry. So...when you're not baking, what do you like to do?"

I paused, realizing this was beginning to sound a lot like a date. Was it just a coincidence two handsome men had taken an interest in me today? Or was something going on?

"Oh, lots of things—reading, traveling, heading out to restaurants. The usual stuff," I said, wiping down the counter again. "It's been lovely chatting with you but I really need to get to work now. I'm sure you do too."

"Yes, of course," he said, shoving the cookie into his bag. "I'll save that for my lunch. Sometimes I need a sugar rush when the kids drive me crazy."

"Sounds good. There's a fortune in the cookie too—edible in case you eat it."

"Perfect, I'll look for it. Anyway, I'd like to see you again. Would it be all right if I gave you my number?"

And yet another man wanted to give me his number. Now I was starting to grow even more suspicious.

"Uh, sure," I said with a nod. "That'd be nice."

The man reached into his bag, pulling out a notebook and pen. It looked like he was using it to plan out his lessons. MR. WILSON'S EPIC GRADE FIVE CLASS was engraved into the side. He ripped out a paper, scribbling down his phone number before handing it to me.

"Here you are," he said with a smile. "Hope to hear from you soon."

"Great, thanks. Have a good day at school—and enjoy that cookie."

He smiled. "Will do. See you around, Angie."

He turned, heading toward the door. I watched him get into a small car outside and drive off before Grandma walked out of the kitchen.

"Ooh, who was that?" she asked. "He was quite handsome."

I turned to her, crossing my arms. "What have you done?"

She paused. "What on Earth are you talking about, dear?"

"Oh, no—don't play coy with me. Two men in one day

gave me their numbers? That never happens. Spill the beans. I already know something's going on."

Grandma laughed nervously. "Honestly, sweetie, I have no idea what—"

When her phone buzzed in her pocket, I lunged forward, grabbing it from her. I ran around the counter to create some distance between us. I saw the notification on her phone as she scoffed.

"Hey, give that back!" she cried.

All the notifications were from Bumble, one of the many dating apps. I briefly wondered if Grandma was getting back into the dating scene until I saw one of the messages. And it was from a man named Ty, probably the same guy I had just met. It read: *I see her by the dumpster. Heading over now. Thanks for all your help!*

I held up her phone. "Okay, what's going on?"

Grandma sighed. "Drat, I suppose my plan's been found out. All right, I'll tell you. Unlock my phone and see for yourself."

I already knew Grandma's phone password—it was the day she and Grandpa met. I inputted the old date, then unlocked her phone and opened the Bumble app. To my surprise, it wasn't a profile for herself, but for me. She had uploaded a picture of me, along with my age, name, and profession.

The profile read: *Hi there, I'm Angela's grandmother, Esther. She's been going through a rough patch with love after her boyfriend broke up with her. She deserves a kind, good man, one who is interested in something serious. Please don't break her heart. Her interests include baking at our family bakery, reading, and going on adventures. She'd be your perfect partner—and I know you'll love her as much as I do. If interested, please text me and I'll set it all up.*

After reading that, I felt my anger fading. "Oh, Grandma...that's really sweet of you."

She paused. "So, you aren't angry at me?"

"I was until I read that. It was lovely," I said, handing back the phone. "No, I'm not mad. I just wish you would've told me what you were up to."

"But then you might've said no. And I really wanted you to give love another shot," Grandma replied. "I only want the best for you, dear. The same kind of love your grandpa and I had. You deserve that and so much more."

I smiled. "Thanks, Grandma. So, those men I met today were all from the app? Including Henry?"

"No, not Henry. I've never met him before. But Jack, Ty, and a few other men are. I sent you to the grocery store and the back of the bakery to meet with them. I set up that profile after your date with Adrian last night. They seem like nice boys, Angie. Will you give them a chance?"

I shrugged. "Maybe. I don't know yet."

"Well, you have time to decide. I'm not saying you have to marry them—just hang out and get to know them. They might surprise you. And make you believe in love again," Grandma said, checking her watch. "You know, Mackenzie and I can handle the bakery today. You should probably head home to relax before tonight."

I frowned. "Tonight? What's happening tonight?"

"I've set up a round of speed dating for you with some eligible bachelors from around New Harbor and the surrounding towns," Grandma said with a wink. "And you want to look your best."

"What? Speed dating?" I asked. "Oh, Grandma, I don't know. I'm barely sure about Jack and Ty—"

"But so many men are looking forward to meeting you. And there's no harm in talking—and we can promote our business as well. So go ahead home and relax before your big night!"

As Grandma guided me toward the door, smiling politely at the customers, I almost groaned.

What kind of elaborate plan had she gotten me into now?

I just hoped it wouldn't be as ridiculous as the time she kept faking illnesses so I would take her to see a cute doctor around my age.

We later found out he was gay.

Chapter Five

On the drive home, I wondered if Grandma was meddling too much. Sure, she meant well and only wanted me to find love, but maybe she was taking it too far. And I wasn't so sure I was ready to throw myself back into the dating ring anyway.

I got home ten minutes later, pulling into the driveway. I flicked on the light as I entered and headed upstairs. I petted Nutmeg who was sleeping on Grandma's bed as usual. She purred and stretched out.

"You're a lucky cat, you know," I whispered to her. "All you have to do is eat, sleep, and play all day long. You don't have to wonder if you'll find love or not. What I wouldn't give for that to be me..."

I let Nutmeg continue sleeping, heading to my room to change into my pajamas. I wanted to take a shower, shave, and get ready for tonight. As I removed my apron and work clothes, I felt something sticking to me. I pulled it off and stared at it in the full-length mirror I had in my room.

"What the...?"

When I pulled it around, I realized it was a piece of

paper with some wet dough on the back. It created an adhesive, sticking to my clothes. It must've gotten stuck to me when I was making cupcakes and writing fortunes to stuff inside. I looked closer, reading the inscription.

"Never fear, you will find great love soon," I read aloud. "Yeah, right..."

I chucked it into the nearby garbage can, then took a shower, shaved, and put on my pajamas. Grandma didn't often give me days off so I wanted to take full advantage. I spent the day reading, catching up on sappy romance movies on TV, and doing chores. I played on my phone, realizing I still had Jack and Ty's numbers in there.

Could I call them? Could I get back into the dating game this soon? I stared at their numbers for a while, wondering about it until my phone rang. The caller I.D. read Sonya Livingston—my best friend since elementary school.

A stab of jealousy tugged at my heart when I saw her name. We had been so close growing up—hanging out constantly, sleeping over at each other's houses, and doing everything together. Her family had been practically my own and I thought we'd be close friends forever. That is, until she met her boyfriend in college and had less time for me. I tried to understand—she was an adult now, much busier than when we were kids—but it still stung.

I picked up the phone, anyway, holding it up to my ear. "Sonya! How are you?"

"Good, good. It's so nice to hear your voice, Angie," she said, and I could hear her smiling through the phone. She sounded so happy. "I'm sorry we haven't spoken in a while. Things have been busy with work. And James and I just got back from a trip to London. We got to see Buckingham Palace and everything!"

I already knew about that—I followed her on Instagram and saw all her lovely couple photos. I didn't know whether I was more jealous that she found love or that she had practically abandoned me for it. Still, I tried to be happy for her.

"Oh, no worries," I said, flipping through the TV channels. "I've been busy with work too. There's always something to do at Grandma's bakery."

"Ah, your grandma. She was always such a nice lady. How is she doing since your grandpa passed? How are you doing?"

"We're...okay," I said, sighing. "As much as we can be. You can really feel his loss at the bakery. He loved that place."

"I know. I'm so sorry," she said, softly. "He was a great man. I'll never forget when he taught us how to make lemon meringue pie. I bake it for James all the time. I did on our second date. In fact, I'm pretty sure that's what made him see me as girlfriend-material!"

I laughed. "Well, I'm sure Grandpa would love to hear that. He was always a big supporter of love. Grandma too. Anyway, why are you calling? Just to catch up?"

"I wanted to see how you are, of course. Since we haven't spoken in a while. And I have some big news. Are you free for lunch tomorrow?"

I thought for a moment. "Yeah, I think so. What's going on? Everything okay?"

"Oh, yeah—everything's great. Perfect, actually. I just wanted to tell you this in person. Want to meet at *Estelle's* tomorrow at noon?"

"Sure, I think my grandma will let me sneak away. Especially if I tell her I'm meeting up with you."

"Great! Looking forward to it. We can catch up on everything we've missed," Sonya said, and I could hear people talking in the background. "Oh, gotta go—a new client's here. See you tomorrow, Ang!"

I said goodbye, then hung up. What big news could Sonya have? I was curious. She worked as a wedding planner, running her own business just outside of town, and I hoped everything was okay with work. My grandparents were actually the ones who encouraged her to become a business owner and follow her passion. Back in the days when we were inseparable.

I sighed, turning the TV off. It was almost dinnertime—almost time to head back to the bakery and see what men Grandma had found for me on Bumble. I had never used a dating app before. A part of me was surprised Grandma had figured it out before me.

After putting on a red dress—one that was modest and pretty, not too sexual so these guys wouldn't get the wrong idea—I paired it with diamond earrings and black heels. I quickly fed Nutmeg her usual tuna dinner and grabbed my keys before locking the front door. As I reached my truck, I felt my phone buzzing.

Showtime, Grandma had texted. *I hope you're ready to find the love of your life tonight!*

I just texted back *lol* and hopped into my truck. As I sped off down the street, heading toward the bakery, I passed Henry in his black SUV. He didn't notice me as he sped off into the distance. I sighed, wishing a man like that was single. Now *he* would've been worth risking heartbreak for.

When I arrived at the bakery, pulling into the back parking lot, I realized Grandma had gone all out with the decorations. She had put up a sign—in neon lights—that read SPEED DATING FOR ANGIE. She had taped love fortunes to the window and drawn little hearts in washable marker.

Oh, Grandma. She was always going the extra mile.

I stepped out of the truck, heading toward the front doors. I opened it with a chime, entering the empty bakery. Mackenzie was leaving for the day. She was covered in flour, something that was pretty typical at the bakery. Grandma was sweeping the floors in her apron and looked up when she heard me.

"There you are, dear!" she said with a smile, setting her broom aside. "Ah, you look so beautiful. You clean up nicely!"

"Thanks, Grandma. What's with all the decorations?"

"Just wanted to make the speed dating feel more comfortable, that's all. Please, have a seat. I sent the customers home and prepared some tea and snacks for you."

"Oh, you didn't have to do all that," I said, sitting down at a nearby table. The napkins had little heart designs on them. "But thanks."

"Of course, dear. Anything for love," Grandma said with a wink. "The men should be here any minute now. Watch for them, will you?"

I nodded, staring out the window as Grandma scurried into the kitchen. She returned with coffee, tea, and fresh desserts she had made while I was gone. She started to assemble them at every table.

"I fed Nutmeg before I left, by the way. She was sleeping—as usual," I said, still looking out the window. "And Sonya wants to meet for lunch tomorrow. Says she has big news. Is it okay if I sneak away?"

"Absolutely," Grandma said, fixing the napkins at a

nearby table. "You haven't seen her in a while. How is she doing?"

"Good, I think. I'll find out more tomorrow. I know she's still dating James."

Grandma smiled. "Wonderful—I'm happy for her. She's a nice girl. She deserves a nice man too."

"Yeah, I agree. I just...I wish it wouldn't have come at the expense of our friendship. I feel like once she started dating James, I was history."

Grandma frowned. "I'm sorry, sweetie. I wish you two would've kept in contact more. But that's life, I suppose. You grow up, find love, start working, and suddenly, you don't have the time you used to. That happened to your grandfather and I. We kept some friends, but we lost a lot of connections. Mainly because we were busy raising a family and running our business."

I sighed. "I get that. Being an adult sucks. Sometimes I wish I had never grown up."

Grandma fixed a vase on a nearby table, laughing. "You and me both, dear. To be twenty-four again like you would be a dream! Make sure to enjoy it before it's gone."

"I'm trying," I said, "but stupid boys keep breaking my heart."

"Well, maybe tonight will be different. You never know. Try to keep an open mind, dear."

I promised I would, still watching the window as Grandma piddled around behind me. I froze when I saw Adrian approaching the bakery, without his blonde friend this time. No, no, no. Was he one of the guys in the speed dating round?

When he entered the bakery, I rose to my feet. "Adrian, what are you doing here?"

"Sorry, didn't mean to intrude," he said, glancing

around. "I was just heading home when I saw all these bright lights at your bakery. What's going on? Some kind of party?"

"Speed dating, actually," Grandma said, turning around. "For my granddaughter. I'm going to help her find love tonight."

"Oh," Adrian said, his face falling. "That's...that's nice."

Was he jealous? I didn't know why—*he* had broken up with *me*, not the other way around. He had no right to be upset.

I gestured at the clock on the wall, a giant cupcake. "And it's about to start soon, so, if you wouldn't mind..."

"Of course, of course," Adrian said, backing up toward the door. "Sorry, I'll be going now."

He left the bakery, taking one last glance over his shoulder. I watched out the window as he scurried to his car. It had started to rain now, dark clouds appearing in the sky as he drove off. I hoped that wasn't a bad omen.

"The nerve of that man to come back here," Grandma muttered, still moving vases around. "He seemed a bit jealous."

"Yeah, I got that vibe too," I said, sighing. "Well, too bad, so sad. We're over."

"That's the spirit, dear," Grandma said with a smile. "He's old news. Maybe the man of your dreams will show up tonight. Or it could be Jack or Ty. Have you called them yet?"

"No," I said, sitting down at my table again. "Still thinking about it."

"Well, take your time. But they did seem like nice men when I chatted with them online," Grandma said, walking over to me. "You never know."

"Maybe you should date them, then."

Grandma laughed. "Ha! You're too funny, dear. No, I could never date again. Your grandfather was the only one for me. My true love. But yours is still out there—and I'm going to reel him in for you. Hook, line, and sinker."

"Nice fishing pun. I hope you're right—that we're not just wasting our time tonight."

"Oh, sweetie," Grandma said, placing a hand on my shoulder. "Love is *never* a waste of time. And look—I think I see our first guest arriving."

When Grandma pointed out the window, I looked, noticing a van pulling up to the street. A dark-haired man in jeans and a t-shirt with stains on it jumped out. He waved at an elderly woman sitting in the front seat, then opened the door to the bakery. He looked me up and down and held out a hand.

"Um, hi," he began. "I'm here for the speed dating thing. Are you Angelina? You look just like your pictures."

I shook his hand. It was very sweaty. "Angela, actually, but yes, that's me. Come on in. What's your name?"

"Karl," he began, sitting at a nearby table. "My mom drove me. She's my best friend. The only woman I've ever really loved."

I blinked. "Uh-huh. Well, make yourself comfortable and enjoy some snacks. I think I see someone else arriving..."

The man named Karl nodded, eating some of the muffins Grandma had made for the round of speed dating. The next guy to arrive came in a sports car, parking in the spot for disabilities. That made my blood boil.

He opened the door to the bakery, entering and reaching for my hand. "Angela, right? Damn, you look even better than the photos."

I cleared my throat. "Uh, thanks. Did you know you're

parked in the handicapped spot? I don't see a sticker in your window."

He shrugged. "And? I got here first. Oh, muffins—my favorite."

I shook my head as he sat at a vacant table, stuffing his face with Grandma's muffins. I glanced over at her and she winced. Suddenly, this felt very much like a bad idea.

The next guy to arrive was blond and came on a motorcycle. He shook my hand, then looked down at my dress. "Hey, I'm Mark. That dress...it's a bit revealing, don't you think?"

"Actually, I thought it was pretty tame," I said, looking at my clothes. "You don't like it?"

He shook his head. "Nah, not really. I like my women to dress traditionally. I want them to act that way too."

Somehow, I didn't think we would work out. "Right. Well, have a seat, please."

He nodded, pushing past me as he sat at an empty table. For the next twenty minutes, one guy after another showed up. One man looked way too young—freshly eighteen and out of high school. I felt like a cougar just talking to him. The next guy was way too old, probably in his mid to late fifties. He could've been my father. That gave me the ick factor very, very quickly.

One guy entered on a phone call, something to do with work. He whispered his name and sat down at a vacant table while still chatting on the phone. The next came in swigging a flask, his breath reeking of alcohol. I tried not to make a face as we chatted. Another guy entered who was ripped and kissing his muscles. (Yes, really.)

After a few more trickled in, Grandma rang a bell. "All right, everyone—time for the speed dating. Angie will have two minutes at each table to chat with you. On your mark, get set...go!"

I tried to look enthusiastic, sitting at Karl's table first. He went on and on about his mother for the whole two minutes. "...and she'll be living with us when we get married. She pays all my bills. And makes an awesome casserole."

"Um, okay," I said, playing with my hands. "And what do you do for a living?"

He hesitated. "Uh, I'm kinda between jobs. But I love video games. I stayed up all last night playing Call of Duty..."

Ding. On to the next guy, the one who parked in the handicap spot.

"...and I don't really think I'm looking for anything serious," he began. "Kinda in my playboy era, you know? Playing the field while I'm still young."

I tried not to roll my eyes. "Well, good luck with that."

Grandma rang the bell. "Next table, Angie!"

Saved by the bell. I spoke with the anti-dress guy next who went on and on about how giving women rights was a bad idea. I was barely listening, watching the candle burn on the table instead. I was never so grateful to hear a bell ringing in my life.

I spoke to the drinking guy, the workaholic guy, the too young guy, the too old guy, *and* the work-out obsessed guy but I didn't feel a spark with any of them. None of them felt right—and I quickly forgot their names.

At least I still had Jack and Ty's numbers in my phone, but what if they were just like these guys too? I glanced at Grandma who gave me a hopeful smile, but her idea of speed dating to cheer me up had the opposite effect.

I had never felt more miserable in my life—and more convinced that love just wasn't for me.

Chapter Six

After another painful hour of chatting with the guys in two-minute intervals, Grandma rang a silver bell she held in her hand. "All right, that's all we have time for tonight! I hope you enjoyed your time with my granddaughter."

The guys nodded and smiled, though I still felt pretty lousy. Grandma nudged me to make a speech so I cleared my throat and rose to my feet. "Yes, thank you for coming. Get home safely. Goodnight!"

The guys looked disappointed, especially the man with the biceps. "That's it? Not even going to give us your number?"

I hesitated. "Sorry, no. I didn't agree to any of that—"

"Typical," the man sneered. "I'm outta here."

He stormed out of the bakery, the bell chiming loudly above me. The other guys said goodbye as they headed to the door. Grandma immediately locked the door behind us, turning around with a sigh.

"That was...something," she muttered. "I'm so sorry, darling."

I sighed. "It's all right, Grandma—you tried. Those guys...I don't want to sound like Goldilocks here, but none of them were quite right."

"Oh, I agree," Grandma said, setting her bell down. "Especially that muscular man. I think his name was Jim or something on the app. He has more brawn than brains, it seems."

"And what about that guy who was totally into his job? He couldn't even put his phone down for a second to talk to me. Can you imagine marrying a person like that?"

"An unhappy marriage, that's for sure," Grandma said, picking up a tray of tea. "Can you help me clean up, dear? Then we can head home."

I nodded, helping Grandma clear the tables and clean up after the guys. The man who still lived with his mother was the messiest of them all—leaving crumbs all over his seat. I was glad I wasn't dating him. I wanted a man, not a boy.

When I heard a tap on the window, I looked over, noticing the last person I wanted to see standing there. It was Lucy Rhett—one of the meanest girls I went to high school with. Since then, she married her high school sweetheart and opened a healthy restaurant a few blocks down called The Green Machine. They served green juices, smoothies, raw vegan desserts, and whole grain bowls and were constantly trying to compete with us.

I thought I'd be free of her after I graduated but life had other plans. She had curly blonde hair, wore cardigans with mom jeans, always had a designer purse, and thought she was better than everyone.

She knocked on the window again. "Excuse me, but are you going to let me in?"

I walked over, unlocking the door and opening it. "What do you want, Lucy? We're closed."

"I'm not here to buy any of your desserts, that's for sure," she said, wrinkling her nose. "All that stuff you sell is really unhealthy, you know. Full of carbs and processed sugar. You're going to give people diabetes."

I rolled my eyes. "Uh-huh. Again, why are you here?"

She pointed up at the sign. "Really, speed dating?"

"Do you have a problem with that?" I asked, crossing my arms.

"It's just so...pathetic," she shot back. "And the lights are too bright. I can see them all the way down the street! You need to turn them off."

"We will soon—we're just about to leave for the night. Happy?"

"For now," she muttered, then her face broke into a smirk. "So, I heard you and Adrian broke up. That's too bad."

See? I knew the news would spread fast around town.

"That's hardly your business," I grumbled. "But what about it?"

She continued to smirk. "I've seen you on a lot of dates. Just can't keep a guy interested in the goods, huh?"

I closed the door, locking it before I spoke to her through the glass. "I don't need to stand here and take this. Goodbye, Lucy. Go back to your lettuce-loving restaurant and leave us alone."

She just scoffed, taking off down the street in the pouring rain. As much as I wished she would've gotten soaked, she had an umbrella to protect her mean little head. I watched her go and turned off the neon lights from the inside while leaning against the glass door. If that round of speed dating wasn't painful enough, Lucy was the icing on the cake.

Grandma came out of the kitchen with a big garbage bag, cleaning up the bakery. "Were you talking to someone?"

"Yep—it was Lousy Lucy from down the block. She came to complain about the bright lights. God, I wish I could get her off our backs forever. Too bad I can't get a restraining order."

Grandma shook her head, tossing a paper plate into her garbage bag. "That woman. She must be truly miserable. You know, last Christmas she complained that the snowman I made outside was ugly. Who is she to decide?"

"She's got a serious attitude problem, that's for sure. Been that way since high school," I grumbled. "We never got along—and for good reason. Good to know she hasn't changed much since her mean girl days. I think she's still stuck in high school."

Grandma nodded, throwing out more garbage. "Yes, you're probably right, dear. Some people just can't move past high school. Say, isn't she married?"

"That's right—to the guy who used to be our football quarterback. Dan something."

"Hmm," Grandma said, tying up the garbage bag. "You think she would be happier, then."

"Just goes to show that you can have love and still be a miserable person," I said, shrugging. "I'd rather be single and happy than married and whatever Lucy is."

"You can have both, darling. Marriage *and* happiness," Grandma said with a twinkle in her eyes. "They're not mutually exclusive."

I chortled. "After the guys I met tonight, I think I'll stay single for a long time, thank you very much. Are you ready to go?"

"Yes—it's getting late. Let's head home."

I nodded, grabbing my coat and heading to the door. Grandma followed as we stepped outside into the pouring rain. We hid under the awning on the sidewalk as Grandma locked the door to the bakery. The sun had set, darkening the sky above us. As we turned around, we heard footsteps coming at us, then noticed it was Chief Teller.

He had been our town's fire chief for decades, someone Grandma and Grandpa had come to see as a close friend. It was the reason we knew Mackenzie so well and hired her when she wanted a bakery job. Chief Rodney Teller was a stocky man with a white mustache, greying hair, and a mole on his upper cheek. He always wore his firefighter's uniform and was much older when he had Mackenzie. His wife, Sandra, was younger than him by a decade.

"Ah, Esther—there you are," Chief Teller said, out of breath. "I was hoping to catch you before you headed home for the evening."

"Well, here I am," Grandma said with a smile. "What can I do for you, Chief?"

"I have an emergency," he replied. "A cake emergency."

"What do you mean?" I asked, raising an eyebrow.

"Well, I don't know if you've heard, but we hired a new firefighter from out of town. Henry Brant," Chief Teller explained as the rain hit the pavement. "It's a good thing I finally found someone. My last firefighter left for maternity leave, and I haven't been able to find anyone since. Anyway, we're throwing him a welcome party at the fire station right now."

Grandma smiled. "That's kind. But what's all this about an emergency?"

"I forgot a cake," Chief Teller grumbled. "My wife even reminded me yesterday and I still forgot. I know this is last minute, but do you think you could whip up something for Henry? Really quickly as he's still at the fire station, celebrating? I'd be in your debt."

Grandma smiled, unlocking the front door. "Of course—and no worries. We'd be happy to. Come on inside, it's pouring out here."

Chief Teller nodded, letting us enter the bakery before following. He brushed the rain off his service medals as I prepared a cup of tea for him. He sat down, sipping it and getting warm as I helped Grandma make the cake in the kitchen.

"Anything in particular you want us to write on the cake?" Grandma called out.

"Yes, please!" Chief Teller said from the dining area. "If you could write, 'Welcome to New Harbor, Henry,' that would be amazing. Thank you."

"You got it!" Grandma called out, turning to me as she picked up her icing bag. "Go keep Chief Teller company, darling. I can handle this. Speed baking is my specialty!"

"All right, Grandma. Let me know if you need any help."

I removed my apron, setting it aside as I entered the dining area. Chief Teller looked up from his cup of tea as I walked toward him.

"Hello, Angie," he began. "How are you? And what's going on with that speed dating sign over there?"

I blushed. "Oh, you saw that, huh? I had a few dates tonight. Grandma's trying to help me find love. It...didn't go well."

Chief Teller's face fell. "Ah, I'm sorry. In my experience,

love is both simple *and* hard to find. So simple to love the right person, so hard to track them down."

"You're telling me. What a paradox. May I sit with you?"

"Of course," he said, gesturing at the other chair. "I'd like the company. My daughter's just starting to date now too. As a father, I'm worried. But hoping the best for her."

"Mackenzie's a great girl—I have no doubt she'll find someone amazing. I have complete faith in her."

Chief Teller grinned. "Thank you, Angie. The same can be said about you. Don't give up, all right? It took me a while to find Sandy but boy, am I glad I did. I wouldn't trade her in for the world."

"You're lucky to have each other, then. Where did you meet Sandra?"

"I saved her from a burning building, actually. What are the odds?" He had a twinkle in his eye. "She's given me a wonderful life and a beautiful daughter."

"That she has. So, tell me about this new firefighter. Henry Brant. Mackenzie filled me in a bit."

Chief Teller took another sip of his tea, wetting his mustache. "As I said, I was really struggling to find a new firefighter. And Henry was pretty insistent about moving here to work. He practically begged, actually."

I frowned. "Mackenzie told me that. Any idea why?"

"No clue," Chief Teller said with a shrug. "He only said he was desperate to get out of Boston. That there was nothing left for him there anymore. It was strange—and I could sense there was a story there—but I didn't want to pry. I hope he'll like his time in New Harbor and stay for a while."

"Yeah, me, too. We already met—he wandered into the

shop. Gave him a free cupcake and spoke to him a bit. He's very nice."

"That he is. And his resume's incredible—commendations and service awards for bravery. Boston lost a great firefighter when he left. He's definitely overqualified for this small town, but hey, I'm not complaining. He's already bonding with the others at the station."

I smiled. "That's wonderful. Do you...do you know if he has any family? A wife, maybe?"

"I don't. He didn't mention anything like that. He was quite mum about his private life, actually. Why do you want to know?"

"Just curious about our new citizen. This town doesn't get many new people," I replied. "Anyway, what's your favorite dessert?"

After chatting with Chief Teller for a bit, Grandma finally walked out of the kitchen, placing the cake in a large box. "Here it is—the congratulatory cake for Henry. I hope he likes it."

"I'm sure he will," Chief Teller said, rising to his feet. "Your desserts are incredible. Thank you so much for making it. What do I owe you?"

"Don't worry about it," Grandma said with a smile. "It's on the house."

He walked over, patting Grandma's shoulder with a grin. "You're too good to me, Esther. And look, about Lou... I'm so sorry he's gone. He's deeply missed around town. You ever need anything, just let me know."

Grandma sighed, looking down. "Thank you for saying that, Rodney. I'm so grateful to have the town's support."

"Oh, you do—people adore you in New Harbor. We want to make sure you stay happy."

"With friends like you, I *am*," Grandma said with a

twinkle in her eyes. "Now, Angie and I should get home. Enjoy the cake and have a good rest of your evening."

"You don't want to come to the fire station?" Chief Teller asked. "We can give you a tour. And that cake smells incredible."

Grandma gestured at me. "It's up to you, dear. Want a tour of the town's fire station?"

And get a chance to see all the hot firefighters up close? Hell yes. And the thought of seeing Henry again put butterflies in my stomach, even though I knew he was married.

"I'd like that," I said, trying not to sound too eager.

Chief Teller nodded, grabbing the cake and leaving the bakery before getting into his truck. Grandma locked the door for the second time and took her own car to the fire station. I followed, pulling into the parking lot of fire trucks. The station was small but capable with firefighting equipment everywhere and plenty of rooms for the firefighters to sleep in.

Chief Teller got out first, carrying the cake and gesturing for us to follow. Grandma and I trailed behind as Chief Teller opened the door and let us inside. I noticed the workout equipment, poles, and fire alarms scattered around. An upper level had the bedrooms and bathrooms. A group of firefighters, including Henry, were sitting around the kitchen table while laughing and drinking beer. I could smell the delicious aroma of chili in the air. They must've eaten that for dinner, the unwashed dishes sitting behind them in the sink.

"I'm back, everyone," Chief Teller said. "And I brought something special. Cake for Henry from the best damn bakery in town!"

All the firefighters sitting at the table cheered, then rose to their feet to shake our hands and introduce themselves.

Chief Teller began chatting with Grandma and Henry, then some of the firefighters joined. I glanced around the station out of curiosity. One of the firefighters, a muscular, greasy-haired guy, walked over and shook my hand with a smirk.

"Name's Devon," he said. "I don't think I've seen you around before. What's your name?"

"Angela Linden. But everyone calls me Angie," I replied. "I run the bakery with my grandma. It was named after my grandpa who opened it, actually."

When I felt eyes on me, I glanced over, noticing Henry staring at us. And he didn't look too happy. Grandma and Chief Teller chatted around him, unaware of his gaze.

Devon smiled. "That's nice—I'm sure you're making your grandparents proud. And I'm sure your partner really appreciates being married to someone who can make incredible desserts."

"Oh, I'm not married. Or seeing anyone. Painfully single, actually."

"Really?" Devon asked, eyeing me up and down. "I find that hard to believe. A beautiful woman like you, single? That's not right. We need to fix that. Say, what do you think about grabbing dinner tomorrow night?"

Before I could respond, I heard footsteps, and when I looked up, it was Henry—and he was walking straight at us with an annoyed look.

Chapter Seven

"Sorry to interrupt," Henry said, butting into our conversation. He put himself between me and Devon. "Just wanted to say hi. Nice to see you again, Angie."

I nodded. "And you too, Henry. Congrats again on getting the job."

"Thanks, I'm eager to start. The cake looks amazing by the way." He turned to Devon. "Why don't you go get a slice? Do the honors of cutting the cake."

Devon looked back at me, then Henry. "Uh, okay. Sure."

He walked away, heading to the counter with the cake while looking confused. I was too. Why had Henry interrupted our conversation like that?

"Sorry, hope I wasn't rude," Henry whispered as he turned back to me. "That Devon guy...I don't trust him. He comes off as a total player. I only met him today but something tells me he's bad news."

"Huh," I said, watching as Devon grabbed a slice of cake and chatted with the other firefighters. "He did come off as a little forward. Was already flirting with me."

"I'd stay away from him if I were you. You deserve

better than a guy like that," Henry said, shaking his head in disgust. Then he looked at my dress. "You look amazing, by the way. What's the occasion?"

I laughed. "Oh, you'll think it's silly, but...my grandma set up a round of speed dating for me at the bakery."

"Oh," Henry said, crossing his arms. "How did it go? Meet anyone special?"

"Sadly, no," I said, shaking my head. "All those guys had issues. And I'm not saying I'm perfect either, but...wow. Those dudes make me never want to date again."

Henry chuckled, like music to my ears. "Yeah, it's a madhouse out there. Dating apps are a special kind of torture."

"I actually wouldn't know. My grandma set it all up—made me a Bumble profile. She's really trying to help me find love. After a lot of disastrous relationships."

"That's nice of her to do," Henry said, looking awkward. "Uh, anyway, thanks for baking the cake on such short notice. That was kind of you and your grandmother."

"Hey, it's what we do," I said with a smile. "Makes me feel closer to my grandpa too. Baking, I mean. That was his thing."

Henry's face fell. "Yeah, you told me about him before. I'm sorry."

I looked down, trying not to cry. Grandpa had died a year ago and yet the wound still felt fresh, especially when I kept talking about him. Would I ever be free of the grief? I glanced at Grandma who was still chatting with Chief Teller, knowing she had to be feeling the same way too.

Maybe some scars were just never meant to heal.

Henry cleared his throat. "Would you like a tour of the station? I just had one this afternoon. I think I remember where everything is."

"Sure, I'd like that. Lead on."

Henry smiled, gesturing for me to follow. He took me upstairs and showed me where all the firefighters slept. He had a bunkbed above Devon, his suitcase sitting on the bed. I noticed he had taped some pictures to the wall above his pillow.

"Hey, who's that woman?" I asked, leaning closer.

Henry noticed the elderly woman in the picture I was pointing at. "Oh, that's my mom. Lynette. She's always been my biggest supporter."

"Moms," I said with a smile, turning to him. "That's what they do. Does she live here in New Harbor?"

Henry shook his head. "Nah, back in Boston. That's where we're all from. My dad lives there somewhere too, but...I haven't seen him in a while. They've been divorced for years."

"Oh. I'm sorry," I said, softly. "For what it's worth, I'm also a child of divorce."

Henry sighed. "Then you get it. My dad...well, let's just say he wasn't the best husband or father. And he's got a lot to answer for. I love my mom though. I'd do anything for her."

"That's sweet," I said with a smile. "You're a momma's boy."

"Guilty as charged," Henry said, chuckling. "Remind me about your parents again. Do they live in New Harbor?"

"No, they're back in Boston too. They separated when I was a child. I've lived with my grandparents ever since. And I'm glad—they've been amazing."

"Well, that's nice. I'm glad you had a safe place. The fire station has always been that way for me—like a second home. We firefighters spend a lot of our lives here."

I sat down on the comfy bed, still looking around. "I

bet. Have you ever had an emergency where you had to get up during dinner?"

"Oh, all the time. I was in the shower once when the fire alarm went off. Got out with soap still in my hair to pull on my gear."

My cheeks burned at the thought of Henry in the shower, soaping up those muscles, but I hid it with a cough. "That's a funny image."

"There've been a lot of silly moments, that's for sure. But that's part of the job. Getting to save people makes it all worth it."

Henry had a lot of pride in his job—I could tell. But as I stared up at the wall of pictures, I noticed there wasn't one with his wife. Why wouldn't he put a picture of his spouse up?

"I'm renting a house a few blocks from here," Henry continued. "Chief Teller helped me find a place. Whereabouts are you?"

"Oh, over on Grover Street. I live with my grandma. It's a small town—we'll probably bump into each other a lot."

Henry shrugged. "I can think of worse things."

Was he...flirting with me? Despite wearing a wedding ring and looking appalled when Grandma suggested we grab coffee together? Huh.

I cleared my throat. "So, I'm curious about you. The mysterious new guy in town. Why did you pick New Harbor to move to? Of all places? It's pretty hard to find on a map."

Henry glanced out the window at the darkening sky, watching some cars drive past. "I don't know, seemed like a nice town. I wanted a change. Boston...it just didn't feel like home anymore, you know? I had to leave."

I had a feeling there was more to the story, but Henry was tight-lipped. What was he so cryptic about?

"Right. And you were a firefighter back in Boston?"

"Yep," he said, turning to me. "Always wanted to save people. I blame it on my mom letting me watch a lot of *Superman* growing up. Christopher Reeve is still the best one, by the way."

I laughed. "Agreed. Chief Teller told me you had lots of commendations for bravery back in Boston. Is that true?"

Henry blushed. "Yeah, I did. I doubt a small town like this will have a lot of emergencies, but you never know."

"And what about your wife or husband? Are they looking forward to it too?"

"My what?" Henry paused, blinking.

"You're wearing a wedding ring. What do they think of moving to a small town like this? What do they do?"

Before Henry could respond, a knock sounded on the door. I glanced over and realized it was Chief Teller. "Sorry to interrupt, folks, but we're all having cake and drinking tea. Would you care to join us?"

"Uh, yes, of course," Henry said, turning to me. "Ladies first."

I nodded, walking toward Chief Teller with Henry trailing behind. The fire chief was telling me about the station, but I was only half-listening. Why had Henry tensed up when I asked about his spouse?

After heading downstairs, we walked into the kitchen where Grandma was serving cake. I noticed the fortune she had baked into it. *You will embark on new beginnings.* I knew she probably put that in for Henry and his new job, but I felt like it was directed at me too.

"This cake is seriously incredible," Devon said, still

eating his slice. Then he winked at me. "Hats off to the chef. And her beautiful granddaughter."

"She *is* very beautiful, yes," Grandma agreed, nudging my shoulder. "Let me cut you a piece, darling. And you too Henry."

"Thank you," Henry said as I blushed, then he glared at Devon.

Devon didn't notice, eating his piece of cake while chatting with the firefighters. Grandma brought us a slice, then we chatted about the bakery. Henry excused himself with his plate of cake in his hands and approached Devon across the kitchen. From so far away, I couldn't hear what they were saying, but it looked tense. Then they stared at me for a few seconds before returning to their conversation.

Were they talking about me? No, they couldn't have been. What was there to say?

"...and Chief Teller asked us to cater his upcoming event," Grandma said, eating her slice beside me. "It's a party at town hall to celebrate firefighters and all the sacrifices they make."

"Oh, okay," I said, my eyes still on Henry. "Did you say yes?"

"Of course. I'd never turn down an opportunity to share your grandfather's delicious recipes. Say, darling...are you distracted by something? Or someone, perhaps?"

"Hmm?" I asked, snapping my head back to Grandma. "Oh, sorry. I was just looking at Henry. What do you think he's saying to Devon?"

Grandma craned her neck, looking over at Henry. He finished speaking to Devon who nodded and walked away.

"I have no idea," Grandma said, turning back to me. "You're quite smitten with Henry, aren't you? I've seen you stealing glances at him all night."

I blushed, setting down my empty plate. "I like him—he seems like a nice guy. But it's a moot point. The wedding ring is a dead-end."

"Hmm. I haven't heard him mention a spouse. Have you?"

I shook my head. "No, not at all. I asked about it upstairs—finding it strange he didn't have a picture of his partner on the wall—and he got all tense. Chief Teller interrupted before I could find out more."

"Strange," Grandma whispered. "Well, not to fear, my darling. Someone else will come along who catches your eye as much as Henry. Perhaps it'll be Jack or Ty?"

"Maybe," I said, forcing myself to look away from Henry. His energy was magnetic. "But no more Bumble dates. I think we should delete my profile. After tonight...I think I'm also done with speed dating forever."

Grandma sighed. "All right, dear, I'll take the profile down. You should've seen how many matches you got though. So many men were clamoring to know you."

"Really?"

She smiled. "Of course, sweetie. You're young, beautiful, kind, smart, *and* a talented baker. Who wouldn't want to know you?"

"Aw, thanks, Grandma. Let's hope I find more guys like Henry soon and less like Adrian."

"You never know what love has in store for you," Grandma said with a wink. "That's the best part."

And the scariest. When I glanced over at Henry, he was already staring at me. I blushed and looked away before Chief Teller grabbed his glass of water and tapped his fork against it.

"If I could have your attention?" he asked, then we hushed and looked at him. "Thank you all for coming and welcoming our latest firefighter, Henry Brant. He's already fitting in well. Your career's been impressive so far, Henry, and it's an honor to have you aboard. Now, would you like to say anything?"

Henry looked nervous, stepping forward. "Uh, thank you for this opportunity, Chief Teller. I've already met some great people in New Harbor and I'm really looking forward to working here. And eating lots of desserts."

Everyone laughed, including Chief Teller. "Yes, Esther's bakery is one of the perks of living here. Anyway, it's getting late and we should let you go home and rest."

"Thanks, I still have some unpacking to do," Henry said, setting his plate aside. "See you all soon. You too, Angie, Esther."

We smiled at him as he walked past, leaving the fire station. He got into his SUV outside and sped off. The firefighters working their shifts returned to exercising and killing time until they got an emergency call. Grandma started helping Chief Teller clean up the kitchen.

But I was still curious about what Henry had said to Devon. He was taking out the garbage so I followed him, stepping outside. The rain had stopped but it was still chilly so I tightened my sweater around my shoulders.

"Hey, Devon," I began as he dumped a bag of trash into the dumpster outside. "Do you have a sec?"

Devon looked uncomfortable, gesturing at the fire station. "I really should get back inside. Excuse me."

I frowned, wondering what had happened. Devon had gone from Flirt of the Year to barely looking my way. Had Henry said something to him?

"Wait!" I said, making Devon stop in his tracks. "I just...I wanted to know what Henry said to you before. It looked tense."

Way to be subtle, I chastised myself. But I really wanted to know.

But Devon didn't turn around. "It was nothing. Let's just say...you're lucky to have him looking out for you."

Devon opened the door to the fire station, disappearing inside. I stood outside in the chilly air and thought about what he had said. I was lucky? Really? I didn't even know Henry was looking out for me. I felt blindsided.

The door opened a second later, then Grandma stepped out with her purse. "Ah, there you are. I just finished helping Chief Teller clean the kitchen. Are we ready to head home?"

"Yeah, I guess," I said with a shrug. "What's on the agenda for tonight?"

Grandma reached into her purse, pulling out her keys. "I was thinking we could watch a romance movie on Hallmark, make some popcorn, and paint our nails. Just like old times."

I grinned. "Nowhere else I'd rather be, Grandma."

I headed to my truck, hopping in the driver's seat, excited to spend a night with Grandma. I followed her home through the dark streets but all I could think about was Henry. From his cryptic comments to the wedding ring and now saying something to Devon, that man was a mystery.

And a part of me liked it. I smacked my steering wheel while waiting at a red light, cursing him for already being married.

When we arrived home, I spent an evening with Grandma, chatting and watching movies like we used to. Nutmeg actually came down from Grandma's bed to cuddle with us. Her old bones were creaky and tired, but she still wanted to be near Grandma. Now *that* was true love.

Grandma deleted Bumble off her phone, taking my profile with it and all the matches I had gotten. I couldn't believe how many guys there were. But who was just looking for hook-ups and who was an actual hopeless romantic? It seemed like looking for a needle in a haystack. I still had Jack and Ty's numbers in my phone as I scrolled through, wondering if I should call them or not.

When morning rolled around, I ate breakfast with Grandma before driving to the bakery. We baked some desserts all morning and sold them before Mackenzie arrived after an early class. She was stressed out from her college course, so we tried to help. She was trying to learn Crème Brûlée—but it kept coming out either too hard on the surface or the pudding was too runny.

"Ugh, this is impossible!" Mackenzie cried. "I'm never going to learn this stupid recipe."

"Take a deep breath, dear. We'll help you figure it out," Grandma said. "The secret to Crème Brûlée is using egg yolks, not whole eggs. I think that's where you're going wrong. Come, I'll show you. Angie, you should get to Estelle's for your lunch with Sonya."

"Oh, crap!" I said, staring at the clock on the wall and removing my apron. "I totally forgot. You going to be okay, Mackenzie?"

She sighed and nodded, wiping flour off her face. "Yeah, I think so. I've got the best baker in town to help me ace this course."

"Hardly, dear, but I'm flattered," Grandma said with a smile. "I'll make you some tea before we try again. Let me know how your lunch goes, hmm?"

I nodded, walking out of the kitchen and heading to my truck. I was eager to see Sonya—and learn what was so urgent.

Chapter Eight

I drove to Estelle's through the afternoon traffic, taking backroads to avoid all the people out for lunch. I pulled into the parking lot behind the busy restaurant and rushed toward the doors. People were always there—morning, afternoon, and night—because of its delicious food. Expensive, but delicious.

When I entered the upper-class restaurant, the host in a black suit behind a desk welcomed me. "Good afternoon, miss. Do you have a reservation?"

"I'm here to meet a friend, actually. Sonya Livingston," I replied. "We're supposed to have lunch."

"Ah, very good. Ms. Livingston's here already. She's just this way," the host said, picking up a spare menu. "Please, follow me."

I nodded, walking down a red carpet through dozens of other tables. People were eating their lunch and gossiping over mimosas. I noticed some familiar faces from the night Adrian broke up with me—and judging by their murmurs, they recognized me too.

Damn small towns. You couldn't sneeze without someone noticing.

The host led me to the back of the restaurant where Sonya was sitting, looking over her menu. The sunlight from the window beside her shone in and made her look even more beautiful. She was always gorgeous—olive skin, honey eyes, and a smooth complexion with dark, shiny hair—but the light made her look ethereal. When you factored in how smart and funny she was, it was no wonder she had a committed boyfriend.

I tried not to be jealous as I sat down, smiling. "Hey, Sonya. Long time no see."

Her eyes lit up. "Angie! God, you haven't changed a bit. It's so good to see you."

She leaned over the table, hugging me as the host left the menu and walked away to check on other guests. Sonya sat back in her seat, grinning at me.

"Same here," I replied, smelling her vanilla perfume. "So, how have you been?"

"I've been great. Work's been busy," she said, then I heard her phone buzzing in the black purse next to her. "See? Probably another client wanting to book my services."

"Wedding planning seems popular around here," I said, placing a napkin over my lap. "I'm glad it's going well."

"Thanks, me too. It's like everyone is getting married and having kids these days."

Everyone except me. Sonya didn't mean to hurt me with that comment, but it still stung a little. Okay, a *lot*. We were going to need some drinks. The strong, alcoholic kind.

"Anyway, we can get back to me in a sec," she said, grinning again. "How are you doing? How's the bakery and your cute little grandma?"

"She's great—as much as she can be now that Grandpa's gone. We've been running the bakery together and it's been doing well. Enough to pay the bills, which is all we really need. And the occasional spa day."

"Aw, that's so awesome. Does she still look the same?"

I laughed. "Oh, yeah—down to the curly white hair. Some things never change. How's your family? And James?"

"Everyone's good. Healthy and happy. James, too," she said, raising a hand as a waitress walked by. "Excuse me? Can we have one bottle of champagne, please?"

The waitress nodded, scurrying away to fetch the bottle in the kitchen as I raised an eyebrow. "Champagne? Wow, that's fancy. What are we celebrating?"

She reached for her purse, beaming. Her pearly-white teeth were almost mesmerizing. "Well, you have to promise not to tell anyone. We're being quiet about it for now."

She pulled something out of her purse, then lifted her hand. My eyes widened when I noticed it was an engagement ring. And the rock was huge—probably very expensive. The light from the window bounced off the diamond and nearly blinded me.

"James proposed!" she whispered, giggling. "His medical practice has been going really well, so he said he could save up for the biggest diamond he could find. Isn't it gorgeous?"

"It really is," I said, reaching for her hand. "That's amazing. I'm so happy for you."

"Thanks," she said, removing the ring and stashing it back in her purse. "But like I said, we're keeping it quiet. My sister, Rachel, is pregnant. Twins. We don't want to announce our engagement right now and upstage her moment."

I gawked. "Your *little* sister Rachel? Who's three years younger? I didn't even know she was dating."

"She eloped last year with her boyfriend on a trip to Maui. Didn't I tell you?" Sonya asked, then I shook my head. "Oh, sorry. Like I said, work's been hectic. I barely have time for myself most days. But yeah, Rachel eloped and now she's pregnant. I'm going to be an aunt."

I smiled. "That's wonderful—I know you'll be an amazing aunt. Totally not the kind to feed their nieces and nephews tons of sugar and send them home to Mom and Dad. That's what I'd do."

Sonya snorted. "Of course you would. But yeah, I'm really happy for Rachel. You'll probably see her at the engagement party and then the wedding. Which I wanted to talk to you about."

The waitress returned, setting down the bottle of champagne with a smile. "Here you go. Care to order?"

"Just give us one moment, please," Sonya said, then the waitress nodded and checked on another table. "I wanted your bakery to cater the engagement party. And the wedding. I pulled a few strings and got the venue set in one month. I know that might be too soon for some of our guests, but we're just so excited."

I reached for a glass of champagne, my eyes wide. "In one month? That's soon. Say when, by the way."

Sonya shrugged as I filled her glass. "Why wait? When. Thanks so much."

I nodded as she lifted her glass, sipping the champagne. I filled my glass and took a long sip, needing it after everything that was happening. So much change. And like usual, I was the last one to find a boyfriend.

"What do you say?" Sonya asked. "Will you do it? I'm

going to pay you and your grandma too—I don't expect it for free."

I smiled. "Well, how could we turn down a paying customer? Of course we'll cater your engagement party and wedding. Whatever you need."

"Eep, thank you!" Sonya said, leaning across the table to hug me again. I nearly ate some of her hair that smelled like strawberries. "That's a big weight off my shoulders. And this way, you'll get to promote your business too. It's a win-win. And you can finally meet James!"

I nodded, glancing down at my menu. "Can't wait—I've heard so much about him."

"Oh, you'll love him. He's so sweet. And a doctor. What more could you want?"

I faked a smile, thinking back to my dating life. Or lack thereof. Why couldn't I find a doctor?

"So, what's good for lunch around here?" I asked, still scanning the menu and changing the subject. "I usually only come here for dinner."

Sonya paused, reading the menu for a moment. "I think I heard someone say the salmon was fantastic. But I'm going to eat light—probably get the tangerine salad. I'm trying to diet before the wedding."

Since I had no wedding, I looked for the meal with the most calories on the menu. The steak sounded pretty good. The waitress returned a second later, taking our orders before she grabbed our menus and headed for the kitchen. I poured myself another glass of champagne.

"Anyway, thanks for agreeing to meet me on such short notice," Sonya said. "Hope I didn't pull you away too much from the bakery."

I shook my head, taking another sip of my champagne.

"Nah, it's all good. My grandma and Mackenzie, our other employee, have it under control."

Sonya sipped her champagne, a smile breaking out across her face. "Are you still putting little fortunes into the desserts? Edible paper, wasn't it? I remember your grandpa being obsessed with it."

"We are—Grandma's mostly the one who writes it all out. She gets a real kick out of it. I think the customers do, too. It keeps them coming back for more. Something that sets us apart from the other bakeries."

"Well, that's good. Glad to hear it's all working out. You know, I miss your grandpa so much. He was a sweet man."

"Yeah," I said, glancing down. "And loyal to Grandma. They just don't make men like him anymore."

"I used to think that too, before I found James," Sonya said, her eyes twinkling. "He changed my mind. I now fully believe that love and good people exist. Speaking of which, how's your dating life going? Are you still seeing Adrian? I remember you telling me about him in passing a while back. When you first met."

My cheeks burned, embarrassed. "No, we aren't together anymore. Actually, he just broke up with me."

Sonya gasped. "Oh. Oh, crap. Angie, I'm so sorry. I didn't know—"

"No, it's okay," I interrupted. "Things with him never felt right, anyway. Even my grandma thinks it's for the best."

"Your grandma's a smart woman," Sonya said, taking another sip of her champagne. "She's probably right. What happened between you two? Unless you don't want to talk about it, in which case I'll shut my mouth."

"He said he wasn't ready for a commitment. But then

the waitress told me he was seeing other women. Even brought in a blonde to our bakery yesterday."

Sonya shook her head. "What a scumbag. Seriously, I agree with your grandma—you're clearly better off. The right person won't treat you like that. James has always been good to me."

"I'm happy for you," I said, swallowing my jealousy. "You deserve the best."

Sonya smiled, placing her hand on mine. "And so do you, Angie. Really. You'll get there—just give it time. Anyone else you're interested in?"

I snorted. "You're not going to believe this, but Grandma set up a Bumble profile for me. I just went to a speed dating thing last night with a bunch of guys. Grandma can barely get her laptop to work so I was surprised she had me on an app."

"Wow, she's dedicated," Sonya said, and I nodded. "I'm sure she just wants you to be happy. Meet anyone promising?"

"Hell no," I said, almost laughing. "All the guys were... just not marriage material. I did meet two other guys, though. Jack, a businessman who works from home, and Ty, a teacher. More men that Grandma tried to set me up with."

"Damn, she's been working overtime," Sonya joked. "Have you gone out with them yet?"

"No, but I have their numbers in my phone. I guess I could call them."

"Yes, definitely!" Sonya cried. "Give it a shot. What do you have to lose?"

I shifted in my seat. "It's just...I don't know. Like I said, none of them seem right. There was this one guy I was interested in, but..."

"But what?"

Before I could respond, the front door to the restaurant opened. And to my surprise, Henry walked in. He spoke with the host who led him past our table. He noticed me, giving me a slight smile as he followed the host and sat down.

"Hello? Earth to Angie?" Sonya asked, waving her hand in front of my face. "You okay?"

"Huh? Oh, right. Sorry," I said, playing with my napkin nervously. "Like I was saying, the guy I have a crush on... he's married."

Sonya cringed. "Oof, that's a big no-no. He's off the market, sorry."

"I agree. Sadly," I said, looking down. Then I gestured across the restaurant. "He's right over there, actually. Just walked in."

Sonya turned her head, noticing Henry sitting at a table by himself. He was looking over the menu quietly.

"Wow," Sonya said, still staring at Henry. "Don't tell James but...damn, that is one fine male specimen. I love the Henry Cavill vibes he's got going on. Real mysterious."

"Funny enough, his name is Henry too," I joked. "Feels cruel that the universe would send him my way only for him to be married."

"I know," Sonya said, reaching for my hand. "I'm so sorry, Angie. But hey, look at it this way—maybe you're meant to find someone even better?"

"Yeah, maybe. I'll be seeing Henry a lot since he just moved to town. He's a firefighter. So I'll have to keep my little crush under wraps."

"A firefighter?" Sonya made a sound of agreement in her throat. "Every woman's fantasy, really. Mmm..."

I laughed. “I don’t even want to know what perverted thoughts you’re having right now.”

“No, you really, really don’t.”

Sonya snorted, then we shared a laugh for a moment. It felt just like old times—two carefree kids with no responsibilities. Back then, there wasn’t anything I didn’t know about Sonya. Now I felt like a stranger in her life.

“I missed this,” I said when the laughter died down. “Us.”

Sonya smiled. “Me too. We really need to meet up more, no matter how much work keeps us busy.”

“Agreed. Well, now that you’re getting married, all the catering I’ll be doing might bring us closer together.”

“True. Your bakery saves the day,” Sonya joked, sipping her champagne. “All right, I want to order now. Where’s our waitress?”

As if on cue, the waitress approached, carrying a notepad with her. We gave our orders—Sonya wanted the salad and I wanted the steak for lunch—before the waitress took our menus back to the kitchen. We passed the time by chatting and catching up, talking about our families and hobbies.

“...and Nutmeg?” Sonya asked. “How’s that old kitty doing? Still alive?”

“Thankfully, yes. That old girl’s still going strong.”

“Aw, I’m glad. She’s a sweet girl. You know, me and James were thinking about getting an animal. Maybe a dog from the shelter...”

As Sonya went on about adopting a pet, I noticed a red-haired woman in a pantsuit enter the restaurant. She was beautiful—and very tall, carrying a briefcase. She glanced around before noticing Henry and rushing to his table. He looked up with a smile as she sat down across from him.

My stomach dropped. Was that his wife? She was gorgeous. But why didn't he have any pictures of her above his bunkbed?

She opened her briefcase on the table, pulling out some paperwork before Henry read them over. I couldn't tell what was written on the papers. When I glanced up, Sonya was still talking, not realizing that I hadn't been listening.

"...and I think it'll be good practice for when we have kids," Sonya said. "Maybe start with a pet. Or, hell, knowing my luck, I'd be better off getting a plant. If I can keep that alive, then maybe I'll be ready."

I smiled. "You'll be a great mother, Sonya. Trust me."

She beamed. "Thanks, Ang. It's really so great to catch up. And hey, there's our food. Good—I'm starving."

The waitress walked over, setting down our plates. My steak looked delicious, but I didn't have much of an appetite. I was still upset seeing Henry with his wife. For some reason, that really bothered me.

When the front doors to the restaurant opened, I groaned, noticing Lucy and her husband walking in. They didn't notice us as the host led them to another table. Sonya noticed my stare, turning her neck.

"What are you looking at?" she asked. "Henry again?"

"No, not this time. Check it out—it's the mean girl of the century," I grumbled. "Lucy. Lucy Rhett. You remember her?"

"How could I forget?" Sonya rolled her eyes. "Homecoming *and* drama queen. I really didn't think she and that high school quarterback would still be together. Guess I lost that bet."

"Yeah, it's surprising. I guess they love each other," I said, trying not to feel envious. "And she's still as horrible as ever. Came over yesterday to tell us our neon sign was too bright. Was a total bitch about it too. She's even been trying to buy our shop."

"Oh my gosh," Sonya said, shoveling lettuce into her mouth. "Can't she mind her own business?"

"Apparently not. Remember when we used to make fun of her?"

"Of course," Sonya said with a smile. "And she deserved it. She was so rude to everyone. I'm so glad we're out of high school."

I nodded, taking a bite of my steak, and I felt a tap on my shoulder. And it wasn't someone I wanted to see when I turned my head.

Chapter Nine

Jim stood there, the muscular guy from the round of speed dating. At least, I thought that was his name—I wasn't really sure since I hadn't felt a connection to him. I had barely thought about those guys again. He wore blue jeans with sneakers and a plain white tee to show off his muscular arms.

"Hey, Angie," he began. "I thought that was you."

"Oh, hello," I replied. "Jim, right?"

He nodded. "That's right. Glad you remembered me. It's good to see you again."

"Um, who is this?" Sonya asked, clearing her throat.

"This is Jim," I said as I gestured between them. "He was one of the men I met at the round of speed dating my grandma set up. Jim, this is my best friend, Sonya."

I didn't really want to introduce them to one another—especially when I had no plans to pursue any kind of relationship with Jim—but it felt rude if I didn't. Sonya narrowed her eyes, having the same reservations about this guy as I did.

"Hey, nice to meet one of Angie's friends," Jim said.

Then he turned back to me. "We didn't have much time to talk at the speed dating event. I'm glad I ran into you—now I can ask for your number in person. Maybe we can grab some coffee or something?"

Sonya looked awkward, sipping her champagne as I sighed. "Jim...while that's a nice offer, I'll have to say no. But thank you."

"What?" he asked, his eyes wide. "Come on—we'd be great together. And I thought we got along well last night. I even made you laugh."

"Well, I'm sorry," I began, "but I'm not sure I really want a relationship. Thanks for coming to the event though, and I wish you all the best in finding a partner."

I thought that would be enough to make him go away, but Jim hung around. "Seriously? That's it? You barely even know me! Look, why don't we just grab one coffee? I'll tell you a little bit more about myself and then you can decide if you want to know me better. It's only fair."

"She already said no," Sonya said. "How many more times does she have to say it?"

"I wasn't talking to you," Jim hissed. "Stay out of it."

I rose to my feet. "Don't talk to her like that. I want nothing to do with you, Jim, so go away. I won't ask you again."

But Jim didn't back down. He got right in my face, close enough where I could smell his breath. He must've had a protein smoothie for breakfast. He was a foot taller than me but I didn't flinch.

"You know, this is so typical," he sneered. "You women wouldn't know what a good man looks like. You're all too busy chasing after playboys who just use you for sex and break your heart!"

As Jim's voice got louder, people in the restaurant began

to look over at us. I was embarrassed. The last thing I wanted was another bad time at Estelle's.

"Look, I'm a good guy," Jim continued. "Why can't you see that? Why won't you go out with me?"

I didn't know what to say. Sonya didn't either, though I saw her reaching for her champagne glass to use as a weapon if things got out of hand. Smart. Before I could respond, I heard footsteps approaching.

"Everything okay over here?"

When I spun around, it was Henry. And he was glancing between me and Jim. Maybe we'd finally get rid of this guy.

"No, everything's not fine," Jim hissed. "All I want is one date with this broad. Why won't you just say yes?"

"Because I don't want to," I replied honestly. "And if this is the way you treat women who say no, I can see why you're still single."

Jim balled his fists, his muscles rippling under his shirt. "You don't know anything about me—"

"I think it's time for you to leave," Henry interrupted, inching closer. "Go work out or something and leave Angie alone."

"And who the hell are you?" Jim asked. "Her boyfriend?"

I blushed, feeling my cheeks getting hot. How I wished.

"Just a concerned party," Henry replied, "and a new friend. So unless you want me to get the police involved, I think you should respect the lady's wishes and leave. Right now."

"Or what?" Jim shot back. "What are you going to do? Hit me? Give me a break. I don't know why you're defending this whore anyway—"

Henry lunged forward, punching Jim across the jaw. He

staggered back and fell into a table behind us filled with old ladies. They gasped and rose to their feet, grabbing their purses before stepping back. Jim picked himself up and spun around. His lip was bleeding hard.

"You'll regret that," Jim said, wiping blood off his mouth. "Trust me."

"What's going on over here?" the host asked as he rushed over. "Do I need to call the police?"

"Nah, our uninvited guest was just leaving," Henry said, his jaw clenching in anger. "Don't let the door hit you on the way out."

I thought Jim might hit Henry back, but he just sneered. He rushed toward the door, vanishing down the sidewalk. Everyone in the restaurant was staring and murmuring when I looked around.

"I'm so sorry about that," Henry said to the host. "He wouldn't leave my friend alone and I just kinda...lost it."

The host sighed. "That's all right. But please, try to keep things civil. This is a respectable restaurant. I'll let the owner know that man is not to be let back inside."

"Thank you," I said with a nod as the host scurried away, then turned to Henry. "That was...something."

Henry sighed. "Yeah, I know. Sorry—it just pisses me off when I see a man disrespecting a woman like that. Especially with...with my history."

I didn't know what Henry was talking about and I didn't want to pry. "Well, thanks. We're grateful you were here. Is your hand all right?"

"Oh, this?" Henry asked, holding up his reddening fist. "Yeah, it'll be fine. Nothing I can't handle. I've hurt myself worse rescuing twin babies from a burning apartment once."

I tried not to swoon. "Wow, that's incredible. Well done."

"Just doing my job. Don't worry about me. You two okay?"

"We're fine," I said with a nod. "Again, thanks for coming to our rescue. We really owe you one."

"Don't worry about it," Henry said, turning to Sonya. "Hello there. I don't believe we've met."

"No, we haven't," Sonya said as she held out a hand. "But I've heard a lot about you. I'm Sonya Livingston, Angie's best friend."

"Henry Brant," Henry said, shaking her hand. "Hope I didn't scare either of you too much. I usually don't use my fists like that—I swear."

"We believe you," Sonya said with a nod. "Thanks for that. That guy was just not taking a hint."

"Yeah, I could see that. I smelled trouble as soon as he approached you," Henry said, turning to me. "Who was he?"

"Oh, one of the guys at the speed dating thing my grandma set up for me. He was mad I wouldn't go out with him. He was pissed off last night too."

Henry shook his head. "He seems dangerous. Unstable. You should stay away from him—just to be on the safe side."

"Trust me, I'll keep my distance. But he threatened you. He said you'll regret punching him. You think he meant it?"

Henry shrugged. "I don't know. If he's smart, he'll keep his distance. Or I'll have Chief Teller get the cops to throw him in a cell. That might knock some sense into him. If my punch didn't do that already."

"I don't know," I said, staring at the door where Jim had

left in a hurry. "That guy didn't look like he had any sense at all. More muscles than brains."

"Fortunately, I have both," Henry joked, making me smile.

"That you do," I replied, checking out his shoulders. I averted my eyes when he noticed I was staring and quickly cleared my throat. "So, um, anyway...what are you doing here?"

"Oh, just some...stuff," Henry said, cryptically. "Chief Teller told me to explore New Harbor for a few days. You know, get familiar with the town. I thought it couldn't hurt."

"If you're looking for a tour guide, Angie could show you around," Sonya piped up. "She knows New Harbor like the back of her hand."

Henry looked uncomfortable, glancing between us. "Oh, uh...I'll let you know if I need any help."

I heard high heels clicking on the tile of the restaurant, heading toward us. The woman with the briefcase walked over and tapped Henry on the shoulder.

"Henry? Is everything all right?" she asked.

He turned to her. "Yeah, don't worry. Just a little misunderstanding."

"With your fists?"

Henry snorted. "Okay, maybe a *big* misunderstanding. But it's all good now."

She eyed him, looking disappointed. "Uh-huh. Anyway, if you're done punching people, we should get going. We have some things to clear up. I already paid our bill so we can leave anytime."

"Right," Henry said, turning to me. "Well, see you around, Angie. If that guy comes back, let me know, all right?"

"Will do. And thanks again."

"Bye, nice meeting you," Sonya said as Henry and the woman left the restaurant, disappearing outside.

I sat back down, reaching for my drink. "Well, this has been a fun lunch."

Sonya snorted. "You're telling me. You know, Henry came to your defense pretty fast. Barely looked my way, in fact."

I blushed. "Please, he's a married man. He was probably just making sure I was okay. And what was with you trying to get me to be his tour guide?"

"Hey, what's wrong with that? There's no harm in being friends. Anyway, think about what I said. Going out with Jack or Ty—or even both—could be good for you."

I shrugged, still thinking about Henry. Maybe going out with someone new was the only way to get him off my mind.

"And don't worry about lunch," Sonya said, setting money down on the table. "It's on me. After everything that happened with that muscular lunatic, it's the least I can do. Now, I have to get back to work, but be careful out there, all right? With dating *and* this Jim guy on the loose. It can be dangerous being a woman in today's world. Lunch just proved that unfortunate fact."

"Got it. I will," I said with a nod. "I'll say the same to you. James better be watching over you."

"He is. My personal Superman," Sonya said with a smile. "See you around, Ang. I promise—we'll keep in touch. Can't wait to see you at the engagement party!"

I waved as she left the restaurant, then I gave the money to the waiter and grabbed my things. People were still murmuring and staring as I left the restaurant. I glanced down the street, looking for Jim, but he was gone—for now. Phew.

Once I'd walked into the parking lot and got into my truck, I pulled out my smartphone. I stared at Jack and Ty's names on my phone for a minute. I chose randomly, landing on Ty, and opened a message.

"This is only to get over Henry," I whispered to myself. "Maybe Ty's the one. As Grandma would say, who knows?"

Before I could stop myself, I typed out a text and sent it to Ty's number. *Hey, this is Angie,* I wrote. *Are you free for coffee or something? Doesn't have to be today. My schedule is flexible.*

Ty's response was almost instant. *I'm at work right now but I'm on my lunch break,* he texted back. *I could see you right now if you'd like? You could meet some of my amazing students.*

A date at school? I had been on worse. I heard both Grandma and Sonya's voices in my head, telling me to go for it, and they became too loud to resist.

Sounds good, I texted back. *Just send me the address and I'll be on my way. I've got some time now.*

Ty quickly sent me the address for his school, then I pulled out of the parking lot of Estelle's. That restaurant was leaving a bad taste in my mouth lately. I drove down the busy street, heading to the elementary just outside town. It was the only one around for miles.

When I pulled into the parking lot of Mae Jemison Elementary, I noticed Ty in the schoolyard, playing basketball with some young students. He looked handsome in his slacks, cardigan, tweed blazer, and dress shoes. I got out, smiling as I headed into the courtyard. I pushed open the gate and walked over.

Ty was obviously bigger and faster than those little kids,

but he still let them beat him. He clapped when one of the girls threw the basketball into the hoop, her team cheering.

"Nice one, Lindsay! You're killing it!" he called out, raising his hand for a high five. "Up top!"

The little girl grinned, high-fiving his hand. Ty was great with kids, I realized. All green flags.

When he noticed me, he gestured at his students. "Hey, kids—I'd like you to meet someone special. This is Angie Linden."

Someone special? I smiled at that.

"Is she your girlfriend?" one of the girls in the crowd asked.

While I blushed, Ty glanced at me. "She's just a friend, Charlotte. For now. Anyway, Angie and her grandma own a bakery called Lucky's Baked Goods."

"I've been there!" one of the boys called out. "My mom takes me there every year when I get my report card. I love their cupcakes."

"Aw, thank you," I said with a smile. "Tell you what? Next time you're there, you and your mom can get two free cupcakes."

"Really? Cool!" the boy cried, looking excited. Then he turned to Ty. "Can we have a field trip there soon, Mr. Wilson? Please, please, please?"

When the other students started to beg, he laughed. "All right—I'll consider it. Just gotta convince Principal Sutter. Anyway, why don't you all play another round? I'll watch from the sidelines. You got this!"

The students nodded, playing basketball amongst themselves. Ty walked over to stand next to me as he watched his students.

"I love my kids," Ty finally said. "Nothing better than watching them learn and grow."

"They seem pretty awesome," I said with a smile. "I think you're doing a great job."

"Thank you. I hope so," he said, turning to me. "Anyway, thanks for coming last minute. I'm sure an elementary school isn't high on your dream date list."

I laughed. "Hey, it's not the worst place to be. It beats getting dumped in a fancy restaurant any day."

"Ouch. I've been there too. So, how have you been?"

"Good, good. Met up with an old friend for lunch. Kinda lost touch when she got a boyfriend but we're hanging out again. How's your day been so far?"

"Great—spending time with my students always makes me happy. And it's really nice to see you again, Angie. I'm glad you texted."

"Yeah, same here. So...when were you planning to tell me my grandma was the one who told you about me?"

Ty laughed. "So you found out? Sorry, didn't mean to keep it from you. Your grandma's a sweet woman—and she really talked you up on Bumble. She wanted me to keep it quiet for now so it wouldn't scare you off. From what I hear, you're a lovely lady. But unlucky in love apparently?"

I sighed. "Yeah, very unlucky. How about you?"

"Well, I had to turn to online dating. So things are pretty dire," Ty said with a chuckle. "My parents have been bugging me to get married and have kids. And it would be nice to have someone. I just turned thirty-two so I'm looking for a real connection now."

"I completely agree. Boy, that wind is chilly..."

I shivered, wishing I had brought something warmer. Ty removed his blazer and slung it over my shoulders. "There you go. Better?"

"Much, thank you," I said, clinging to the blazer. "I really need to start dressing warmer."

"No worries. Why don't we head inside and get some coffee? We can chat a bit more in there. And warm up."

"Sure, sounds great. But what about your kids?"

"They're on recess. See that monitor over there? Should be fine for another twenty minutes," he said, checking his watch. "After you."

He gestured toward the front doors of the school, then I nodded and walked with him. So far, things were going great with Ty. I tried to push all my fears and doubts—and crush on Henry—out of my mind as I entered the school with him, his blazer snug around my shoulders.

Chapter Ten

Ty took me around the whole school, showing me the classrooms and introducing me to some teacher friends. He didn't really know what to label us yet. New friends that might evolve into something more? We were sticking with that. As the students greeted him, high-fiving and fist-bumping Ty, I realized he was very popular.

"All the kids seem to love you," I said as we walked down the hall. "How'd you manage that? Bribe them with chocolate?"

Ty laughed. "No, nothing like that. I just listen—try to be there for them. All these kids want is someone to see them for who they really are. So that's what I try to do."

I smiled. "That's lovely. No wonder you're their favorite."

Whenever we talked about his students, Ty had a big smile on his face. I could tell he loved them—and that was very attractive. There was nothing hotter than a man who was good with kids.

"Thanks. I hope I've made this school a safe place for

them," he began, pausing at a classroom. "School...wasn't always a safe haven for me as a kid. I was bullied a lot."

I frowned. "I'm sorry. Me and my best friend, Sonya, were the butt of people's jokes too. Especially this one mean girl, Lucy Rhett."

Ty paused. "That name sounds familiar. Do I know her?"

"You might—she runs The Green Machine. You know that uber-healthy salad and smoothie bar downtown?"

"Ah, that's right. I think I got a green juice before work one time. And you know what? It wasn't even that good. And very overpriced."

I snorted. "Sounds about right. Is this your classroom?"

"Yep," Ty said, pointing inside. "Go ahead in, I'll give you the tour."

When I stepped inside, I spotted motivational posters everywhere. He also had his kids write summaries of who they were before posting them on the walls. I noticed an LGBTQ+ flag on the wall as Ty sat at his burgundy desk.

"Nice flag," I said, pointing at the wall.

"Thanks. Like I said, I try to make all my students feel welcome. Especially the ones who are different."

"I have no doubt they're very proud to have you as a teacher." He smiled at that. "So, we've already established you're handsome, looking for something serious, and great with kids. You also know how to dress and you're respectful. You seem like the perfect man to me. What's the catch?"

Ty laughed. "Hey, I'm not perfect. I've got flaws like everyone else. Like being obsessed with my job, for starters. I don't feel truly alive unless I'm spending time with my students."

"Unless you just haven't found the right person, yet

who can make you feel that way," I said with a shrug. "Ooh, it's a bit chilly in here. Can I have that coffee I was promised?"

"Absolutely," Ty said, gesturing at the door. "Follow me."

He took me to the break room down the hall, inviting me to sit on one of the leather couches. I looked at the class photos on the wall as Ty poured us both a cup of coffee at the coffee machine. He brought the mug over to me, the steam billowing above it as he sat down across from me.

"Be careful, that's super hot," he said. "Might have to give it a minute."

"Then we can chat to pass the time," I said, setting the cup of coffee down on the nearby table. "What was your upbringing like?"

"Typical. Two parents, lots of aunts and uncles, a little sister. We were happy. I just wish my parents weren't so pushy about me getting married and having kids."

That reminded me of my grandma. "Yeah, I get that. Are you sure you want that, or are you just pressured by them?"

"No, I definitely want to get married and have kids," Ty said, filling me with a sense of relief. "I just wish my parents would let me do it on my own time, you know? I don't think love can be rushed. It's delicate."

"I agree," I said with a smile. "What's your favorite thing about love?"

"Oh, man," Ty said, leaning back. "That's a hard question. Probably...the connection. I think that's what we're all searching for in life. I want a partner who gets me as much as I get them."

Green flags everywhere. The more I talked to Ty, the

more I liked him. I was barely thinking about Henry anymore.

"What about you?" Ty asked.

"Same thing. I want a partner who's my best friend at the same time. It has to be more than just physical."

"Friends to lovers is my favorite romance novel trope," Ty said with a laugh. "How was your upbringing?"

I cringed. "Not that great. My parents had a messy divorce—and they still don't get along to this day. When I was ten, I moved in with my grandparents. They were sweet, though. I love all the time I've spent with them."

"And I heard your grandpa passed away last year, right? I'm so sorry. That has to be hard."

"Yeah, it is. The house and bakery are just so empty without him. I'm hoping he'll send someone great my way —throw me a bone. Who knows, maybe he already has."

As Ty smiled at me, the door to the break room opened and footsteps echoed inside. When Ty turned his head, noticing who it was, he rose to his feet immediately and looked a bit nervous. It was a man—handsome and young in his mid-thirties, wearing a suit with neatly combed black hair.

"Principal Sutter," Ty stammered. "Good afternoon."

"Afternoon, Ty. How're the kids?"

"Doing well. They've been learning nouns and adjectives. They're really getting the hang of it."

"Ah, that's good." The principal noticed me, then gestured at Ty. "Who is this?"

"Angie. Angie Linden," Ty introduced. Then he hesitated, searching for a label. "She's…"

"A new friend," I said, rising to my feet and holding out a hand. "Hello, nice to meet you, Principal Sutter. Ty was just giving me a tour of the school."

"Oh, I see. A pleasure," Principal Sutter said as he shook my hand. "Well, don't mind me. I'm just grabbing a coffee before heading back to my office."

The principal pushed past us, walking toward the coffee machine. He poured himself a mug as Ty stared at his back. The break room turned silent. Once Principal Sutter had his coffee, he nodded at us, then stepped into the hallway and vanished. Ty was still staring after him.

I cleared my throat. "So, that was your principal?"

"Hmm? Oh, yeah," Ty said, tearing his gaze away from the door to look at me. "Principal Craig Sutter. He's the one who hired me. A great man—I really admire him."

"I hope he didn't mind I was in the break room."

"Don't worry—he's pretty cool. You aren't in trouble or anything." When the bell rang above our heads, Ty rose to his feet. "Well, I have to get back to class. I'm teaching math now. But I had a great time with you, Angie."

I smiled as I stood up, grabbing my coffee. "Yeah, same here. And thanks for the free coffee. Hope your afternoon classes go well."

"Thank you. Come on—I'll show you out."

I nodded, following Ty out of the break room. Students were starting to come in from recess and looked excited to see Ty. They all stopped him to chat in the hallway, nearly swarming him. I just laughed.

"Don't worry about walking me out—I'll find my way," I yelled over the crowd of chattering students. "See you later, Ty!"

"Bye, Angie!" he called out, the kids still asking him questions and demanding his attention.

When Principal Sutter walked by, chatting with another teacher, Ty's gaze immediately went to him. Why did he stare at the principal so much? I wondered about that as I followed the directions on the walls to the exit.

I stepped outside, entering the empty courtyard to head to my truck. As I did, I got a text from my grandma. *Can you pick up some chicken at the store? I want to make shake and bake for dinner tonight and I think ours expired in the fridge. If you aren't still with Sonya.*

Sure thing, I texted back. *I'll buy it and bring it home before coming back to the bakery.*

Grandma sent a heart emoji, then I put the truck in drive and headed to the grocery store. I parked in the back, then headed inside and grabbed a basket. As I turned around, I bumped into something tall and strong.

"Oh, sorry!" I called out.

When I looked up, it was Henry, also carrying a basket with some groceries inside. "No problem—I wasn't looking where I was going. Oh, Angie, it's you."

"We run into each other a lot," I joked. "Guess we should get used to it in a small town. You out shopping too?"

"Yeah, just for a few things," he said, gesturing at his basket. I noticed the basics inside—bread, eggs, milk, and flour. "I've got nothing in my fridge at the moment. Chief Teller's given me a few days to get settled."

"That's nice of him. And thanks again for saving me and Sonya from Jim earlier."

"No problem—it was the least I could do. You haven't seen him again, have you?"

"Nope. Have you?"

"Not at all," he said, shaking his head. "Let's hope it stays that way. Or he'll have another punch waiting for him."

I laughed. "Your poor hand. So...are you shopping alone?"

I looked around for the woman he was with at the restaurant, but I didn't see her anywhere. Henry was still wearing the ring on his left finger.

He looked confused. "Yeah, I am. Why wouldn't I be?"

Before I could respond, my phone buzzed. I pulled it out, wondering if it was Grandma telling me something important, but it was only a text from Ty. It read: *Get home safely. Had a great time with you.*

I smiled, texting back that I would when Henry cleared his throat. "Who's that?"

"Oh, just someone I met the other day," I said, putting my phone back in my pocket. "Ty Wilson. He's an elementary school teacher. Spent time with him today."

Henry looked visibly uncomfortable. "Oh...oh, I see. Well, I should get going—"

A group of men turned around the corner, all wearing firefighter uniforms, and I realized they were the men I had met at Henry's welcoming party. It looked like they were buying food and supplies for the fire station. Their eyes lit up when they noticed Henry, patting him on the shoulder. At least they were all getting along.

"Hey, new guy," Devon said. "You settling into New Harbor all right?"

"So far, so good," Henry replied. "Looking forward to joining you on duty in a few days."

"We could always use the help." Devon noticed me, his smile fading. "Uh, excuse me."

He scurried away, heading down another aisle to pick up a can of beans. I found it strange how charismatic Devon had gone with me to barely looking my way. What had Henry said to him?

"So, you and Chief Teller make up yet?" another firefighter asked Henry. "We heard him tearing you a new one on the phone earlier. Sounded brutal."

"What happened?" I asked, frowning.

Henry scratched the back of his neck. "Word spread about how I punched Jim earlier. Chief Teller called me, told me he was angry and disappointed, and said a few choice words."

"Oh," I said, sadly. "I'm so sorry. I didn't mean to get you into any trouble."

Henry shook his head. "It's all right, Angie—it wasn't your fault. I'd do it again in a heartbeat."

"Word spreads fast in a small town like this," one of the firefighters said. "You'll learn that soon. Hope you don't get fired before your first shift. Anyway, see you soon."

Henry said goodbye to the firefighters, letting them finish shopping before heading back to the station. Devon barely looked my way as he left with them. I found it strange, though I still felt bad about Henry getting chewed out by Chief Teller.

"I can talk to him. Chief Teller, I mean," I said as Henry's eyes fell on me again. "I can tell him you were only defending me—"

"No, it's okay. Really," Henry interrupted. "He said everything was fine as long as I promised not to do it again. Said something about how firefighters are supposed to uphold the law and not get into restaurant brawls."

"Well, he does have a good point. But sometimes, restaurant brawls are necessary."

Henry laughed. "I couldn't agree more. Well, I won't keep you. I should get what I need and head home to finish setting up my place."

"Of course. Hey, me and my grandma should throw you

a housewarming party. With some amazing desserts. What do you say?"

"I'll think about it," Henry said. "But that's nice of you. See you around, Angie. Watch out for jealous muscle men."

I snorted. "I'll try. Hey, Henry?"

He paused, turning back to me. "Yeah?"

"Did you…did you say something to Devon?" I asked. "Because that guy is avoiding me like the plague. It's a total one-eighty from how much he was flirting with me last night."

"Oh, yeah. I might've said something to him," Henry said, shrugging. "Just that I thought he should stay away from you. You know, not play you or take advantage of you. I just told him you deserved better than that. Like I said that guy rubs me the wrong way. Seems like a womanizer to me. I told him to have a little more respect."

"Oh. Wow…I don't know what to say. Thanks for doing that."

Henry nodded. "No problem. You've been through enough heartbreak, and I just figured you don't need anymore. Well, see you around."

I smiled, watching as he walked off to the other side of the grocery store to get what he needed. First, he lectured Devon, then he punched Jim. Henry was sure going to a lot of trouble to look out for me. But why? And was he like that with all women or just me?

But then I remembered the ring on his left hand and the beautiful woman he was with at lunch. He had a lovely wife—much lovelier than me. He must've just been being nice and I was reading too much into it. He was taken and that was it, case closed.

I paid for the groceries we needed, then drove home and put them away in the fridge. As I turned around, my shoe stepped in something soft and squishy. I scowled when I looked down and realized it was barf.

"Just my luck," I grumbled, reaching for a paper towel to clean it up. "Now, who committed the crime? I know it wasn't me."

I walked up the stairs, finding Nutmeg lying on Grandma's bed. She looked tired and sick. I petted her head, bending down next to her.

"Hey there, old lady," I whispered. "Did you throw up? Is your tummy upset?"

Nutmeg mewled, rolling over. Poor kitty.

"Just take it easy and drink lots of water," I said, rising to my feet. "I'm sure it was just a hairball. I'll be back later, okay?"

Nutmeg meowed again, then closed her eyes and went back to sleep. I made sure there wasn't any more barf on my shoe before heading to the bakery. As I pulled into the parking lot, I spotted someone hanging around near the front doors.

Jim—the muscular idiot from the restaurant. His lip was black and blue from where Henry had punched him. Once he saw my truck, he took off on foot, running down the sidewalk. As I got out and approached the bakery, I hoped he wasn't up to something.

That was the last thing I needed.

Chapter Eleven

When I entered the bakery, I smelled smoke. I plugged my nose and rushed into the kitchen. I found Grandma and Mackenzie standing over one of the stoves, then watched as Mackenzie used gloves to reach in and pull out an apple pie. It was charred black when she placed it on the table.

"Ugh," Mackenzie cried. "I'm so going to fail my baking test! Why am I so bad at this?"

"You're too hard on yourself, dear," Grandma said. "You're going to get the hang of it. I promise. Do you think my husband was good at baking the first time he started? Of course not. It's a skill like anything else that requires time and patience."

Mackenzie sighed. "Yeah, okay. I hope you're right. Thanks for letting me practice in here."

"Of course, dear. You're welcome anytime. Now, throw out that dessert, please. I'm afraid it's stinking up the entire kitchen," Grandma said, then she noticed me. "Ah, my lovely granddaughter. Did you get what we needed from the store?"

"I did," I said, taking off my coat. "Do I even want to know what happened here?"

As Mackenzie dumped her destroyed dessert in the garbage, Grandma shook her head. "Just a simple mistake —but Mackenzie's already learning from it. So, how was lunch?"

"It went great. Sonya's getting married to James. That was her big news."

Grandma's eyes lit up. "Little Sonya is getting married? Oh, I'm so happy for her. I just know your grandfather would be too."

"I know—she was pretty excited about it. I saw the ring and everything. She wants us to cater her engagement party and wedding, by the way. I told her yes. Was that okay?"

"Of course! I'd never turn down anything for Sonya. That girl practically lived at our house when you were kids."

"I know, I miss those days. While I'm happy for her... sometimes, I wish we could go back to just being kids. When Grandpa was alive and everything was fine."

Grandma frowned, placing a hand on my shoulder. "I know you do, dear. I do too. But we must keep looking to the future. Yours looks bright from where I'm standing."

"I sure hope so. Now, do you need my help with anything?"

"Yes—I've got some desserts to bake for the firefighter's party tonight. Do you think you could make some cupcakes?"

"My specialty," I said with a smile, putting my apron on. "Nutmeg threw up, by the way. Probably a hairball. She seems okay now."

"Oh, no. My poor darling," Grandma said, handing me

a baking sheet. "She's getting old. I hope it isn't anything more serious. Now, Mackenzie, can you help me with this Black Forrest cake?"

Mackenzie nodded, then prepared for another one of Grandma's lessons. She still seemed a little sad about burning her dessert but we tried to take her mind off it by talking about other things. When Sonya was brought up again, I cleared my throat.

"Her engagement wasn't the only interesting thing that happened today," I began, putting icing on the cupcakes. "Henry was there. With some beautiful woman too—probably his wife. And that man named Jim."

"Hold up," Mackenzie said, pausing her blueberry muffins. "Isn't he the guy you told me about from the speed dating thing?"

"Yep," I said with a sigh. "He was angry I wouldn't go out with him. Insulted both me and Sonya and got right in our faces. When he got worse, Henry just...came out of nowhere. Punched him in the face."

Grandma gasped. "Oh my gosh! Henry doesn't seem like the type to do that. To use his fists."

"I was glad he did," I said, gesturing at the cupcakes. "These are ready, by the way. Without Henry, Jim might've not left us alone."

"Then maybe it was a good thing he was there," Grandma said, placing the cupcakes in a paper box. "You can get started on the sweet potato pie now, dear. We're going to honor the firefighters by bringing the best desserts tonight."

"Yum," I said, reaching into the fridge and pulling out the sweet potatoes. "But speaking of Jim...I saw him poking around outside. Be careful, all right? Let me know if you see him again."

"Will do," Grandma said, looking concerned. "Do you think he's dangerous?"

"If you saw him the way I did at the restaurant, you might think so, yeah. Let's just be cautious."

Mackenzie shook her head, decorating the muffins with sprinkles. "This is why I'm glad I'm attracted to women. I don't have to put up with men's bullshit."

"Speaking of which, have you told that lovely girl at the coffee shop that you like her?" Grandma asked, cracking a smile.

Mackenzie blushed. "No...no, not yet. I've been meaning to though. Maybe one day when I work up the courage. Maybe I can even bake her something—as long as I don't burn it."

"Like I said, practice makes perfect," Grandma said with a sweet smile, putting a cake in the oven. "In baking *and* relationships. So, other than that little hiccup with Jim, everything went okay? Sonya is doing well?"

"Oh, yeah—business is good. She said she's really busy at her wedding shop. Seems everyone is getting married or pregnant. Like her little sister, Rachel. She's pregnant with twins after eloping last year."

"My goodness," Grandma said with wide eyes. "I'll have to send them a congratulations card in the mail. Well, I'm happy everything's worked out."

"Yeah," I said, leaning against the counter with a sigh. "I just wish my relationships didn't suck so much. I did spend some time with Ty today, though."

"Which one is he again?" Mackenzie asked from her counter.

"The teacher. He was very nice when I spoke to him online," Grandma said, turning to me. "Where did you go? What did you do?"

I laughed, realizing Grandma was living vicariously through me. She obviously missed going on dates with Grandpa.

"Well, it was short notice so he invited me for coffee at his school. Showed me around too. I met his principal, teacher friends, and students. They all love him," I explained. "He's great with kids."

"Clearly husband material," Grandma said with a smile. "Things may go well with him, then. What about Jack? Are you still going to see him?"

"Should I? Especially now that I've connected with Ty?"

"Hey, you never promised yourself to that guy," Mackenzie said, eating icing out of the container with a spoon. "I say you should play the field. Go out with Jack too."

"Agreed," Grandma said, then paused. "Are you...eating icing like it's yogurt?"

"Yep," Mackenzie said. "So, what next?"

Grandma gave us a list of things to do—which included the usual from baking to cleaning the shop. We served a few customers that trickled in while we prepared for the firefighter's party. Then I texted Sonya, asking what her favorite desserts were before me and Grandma sat down to plan out her engagement party.

"...and chocolate balls are always a big hit," Grandma said, writing it down on her list. "I think Sonya and James will love that. Oh, and a reporter from the local news will be here tomorrow. He'll be putting a spotlight on our bakery."

"Wow. Okay, I'll be ready," I said with a nod. "That's good for exposure."

"Definitely," Grandma said, checking her watch. "Well, we've made good progress. I think we're ready for the party later. I have a few errands to run so I think I'm going to close the shop early. Mackenzie, you're free to leave for the day."

Mackenzie came out of the kitchen, reaching for her bag. "Okay, cool. Going to keep practicing that stupid recipe. I'm going to pass this course even if it kills me!"

"Let's hope it doesn't come to that," Grandma joked. "Get home safely, Mackenzie."

We both said goodbye, watching Mackenzie leave from the window. Grandma got up to put the CLOSED sign on the door. As she piddled around, I rose to my feet.

"Need me to do anything?" I asked. "We've got a few hours to kill before the party."

Grandma shrugged. "No, not really. Why don't you take the afternoon off? You do so much for me. You should rest. Or, if you wanted to call Jack for a date…that would be a good idea too."

I crossed my arms. "Are you only giving me the afternoon off so you can set me up with more men?"

"Maybe," Grandma said with a smile. "Would that be so wrong? You're doing well, Angie. You've come a long way from when Adrian broke up with you. And it's only been a few days. I think you're on the right path—that love is coming soon. Don't forget the cupcake messages."

Grandma picked up a piece of paper off the counter, showing me the fortunes. They were all some variation of *love is coming your way.* So cheesy, but it did make me smile.

"You really believe in those things, don't you?" I asked.

"I do. And more importantly, so did your grandpa," Grandma said, setting it down on the counter. "He was a smart man. Anyway, I'll see you at home for dinner, dear. Enjoy yourself, hmm?"

I hugged her and said goodbye, leaving the bakery to get into my truck. After Grandma locked up, leaving to run her errands, I looked through my phone again to find Jack's number. I guess it couldn't hurt to go out with him. Mackenzie was right—I hadn't promised myself to any man.

I decided to call Jack, wanting it to be more personal. He answered on the third ring. "Hello?"

"Hi, it's Angie. Angie Linden," I replied. "We met at the grocery store?"

"Of course! I remember you. Hi, Angie." I could hear typing in the background. "I was just finishing up some work for the day. What's going on?"

"Well, if you aren't busy...I was hoping you might like to go out. Maybe to a local coffee shop. I know it's last minute, but I'm so busy these days that I have to fit things in when I can—"

"No problem, I completely understand. Like I said, my schedule's flexible since I work from home. I can definitely meet you. What's the name of the coffee shop?"

"Cool Beans," I replied. "It's the best coffee in town. With a really cute name."

"All right, I'll meet you there soon. Say, in fifteen minutes?"

I smiled. "Sounds great, see you soon."

After we hung up, I drove to the coffee shop, waiting in my truck for a bit. When it got closer to fifteen minutes, I walked inside, finding it busy as always. People of all ages wanted their coffee. I waited in line, then approached the cash register when it was my turn. A beautiful girl stood there in the shop's yellow uniform.

"Hello there," she began. "What can I get you?"

I realized her name tag read MELISSA. That must've been her—Mackenzie's crush.

I cleared my throat. "I'd like a medium latte, please. With oat milk."

"Perfect," the girl said, punching it into her machine. "I'll make that for you right now. Your total is five fifty-seven."

"Thank you. Here you are," I said, handing over the change. "Hey, can I ask you a quick question?"

"Sure," the girl said as she walked to the nearby latte machine, making my drink. "What's up?"

"Do you know a girl named Mackenzie? Mackenzie Teller? Close in age to you, red hair with freckles?"

She handed me my latte. "Yeah, I've seen her around. The last name does sound familiar."

"It should—she's the fire chief's daughter. She works at my bakery, Lucky's Baked Goods. Anyway, when she comes in here next, you should chat with her. Maybe get to know her a bit."

"Really?"

"Yeah—I just think you two would have a lot in common. Anyway, thanks for the latte. See you around."

The girl looked puzzled as I walked away, heading for an empty table. I tried to help Mackenzie get the girl she wanted. I only hoped it worked. I sipped my latte, relaxing in my seat while waiting for Jack. I felt an arm on my shoulder a minute later.

When I spun around, it was Jack—much to my relief. No Jim this time. Jack smiled, looking down at me.

"Hi, Angie," he began. "You look beautiful today."

"Aw, thank you," I said. "Care to join me?"

"Of course, I'll just grab a coffee. You haven't been waiting long, have you?"

He was thoughtful. That was a good sign.

"Not at all," I said, shaking my head. "Just got here. You should try the latte with oat milk—it's delicious."

Jack nodded, walking toward the cash. He ordered the same thing and paid Melissa before joining me at my table. It was nerve-wracking going on all these dates, but I figured I owed Jack a shot. He was already a lot better than the guys at the speed dating round.

"So, what have you been up to?" he asked, sipping his latte.

Oh, just dating around and watching a married guy I have a crush on punch a guy to protect me. Nothing much.

"This and that," I said. "Mostly working at the bakery. My grandma needs help running the place."

"I bet—it seems very popular. Now, do you actually like baking, or do you just do it for your grandma?"

"No, I really do enjoy it. It's fun baking treats for people and then slipping in fortunes. My grandpa started that tradition. But hey...were you going to tell me my grandma was the one who helped us meet? You met her on Bumble, right?"

Jack laughed. "You caught me. Yes—I spoke with her on Bumble when she made your profile. I thought to myself, how could such a beautiful woman be single? I didn't need much convincing to meet you, that's for sure."

I blushed. "Well, thanks. Do you have any interest in baking?"

"I do—if you can believe it. It's one of my passions. I was actually hoping you could show me the ropes."

"Yeah, I'd like that. You'll be a regular baker in no time."

He grinned. "I'm holding you to that. Don't worry—I'm a fast learner."

When a breeze blew by, I realized the door had opened. I scowled when Lucy walked by to grab a coffee. Fortunately, she hadn't noticed me.

"Not a fan of that woman?" Jack asked, studying me.

"Can you tell? She's just...awful. The queen of the mean girls back in high school. And nothing's changed."

"Oof, I can't stand mean girls," Jack said, shaking his head in disgust. "I'm sorry you had to deal with that."

Lucy grabbed a coffee, then headed to the door. But not before she noticed us sitting there. She walked over with her coffee in hand, smirking.

"Oh, look who it is. The town's little baker," she mocked. "I'm glad you finally took down those God-awful neon lights. They were an eyesore. Who's this?"

"I'm Jack. Jack Hawkins," Jack introduced, turning to her. "A new friend of Angie's."

Lucy snorted. "Angie Linden has friends? Other than that super dorky Sonya Livingston? That's a surprise."

Typical Lucy—always bringing people down to her level to make her feel better about herself. It was getting old in high school, and it was downright ancient now.

"Excuse me, but we're trying to have coffee here," Jack said. "I don't know what terrible hole you crawled out of, but if you could go back there and leave us alone, that would be great, thank you. Goodbye."

Lucy looked appalled that Jack had spoken to her that way. Just as she opened her mouth, I cleared my throat. "Goodbye, Lucy. That means go away."

Lucy just scoffed, turning on her heel and leaving the coffee shop. I turned back to Jack.

"Thanks for telling her off. She's been a thorn in my side since ninth grade."

"Hey, anything I can do to help a pretty lady," Jack said

with a smile. "She was a total bitch so it was my pleasure. Anyway, let's forget all that nastiness and move on. She's clearly not worth your time. So, when you aren't baking, what do you like to do? Travel anywhere fun?"

As Jack and I spoke, trading information about our lives, I was beginning to like him too. And Ty.

If things kept going like this, I'd forget about Handsome Henry in no time.

Chapter Twelve

After chatting for a while, we were the only two left in the coffee shop. I checked my phone with wide eyes. "Oh, wow—we've been talking for a full hour now. Doesn't feel like that long."

"You're right," Jack said, flashing me a pearly-white grin. "But I guess time flies when you're having fun. I had a great time."

I blushed. "Yeah, me too. I have to get going now—there's a firefighter appreciation dinner happening tonight at city hall. My grandma and I are catering."

"That's exciting. Hope it goes well."

I rose to my feet, reaching for my jacket. "Thanks—me too. My grandma was baking all day for it. Hey...do you want to come?"

"Like a date?" Jack asked as he stood up. "Because I'm onboard."

I smiled. "Great—I'll see you at five o'clock. Looking forward to it."

"Me too. You're a delight to talk with, Angie," he said, reaching for my hand. "Until we meet again."

I could only smile, watching as Jack left the café. Despite how sad I was that Henry was taken, things were going well with both Jack and Ty. Maybe love was going to work out for me after all.

I grabbed my things, then headed to the door to get into my truck outside. I passed the bakery and found it closed, Grandma focusing all her energy on the party. When I got home, parking in the driveway, I noticed Grandma's sedan was already there.

After I unlocked the door, I entered, glancing around. "I'm home, Grandma!"

"In the kitchen, dear!" Grandma called out.

I entered the kitchen, finding her cleaning something up on the floor. "What happened? Flour emergency?"

"No—I think Nutmeg barfed again. Poor girl," Grandma said sadly, throwing a paper towel in the garbage. "I called the vet. She's got an appointment tomorrow morning to make sure everything's okay."

"Okay. Smart idea," I said, glancing at the stairs. "She *has* gotten really old."

"Yes, I know," Grandma said as she sat down at the living room table. "That's the hardest part of life, dear. Watching the ones you love get old and sick. Seeing your grandpa suffer...it tore me apart."

"Oh, Grandma," I said, walking over and hugging her. "I'm so sorry."

"It's all right, dear. That's life, I suppose," she said, looking up at me. "Let's talk about something more positive. How's your search for Mr. Right going?"

Typical Grandma.

"It's been okay. I went out with Jack to a coffee shop," I said, walking toward the fridge. I removed the chicken and placed it on the counter. "We got along really well. I invited him to the firefighter appreciation event tonight."

"Oh, lovely—I can meet him in person. I already chatted once with him on Bumble and he seemed nice."

I turned to her, laughing. "All right, but don't do anything embarrassing. We're still getting to know each other."

"Of course, dear. And what about Ty? Which man are you leaning toward?"

I paused, thinking. "I don't know. I think I should take it slow—see what happens. Let things progress naturally. Now, could you help me boil the potatoes?"

Grandma nodded, rising to her feet to grab the bag of potatoes we kept in the cupboard. She got the mashed potatoes and fried green beans ready as I coated the chicken in breadcrumbs and spices and baked it in the oven.

"So, what did you and Jack talk about the whole time?" Grandma asked. "You were gone for a while."

"Tell me about it—the time just flew by. We chatted about everything, really. Our lives, jobs, what we like to do. He was really interested in the bakery. Kept asking questions about our recipes."

Grandma smiled, stirring the mashed potatoes. "I always said that the way to a man's heart is through his stomach. Perhaps that'll be true for you and Jack—and possibly even Ty. Ah, I think the mashed potatoes are ready. Let's eat!"

After setting the table, Grandma and I ate our dinner, chatting about the bakery and things we needed to do. Grandma was excited about the interview tomorrow and I hoped it would help our business grow even more. Nutmeg came down, eating a little bit of her food and getting a drink of water before heading back upstairs to sleep. I vowed to keep an eye on her and make sure she didn't get any worse.

After doing the dishes, Grandma grabbed her keys, then I followed her to the bakery. I offered to drive her, but she insisted on being independent and taking her own car. When we arrived, we unlocked the door and entered to collect all the baked goods Grandma had prepared for tonight.

"Wow, you went all out," I said, peeking into the kitchen. I noticed tables full of cupcakes, muffins, cakes, and pies. "You're going to give everyone a sugar rush."

Grandma laughed. "Chief Teller asked us to cater, and I didn't want to disappoint. Grab a few containers, will you, dear? I can't carry all of this myself."

I nodded, picking up the muffins and cupcakes and bringing them out to the truck. They looked delicious as Grandma locked the door. She took the rest of the desserts, then followed behind in her sedan as we headed to city hall. It was a small, round building in the heart of downtown with a neatly trimmed lawn. A sign that read FIREFIGHTER APPRECIATION NIGHT was posted in the grass.

Chief Teller was chatting with a few firefighters on the lawn as we pulled into the parking lot. I didn't see Henry anywhere yet—or Jack. Grandma and I stepped out of our vehicles, carrying the desserts she made for tonight. Chief Teller smiled as he noticed us, then the firefighters he was chatting with headed inside.

"Ah, there you two are!" Chief Teller said. "Our lovely bakers. And you came prepared!"

"Of course," Grandma said with a smile. "Anything to show our appreciation for our town's hard-working fire department."

"You're too kind, Esther. Head on inside—I've set up tables where you can put the desserts. They look amazing, by the way. Can't wait to try them."

"I made them with extra love and care," Grandma said, still smiling. "Come on, Angie—let's put these inside."

"You go on ahead. I just have to talk to Chief Teller for a sec," I said, glancing between them. "It's important."

Grandma nodded, heading through the double doors into the town hall building. Dozens of other citizens from New Harbor and the surrounding areas began to arrive in their cars and follow her inside. Chief Teller glanced at me in confusion.

"What's going on, Angie?" he asked. "Everything all right?"

"Oh, yeah—I'm fine. I wanted to talk to you about Henry. I know you scolded him for what happened at the restaurant."

Chief Teller sighed. "Indeed, I did. I heard reports that he punched a man earlier. News travels fast in a small town like this. Anyway, I reprimanded him for it. Told him if he did it again, he'd be suspended for a few days without pay. We have to maintain a good reputation. I won't let my firefighters get into petty brawls."

"I know, Chief Teller, but he only did it for me. Did he mention that guy was harassing me and my best friend? Getting in our faces and threatening us?"

Chief Teller nodded. "Henry mentioned something along those lines, yes. But—"

"Go easy on Henry," I urged. "He's a good man. And I'm grateful for what he did. You should be proud to have someone so brave on the force."

"Well, I'm glad he's made such a good impression on you," Chief Teller said. "I've already given him a second chance. While I understand why he did it, I hope it won't happen again."

"Me too, Chief. I hope that Jim guy learned his lesson," I said, shaking my head in disgust. "Speaking of Henry, is he here yet?"

"He should be—he was invited. He said he had something to take care of and then he'd be here. Anyway, I should get inside and mingle. Enjoy the evening—and thank you again for baking the desserts."

I nodded as Chief Teller entered the town hall, chatting with more people who had arrived. I spotted the mayor in the crowd, surrounded by her bodyguards and supporters. I was just about to enter the building when I heard an SUV pull up.

When I turned around, it was Henry, pulling into a spot in the parking lot. He looked handsome in a blue suit with his hair combed back. But he always looked handsome—that was nothing new. Once he parked, he called someone on the phone, then his face completely changed. He looked angry—and tense. After talking for a few minutes, he rolled his eyes then hung up, getting out of the SUV.

I waited for him by the curb. "Hi, Henry. You look nice."

"Hey, thanks," he said, walking toward me. He still had a stressed out look on his face. "Chief Teller told us to dress up for tonight. I wanted to make a good impression."

"I'm sure you will," I said with a smile. "Everything all right? I didn't mean to spy on you, but I saw that phone call you had in the car. Looked…intense."

Was it trouble in paradise, I wondered? Problems with his wife? Or something worse?

Henry sighed. "Yeah, it was. I'll be all right though. So, you and your grandma baked everything for tonight?"

"We did. Well, it was mostly my grandma. She's a pro in the kitchen," I said, opening the container. "Want a cupcake? I'll let you have the first bite."

"Definitely. I could use the sugar high," he said, reaching into the container to grab a cupcake. "Thanks."

As I closed the container, our fingers brushing against each other, I cleared my throat. "You're welcome. Well, I guess I'll see you inside—"

When I felt a tap on my shoulder, I spun around, noticing Jack standing there with a smile on his face. He had put on a blazer and dress pants with dark boots.

"Hey, Angie," he began. "Hope I'm not late."

"Nope, you're right on time," I replied. "Glad you could make it, Jack."

"Of course," Jack said, eyeing Henry. "Oh, sorry. Were you two in the middle of something?"

"It's all right," Henry said as he held his cupcake. "I don't think we've met yet. Are you Ty?"

Jack looked uncomfortable. "Uh, no, sorry. Not me. My name's Jack. Jack Hawkins."

I felt my cheeks reddening, feeling embarrassed. I hoped Jack wouldn't mind that I was seeing someone else.

"Oh, I see. My bad," Henry said, shaking Jack's hand. "What do you do?"

"I work from home. Boring accountant stuff. I don't get out much. And you are?"

"Henry Brant, the town's newest firefighter. Just moved here a few days ago. So, how do you know Angie?"

Why did Henry want to know? I wondered what he was getting at. Henry glanced between us both, then his gaze landed on Jack. And he didn't look happy. But it could've just been leftover anger from that tense phone call.

"It's a bit of a long story," Jack said with a smile. "Angie's grandmother made a Bumble account for her. You know that dating app? I saw Angie's picture and thought she was beautiful and wanted to meet her. Her grandma made it all happen, really."

"How nice," Henry said, gripping the cupcake hard. He was beginning to crush it in his hands.

"Um, that cupcake's going to explode," I pointed out.

Henry looked down at the cupcake in his hand, easing his grip. The fortune was beginning to fall out from where he had grabbed it. "Whoops. Sorry, didn't mean to squish it that hard."

"At least you found your fortune. What does it say?"

Henry grabbed the small paper, reading it. "It says... there's always time for second chances. Hmm."

"Interesting. Grandma sure loves her cryptic fortunes. My grandpa was the one who started it, actually."

Henry tucked the fortune inside his breast pocket. "I guess time will tell if it comes true. Anyway, I should get inside and check in with Chief Teller. See you around."

"Nice to meet you, Henry!" Jack called out.

Henry nodded but didn't say anything, pushing through the crowd to head inside. I turned to Jack when we were alone on the grass.

"Well, that was fun. Sorry he confused you with someone else."

"No worries. Who's Ty, anyway?"

I hesitated. "He's...another guy I've been seeing from Bumble. I hope you aren't upset I've been on a date with someone else—"

Jack interrupted me. "Really, Angie, you don't have to apologize. This is only our second date, and we never said we're exclusive. So don't worry, okay? I'm cool with taking it slow and seeing where it goes."

I breathed out. "Great, thank you. I was worried for a sec."

"Hey, no problem. You've got nothing to be sorry for. I don't mind if you go on dates with other people—play the field a bit. How else are you going to find your perfect partner?"

I felt a bit better. "Yeah, I agree. Are you seeing anyone else?"

"No, just you. I want to see where this goes first. But like I said, I won't judge you if you're different. Really, there's nothing to worry about. So, should we head inside?"

"Yes, please," I said with a nod. "It's cold out here and I'm sick of holding these cupcakes."

Jack agreed, opening the double doors for me before we entered town hall. We walked down a long corridor before we found the main room where the firefighter's appreciation party was being held. As we entered, I noticed dozens of tables with chairs, balloons and banners hung around, plus a stage with a microphone. Grandma had placed the desserts on a side table as people mingled and helped themselves to drinks.

"I'll just set these down over here," I said, gesturing at the table. "People can take as many as they'd like."

Jack followed, grabbing a cupcake. "Seriously, your desserts are amazing. You're going to have to share your recipe one day. I'd love to bake it for my stepsister."

"Our recipes are top secret, but I'll see what I can share," I said with a smile. "What's your fortune say?"

"Love is always worth taking a chance on," Jack said, holding it up with a sheepish grin. "I completely agree. So, I have to ask—did you and Henry date?"

I blinked. "What? No, we didn't. I just met him a few days ago. Why?"

"Well, he was staring at you pretty hard," Jack said as he bit into his cupcake. "Like you were the only thing around, actually. I was just curious."

"I think that's just Henry's gaze. I'm pretty sure he's married."

"Really? Hmm," Jack replied, finishing his cupcake. "Then I hope his partner won't be mad at how much he was checking you out."

I cleared my throat. "Checking me out? I doubt that. Anyway, why don't we mingle? And we can find my grandma."

"Perfect—I'd love to say hi, and thank her for setting us up. Do you think she'd be willing to share the secret of what makes your desserts so amazing?"

I laughed. "Maybe—if you earn her trust. Come on, she's over here."

We pushed through the crowd, heading to one of the tables where Grandma stood. She was chatting with the mayor and trying to promote our business. We butted in, saying hello before the mayor walked away to chat with some of her constituents.

"Hi, dear. Ah, you must be Jack. Angie mentioned she invited you," Grandma said, holding out a hand. "Nice to meet you in person."

Jack shook her hand. "Thank you, Mrs. Linden. I'm glad you made a Bumble profile for Angie. If you hadn't, I never would've been able to meet such an amazing woman."

I blushed. "Yes, thank you for meddling in my love life, Grandma."

Grandma laughed. "Not meddling—just trying to give you a push in the right direction. You're very welcome, Jack. And please, call me Esther. Everyone else does."

"All right, Esther. Thank you. So, everyone in town knows how amazing your desserts are. I'm dying to know —what are your baking secrets?"

"Oh, I'm afraid I can't tell," Grandma said with a grin. "Those are private. I keep my recipe book at home so no one can take a peek. My husband worked hard to perfect his desserts, you know."

"I see, I see. That's too bad—I'd love to make them for my step-sister and impress her. Can you give me any baking tips? I've been wanting to get into it for a while."

"Of course, of course. Now, you wouldn't believe how important the right pan sizes are for making perfect desserts..."

As Grandma shared some advice with Jack and he listened intensely, I spotted Henry across the room. He looked a bit uncomfortable and out of place chatting with people he didn't know. He reached into his pocket, rolling his eyes and answering his phone before heading outside.

What was going on with him? I decided to follow and find out.

Chapter Thirteen

I left Jack and Grandma, still talking about baking tips in the conference room, and followed Henry out the back door. No one noticed as I slipped away from the party. As I walked outside, I heard Henry nearby, talking on the phone.

"...and you know I'm devastated," he was saying. "I didn't want it to happen like this, but you left me no choice. You'll get the papers soon. Goodbye."

He hung up, running a hand through his hair. Then he raised a hand and stared at his ring in the light. What was he doing?

When he turned around in a huff, he noticed me standing there. It was too late to run or hide. I forced a smile, creeping toward him as he stared at me. He didn't say anything so I figured I should.

"Um, hi," I began. "Sorry—didn't mean to eavesdrop. But I saw you run out of there and, well...I wanted to make sure you were okay. Are you...are you okay?"

"Yeah. Yeah, I'm fine," he said. "Excuse me."

Henry pushed past me, looking upset as he entered the

building. I stood there for a second and thought about everything. Was Henry in some kind of trouble?

When I entered the side door to the convention room, Henry was helping himself to some snacks, avoiding everyone. I spotted Jack standing a few feet away, sipping punch and looking around. He must've finished speaking with Grandma because she was chatting with other people. I walked over to Jack, smiling at him.

"Hey," I began. "What'd I miss?"

He shrugged. "Nothing much. When I was done talking to your grandma, I turned around and you were gone. Saw you running after Henry. Where did you go?"

"Oh, I just went to check on him. He looked upset. Didn't figure out why, though."

Jack studied my face. "Angie...do you have feelings for Henry?"

Before I could respond, Chief Teller walked onto the stage and tapped the microphone. "If everyone could take their seats, please, that would be wonderful."

"Come on," I whispered to Jack. "We're sitting over here."

Jack nodded, not bringing up Henry again as he followed me over to our table. I sat next to Grandma with Jack on the other side. My eyes found Henry in the crowd as he sat down, sitting at the firefighters' table near the stage. He was already looking at me. I blushed, looking away.

A few more townspeople slipped in through the back door, taking their seats. I noticed Lucy and her husband among them. I tried not to scowl, despising that woman. But then I noticed Jack was staring over at her. I wondered why.

"Thank you all for coming," Chief Teller said from the

stage, beaming at Mackenzie and his wife in the crowd. "And for my lovely family for helping me make this possible. Today, we're gathered here to celebrate the selfless heroes in our community—those who put their lives on the line every day to protect others. I'm, of course, talking about our wonderful firefighters. Give them a round of applause!"

Everyone began clapping, and Grandma, Jack, and I joined in. Henry and the other firefighters sat there and looked a bit awkward to be the center of attention. Chief Teller continued his speech, glancing around the audience.

"This is an event I'm proud to host every year," Chief Teller said, "and this year, we have a new member on the force. Please give a round of applause to Henry Brant, our town's newest firefighter!"

Everyone began cheering, making Henry blush in his seat. Devon and the other firefighters patted his shoulder with smiles and made him blush harder.

"I'm confident he'll fit in nicely. I'd also like to thank Esther Linden and her granddaughter, Angie, for baking this year's desserts. Which are wonderful, by the way."

Everyone's gaze turned to us. Me and Grandma smiled, waving. Henry was staring at me again.

"And before we get back to eating those amazing desserts and mingling," Chief Teller continued, "I'd like to make a personal announcement. Next year, I'll be retiring. As you all know, I'm getting up there in age, and I'm ready to pass along the title of chief to a deserving firefighter. I'm still determining who would be the best candidate."

"Wouldn't it be wonderful if it went to Henry?" Grandma whispered, turning to me. "I think he'd make a great chief. He's clearly brave—he proved that when he punched Jim."

"Who's Jim?" Jack asked, leaning forward with a furrowed brow.

Before I could respond, Chief Teller continued speaking. "But anyway, enough of my rambling. My daughter says I like to hear the sound of my own voice sometimes. Oops."

Mackenzie, his wife, and everyone in the audience laughed at that. Jack was still staring curiously between me and Henry.

"Without further ado, let's get back to the party," Chief Teller said. "I've hired a local band to play for us. And for the firefighters in town who make this place safer, I thank you. We're truly grateful for your service."

Everyone clapped as Chief Teller stepped off the stage, walking over to Mackenzie and his wife. A small band approached the stage and began playing a soft jazz melody. People rose to their feet, chatter filling the hall again, as everyone returned to eating and mingling. Our desserts were vanishing off the table at warp speed.

"Well, I guess everyone likes our desserts," Grandma said, glancing over at the table. "I hope they'll show their appreciation by donating. It isn't cheap running a business by yourself, you know. Especially these days."

"I'd like to contribute," Jack said, reaching into his wallet. He pulled out a twenty-dollar bill. "It isn't much, but I want to support you. Please—take it."

Grandma grinned, taking the bill. "Jack, you're too sweet. I knew I had a good feeling about you. You and my granddaughter look lovely together, by the way."

"Agreed," Jack said, glancing at me.

I blushed. "Grandma, please..."

"All right, all right. I'll butt out," she said with a wink.

"Anyway, I'll let you two chat. There are a few more people I want to say hello to."

"Good luck, Grandma," I said, as I stood up. "Once they taste your amazing cupcakes, I have no doubt they'll fully support us."

"Fingers crossed, dear," Grandma said, as she slipped the money in her pocket. "See you two later."

We nodded, watching as Grandma crossed the convention hall to continue mingling. I turned to Jack. "Sorry about her. She can be...embarrassing sometimes."

"Aw, I think she's cute. I'm glad she's so supportive," Jack said with a smile. "I think she's a fascinating woman, actually. What was the first recipe she and your grandfather taught you to make?"

I paused, thinking. "Hmm...probably cinnamon cookies. They added some nutmeg too. And white chocolate chips."

"I see," Jack said. "I wouldn't have thought of that. What's been your favorite recipe so far?"

"Oh, I can't choose. Everything my grandparents baked was always wonderful. But...chocolate cake *does* have a special spot in my heart."

"I'd love to learn that one," Jack said with a smile. "Maybe we could make it together? Say, tomorrow at your place after dinner? I'll look online and get all the ingredients we need."

I didn't see the harm, and I had no plans after dinner, so I nodded. "Sure, I'd like that. Always good to brush up on my baking skills."

"Then it's a date," he said with a wink. "No need to buy anything—I'll bring everything we need to your house. All I need from you is your beautiful self."

I tried not to blush. "Sounds good. Now, I don't know about you, but I'm hungry again. Want to grab more snacks?"

"You must've read my mind," Jack said, as he held out an arm. "Let's go."

I laughed, taking his arm as we pushed through the mingling people to reach the dessert table. A lot was gone already, but we managed to get the last slice of cheesecake. Jack and I shared, then he tried to guess all the flavors inside.

"Strawberry, obviously," he said. "And cream cheese. But there's something else I can't put my finger on..."

"Even I don't know what it is. Grandma's cheesecake recipe is special—secret. Who knows what she puts in there."

"Too bad. I'd love to make this at home," Jack said as he finished the cheesecake. "It's too good. I just have to use the bathroom. Wait for me?"

"Of course—take your time."

Jack nodded, heading down the hall to use the restroom as I glanced around. The citizens in town were thanking Henry and the other firefighters for their service. I was about to do the same when I heard footsteps behind me.

When I spun around, Lucy and her husband were standing there, trying the desserts. She wrinkled her nose at a cupcake. "It's way too sweet. And it's got something in it that I can't identify. Why do people like the Linden's again?"

Her husband just shrugged as I approached, crossing my arms. "Maybe because we're kind to people? And we love what we do? You should try it sometime."

Lucy rolled her eyes. "Or maybe everyone feels bad for

you after your grandfather died. It can't be because your desserts are good—trust me."

"I think everyone here would disagree with you. Including Chief Teller who asked us to host the party, not you and your green juices."

"Always so smug," Lucy sneered. "You'll get yours. Get the car, babe—I've had enough of this place. I just need to use the bathroom first."

Her husband nodded, giving me a look of pity as he reached for his keys and left the room. I felt just as much pity for him for being married to that. Lucy glared at me once more, then vanished down the hall to use the bathroom. She wasn't missed—at all.

I glanced around, realizing Jack still wasn't back yet. I was getting bored so I decided to find Grandma in the crowd. She was speaking to Chief Teller again. I pushed over, clearing my throat.

"Sorry, hope I'm not interrupting," I began.

"Oh, nonsense. It's nice to see you, darling," Grandma said, turning to me. Then she frowned. "Where did Jack go?"

"He's just using the bathroom. He'll be back soon." I turned to Chief Teller. "So, retirement. We had no idea you were planning that."

"Yes, it was a big surprise to me too," Grandma said. "Do you have anyone in mind to take your place?"

"Still thinking about it," Chief Teller said, glancing at his group of firefighters. They were speaking with people in the crowd and answering their questions about fire safety. "I'm keeping my options open."

"Well, if you ask me, I think you should consider Henry," Grandma said. "Even though he's new, he seems like a good, earnest young man. And I'm sure my granddaughter would agree. Isn't that true, Angie?"

I blushed. "Oh, yeah—totally. He's got my vote."

"I'll keep that in mind, thank you," Chief Teller said with a nod. "I'm looking forward to seeing him in action before deciding. Some of my other firefighters...well, they mean well, but they're awfully young. They can be immature sometimes. Henry is older—more experienced. He would make a good candidate. I'm eager to see him in action in the coming weeks."

"I'm sure he won't disappoint. Hey, Chief—do you have Henry's address? I'd love to do a surprise party for him. You know, bring him desserts to welcome him to town."

"That's a nice idea. Yes, I do," Chief Teller said, reaching for his smartphone in his suit pocket. "I've got it saved in my phone...ah, yes, he owns 63 Maple Ridge Road. I helped him find that place."

I grinned. "Perfect—thank you."

I tried not to let it show, but I was eager to learn more about Henry. He was so quiet—so elusive. And I was still curious about the phone call.

"I'm sure he'll appreciate the warm welcome," Grandma said, then turned to Chief Teller. "Now, if you're going to retire, that means a retirement party. I can start writing out a dessert menu for you if you'd like. My granddaughter and I would love to cater..."

As Grandma tried to convince Chief Teller to hire our services, I shook my head, trying not to laugh. She was always thinking about the family business. When I glanced around, still not seeing Jack, I decided to go looking for him. Just in case he got lost.

I pushed the door open to the hallway, walking down the long corridor of offices. Town hall was always busy hosting different parties and meetings. When I turned down another hall, following the signs to the bathrooms, I heard whispering. They were too faint to make out.

As I turned the corner, I noticed it was Jack—and he wasn't alone. He was whispering with Lucy. I frowned, trying to get closer when I stepped on a noisy part of the old wooden floorboard. It cracked underneath my heel.

I almost scowled. Busted.

Both Jack and Lucy's heads shot over, noticing me standing there. No one said anything for a few seconds. I waved, trying not to make it awkward.

"Hi," I began. "What's going on over here?"

"Oh, nothing. Lucy was just yelling at me for knocking into her shoulder," Jack said, stepping back from her. "Really, it was an honest mistake."

"Whatever," Lucy huffed. "Just be more careful next time."

Lucy rushed past me, then ran outside. The room turned quiet as Jack approached. "Sorry I took so long. Like I said, I was coming out of the bathroom when I walked into Lucy. She wasn't too happy about that—chewed me out for a good few minutes."

"Yeah, that's Lucy," I said, shaking my head in disgust. "She's like that. But why were you two whispering?"

"Were we?" Jack asked. "I didn't think so. I'll do my best to stay away from her in the future. Anyway, I should get going now—I have some work to do tomorrow. Looking forward to seeing you afterward."

I smiled. "Me too. Here, I'll give you my address. You should wear something casual. Baking can get pretty messy."

"Will do," Jack said, taking down my address into his phone. "See you then, Angie. Get home safe."

I promised I would, then watched Jack leave the town hall building and get into his car. After he drove off, I headed back into the hall, searching for Grandma. She was packing up her containers.

"Here, let me help," I said, walking over. "Jack just left —he had work in the morning. We should probably head home too."

"Yes, good idea. We've got a busy day tomorrow with the TV interview and then Nutmeg's vet appointment. Chief Teller seems to be leaving too. I was just grabbing our things," Grandma said, collecting everything. "Did Jack have a good time?"

"I think so. He's coming over tomorrow after dinner—we're going to bake. I'm going to teach him how to make chocolate cake."

Grandma smiled. "That's such a sweet date—no pun intended. Don't worry, I'll stay out of your hair. I can even go out to give you two some privacy. Perhaps I'll head to the coffee shop and enjoy some tea."

"Would you? That would be great, thanks."

"Of course, sweetie. However I can help. Say, do you know what's wrong with Henry? He left a few minutes ago. And he didn't look too happy."

I shrugged. "I have no clue, but he's been acting weird all night. Had an intense phone call when he got here and another during the event. Something's going on. Maybe it's about his wife."

"Poor guy. He looked very stressed," Grandma said, balancing all the empty containers in her arms. "Anyway, I'm ready to leave if you are, dear." She turned to the fire chief. "Goodbye, Chief Teller. Thanks for having us!"

Chief Teller waved, yelling goodbye as he was leaving with Mackenzie and his wife, Tabitha. Most of the partygoers were clearing out. As I headed into the parking lot with Grandma, helping her carry everything, I thought about Henry and how I could cheer him up. For some reason, it was very important to me.

I had a specific dessert in mind—and now that I had his address, I could surprise him. I hoped he wouldn't mind.

Chapter Fourteen

After Grandma and I drove home, unlocking the front door and heading inside with our empty containers, I noticed Nutmeg lying on the kitchen floor. And she didn't look too good. Her eyes were half-open, her breathing labored.

"Nutmeg!" I cried, setting down the containers on the counter. "Oh my gosh. Grandma!"

Grandma rushed over, bending down next to Nutmeg. "We need to get her to the emergency vet—right away. Angie, bring me her cat carrier from the basement, please."

I nodded, nearly tripping over my own feet as I ran downstairs to grab her cat carrier. When I returned, Grandma was holding Nutmeg, lightly stroking her head. If Nutmeg died, I knew I'd miss her—but Grandma was going to be devastated. There was just too much loss these days.

"Thank you, dear," Grandma said, looking up at me. "Let's get her inside."

I nodded, setting the carrier down on the floor. Nutmeg didn't put up a fight—too weak to resist—as Grandma gently slid her inside, then zipped up the carrier. I should've known something was wrong when she kept throwing up everywhere.

"The vet in town will be closed right now but there's an emergency vet just outside the city," Grandma said, reaching for her purse. "We'll take my sedan. You sit in the backseat with Nutmeg and comfort her, all right?"

"Okay, Grandma," I said, lifting the carrier. "Do you... do you think she'll be okay?"

Grandma looked like she was on the verge of tears but held them back. "I hope so, dear. I really do. Hurry—there's no time to waste."

I left the house, getting into Grandma's sedan as she locked the front door. I buckled Nutmeg in her little carrier before sitting next to her in the backseat. Grandma joined us, pulling out of our driveway and barreling down the street. We hit a bump, and I realized Grandma was driving well over the speed limit.

We sped out of town as I held onto the carrier, glancing out the window. I spotted the WELCOME TO NEW HARBOR sign growing smaller behind us. Boston was the closest city to where we lived, so Grandma decided to take us there.

"Okay, I know the vet hospital is around here somewhere," Grandma said, turning the corner down a busy street. "Ah, there it is."

Grandma parked in the lot around the back, the sky growing dark. I saw a light on inside the vet hospital and hoped they could help Nutmeg. Through all the stress, I had completely forgotten to text or call first. I opened my door, unbuckling her cat carrier and rushing inside with Grandma hot on my heels.

The vet clinic was mostly empty so late at night, though I could hear animals in the kennel barking and meowing.

A lone secretary sat at the front desk while typing on her computer. She looked up when she saw us, then spotted Nutmeg.

"Oh, my. That poor kitty doesn't look too well," she said. "What happened?"

"Nutmeg—that's our cat—has been throwing up the past few days," I explained quickly. "We had a vet appointment for her tomorrow. But when we came home tonight, we saw her lying on the kitchen floor, her breathing labored. We rushed her here to get looked at."

"Good call. I'll let Dr. Bentley know right away," the secretary said, rising to her feet and reaching for the cat carrier. "We'll take good care of Nutmeg—don't you worry. Please, have a seat in the waiting room while we examine her."

I nodded, gesturing for Grandma to follow. We passed a wall of pet toys for sale before finding our way to the waiting room. The chairs were comfy and soft as we sat down, noticing a coffee machine on the table near a vending machine. We were too nervous to eat or drink anything.

"Oh, I hope Nutmeg will be all right," Grandma said, sitting next to me and placing her purse on her lap. "I can't lose her too."

I gave Grandma a side hug. "It'll be okay—I promise."

I didn't know that for sure but I had to comfort Grandma somehow. We waited silently in the empty room, hearing muffled voices from the veterinarian and secretary talking down the hall. I eventually got up to pace to pass the time before the vet walked out of the side room to speak with us. He was handsome—sparkling green eyes, blond hair, and muscles under his vet coat—but then I noticed the glimmer of his wedding ring under the light.

Of course. All the good ones were already taken, like Henry. Why was life so cruel?

"Hi there," the handsome vet said, approaching us. He shook Grandma's hand and then mine. "I'm Dr. Bentley, the emergency vet on call."

"Nice to meet you, Doctor. How is Nutmeg doing?" Grandma asked as she rose to her feet.

Dr. Bentley sighed. "Not good, I'm afraid. We performed an x-ray and discovered she has a blockage in her stomach. You mentioned to my secretary that she's been throwing up? That blockage is most likely the cause."

"Oh no," I murmured. "Can you clear the blockage?"

"Yes, we can—but it'll require surgery. And it can be expensive."

"How expensive?" Grandma asked, nervously.

"Five grand, I'm afraid."

Grandma turned to me, on the verge of tears again. "I… I don't think we can afford that. The life insurance money from your grandpa went to fix that leak in the bakery's roof last month."

"We don't have money anywhere else?" I asked. "No savings?"

Grandma sighed. "I'm afraid not, dear. Everything goes to the bakery—and it isn't cheap running a business these days."

Dr. Bentley looked awkward. "I'll let you two discuss this in private. I'll be in the exam room at the end of the hall, giving Nutmeg some IV fluids. She was also dehydrated."

"Wait a minute," I said, making the vet pause. "If we don't remove the blockage, will…will Nutmeg die?"

The vet hesitated, then nodded. "Yes, I think so. It's deadly for a cat of any age."

"Poor Nutmeg. She's sixteen, you know," Grandma replied. "She was a stray we adopted when my granddaughter was a child. My husband—who passed away last year—just loved Nutmeg. He would've done anything for her."

"I'm sorry for your loss," the vet said softly. "Please, take all the time you need to talk things through. No rush at all."

The vet walked away, and the secretary followed. Grandma sighed. "I just don't know what we'll do..."

"We have to be able to find five grand somewhere," I said, crossing my arms. "I could get another job. Or take out a loan. Maybe Sonya could help—"

"No, I don't want to burden her. Or anyone else. There's only one solution. I'll have to sell the bakery."

My face fell. "What? You can't do that! That place is Grandpa's legacy."

"Yes, but he loved Nutmeg deeply. He wouldn't want her to die. Lucy's been inquiring about our business, you know. She wants to buy the lot. Perhaps she'd be interested."

I scoffed. "Lucy? No way. She wants to destroy us, Grandma. If you sold her our bakery, she'd never let us live it down. She'd taunt us about it forever."

"I...I don't know what else to do," Grandma stammered, and I'd never seen her look so desperate. "We don't have money anywhere else. It'll have to be the bakery who dies instead of Nutmeg."

I sighed. "Grandma..."

"Wait here. I'm going to tell Dr. Bentley that we'll get the money soon," Grandma said, taking a deep breath. "We'll do what needs to be done."

I watched as Grandma walked away, heading into the room where Nutmeg, the vet, and the secretary were waiting. Nutmeg was lying on a table with an IV attached to her arm. She looked tired and sad, lying there quietly. Grandma stroked her head before she began speaking with the vet.

I couldn't believe this—we were actually going to lose the bakery. I didn't want Nutmeg to die but I couldn't bear to live without Grandpa's shop either.

To clear my head, I walked outside, standing on the dark street. I closed my eyes as the breeze tousled my hair. As I thought about the bakery—and having to say goodbye —I heard a car stop a few feet away.

When I opened my eyes, it was Henry. What was he doing here?

"Angie, is that you?" he asked, rolling down the passenger side window to look at me.

"Henry?" I asked, walking toward his car and leaning in through the window. "What are you doing out here so late?"

"Came out here to clear my head. Driving helps me think," he said. "But what are you doing here?"

Before I could respond, the door to the vet clinic opened behind me. Grandma came out with a sigh. "It's done—I signed the paperwork. We owe them five grand. Oh, who is this?"

"It's Henry," I said, gesturing at his car. I stood near the door and pointed at the vehicle. "He was out for a drive."

"Hello, Mrs. Linden," Henry said as he waved at her. "What's going on?"

"We found our cat, Nutmeg, on the floor earlier. We rushed her to the emergency vet."

"Oh, no. I'm sorry to hear that. Will she be okay?"

"Well, she's got a blockage that'll cost five grand to fix. If we don't do it, she'll definitely die."

Henry winced. "Ouch, that's a lot of money. Are you going through with it?"

"We are," I said, sadly. "But we don't have that kind of cash. Grandma...she's going to sell the bakery. To one of our competitors."

"Really?" Henry asked, his eyes widening. "But don't you two love that bakery? Isn't it the shop your grandfather opened?"

Grandma cleared her throat, then I glanced at her. It looked like she was trying not to cry.

"It is," I said, turning back to Henry. "But we don't have any other choice. There's nowhere else we can get five grand."

Grandma placed a hand on my shoulder, her bottom lip quivering. "I'm sorry, Angie. I always envisioned you running the bakery in the future—perhaps with a husband and a family of your own. I'm so sad that won't happen now."

"Me too. But...Nutmeg is important. She needs that surgery, so we don't have any choice."

"Damn. I'm so sorry," Henry said, glancing between us both. "This is awful. Your desserts are amazing—and popular from what I've seen. It'll be devastating to New Harbor to lose that."

Grandma and I said nothing, quietly nodding. We knew it would be. So much had changed in the last year with Grandpa's death. Working at the bakery was the only thing I had of him, my last shred of normalcy. I wasn't ready to let it go.

The door to the vet clinic opened behind us, then Dr. Bentley stuck his head out. "We're prepping Nutmeg for surgery. It's risky due to her age but if that blockage isn't removed, she'll die. Would you like to see her one last time before we put her under?"

"Yes, we would," Grandma said, glancing at Henry. "Nice to see you, young man. Thanks for listening."

Henry gave her a sympathetic smile as she headed inside, following Dr. Bentley. I looked back at Henry and said goodbye before following. I glanced out the vet clinic's window, noticing him lingering before I followed Grandma into the exam room. We both petted Nutmeg, trying to comfort her before surgery. Dr. Bentley promised he'd do his best to save her as he took her away to the surgical room.

When Grandma and I returned to the waiting room, the secretary came running up to us. "Excuse me, but this was just dropped off. A man walked inside the clinic and said it was for you."

"Did he give a name?" I asked.

"No, just that he was a friend. He was very handsome."

Henry. It had to be. Just what was he up to?

She handed us an envelope. I took it, noticing nothing was written inside. But there was money in the envelope. When I took out the green bills, counting them, it amounted to five grand.

"Oh my gosh," I murmured.

"What?" Grandma asked, peering over my shoulder. "What is it?"

"Henry...I think he left us the money for Nutmeg's surgery," I said, showing the envelope to Grandma. "It's exactly the five grand we need. Look!"

Grandma took the envelope, noticing the money inside. Her eyes widened. "Oh, my. Why would he do that?"

"I...I don't know." I glanced toward the window. "Let me go see if he's still out there."

I ran outside, looking in both directions down the dark street, but no one was there. Henry had driven off. Why did he have all that money on him? And why would he just give it away to help people he barely knew?

When I walked back inside, Grandma was still holding the envelope, looking puzzled. "So? Did you find him, dear?"

"No, he must've driven off already. Too bad. Well, I'm definitely going to his house tomorrow with some desserts. He deserves it."

"Definitely. I feel bad taking his money," Grandma said, looking at the envelope, "but we have no choice. I'll go give this to the secretary and pay our bill in full."

"And we can keep our bakery," I said with a smile. "No need to sell it to Lousy Lucy. This is awesome!"

"Indeed. Henry will have free desserts for life now," Grandma said, grinning. "He's truly a wonderful, wonderful man."

As Grandma walked away to the front desk to pay, I nodded. "He really is. Too bad he's married…"

The secretary took the money, shocked we suddenly had it in full, then paid off Nutmeg's vet bills. Grandma joined me in the waiting room where we read magazines and drank coffee to pass the time.

"We'll have to pay Henry back at some point," Grandma said. "I can try to put some money aside every month. I hope he'll accept monthly payments."

"Here's hoping." When I saw Dr. Bentley coming out of the surgery room, I rose to my feet. "Doctor, there you are. How is Nutmeg doing?"

"She survived the surgery. She's stable for now," he said. We sighed in relief. "For her age, that's pretty incredible. She has a fighting spirit."

"That she does," Grandma said with a smile. "She's a true Linden. Can we see her?"

"Absolutely. We need to keep her here overnight for observation, but based on what I've seen, I think she'll make a full recovery. We removed the blockage and she already seems a bit more alert. It must be such a relief for her."

Grandma reached for my arm, grinning wide. "Thank goodness! Oh, this is truly a miracle. My sweet little Nutmeg!"

Grandma rushed into the surgery room where Nutmeg was recovering, petting her furry head. Nutmeg was already looking much better. She even lifted her head, meowing at Grandma.

Dr. Bentley was watching with a smile as I turned to him. "Thank you, Doctor, for saving Nutmeg. You don't know how much that cat means to us—especially my grandma."

He nodded. "I can see that. I'm just glad this story had a happy ending. And my secretary said you paid the bill in full?"

"We did. A friend helped us out—a very good friend. We owe him."

"Well, I'm happy it all worked out. Would you like to see Nutmeg as well?"

"Of course," I said, heading to the surgery room. "Poor kitty..."

As I petted Nutmeg with Grandma, I was thanking the Heavens that Henry Brant had decided to move to New Harbor. Where would we be without him?

Chapter Fifteen

We left Nutmeg at the vet, giving her time to recover after surgery. I got into Grandma's car, then we drove back to New Harbor and headed straight for bed. We were both exhausted after a long, stressful night of many emotions.

I fell asleep quickly and woke up early to get dressed, cooking eggs for Grandma and me while getting a head start on Henry's desserts. It was the least he could do after saving Nutmeg *and* our bakery in one night. I baked him chocolate chip cookies—everyone's favorite—and put smiley faces on them in icing. I called them Happy Cookies, used to thank or cheer someone up. They were my own creation.

"My, you're up early," Grandma said, yawning as she walked into the kitchen and tightened the robe around her body. She took a seat with a smile. "Aw, you made breakfast."

"Of course," I said, kissing her cheek and putting eggs on the table in front of her. "Any news on Nutmeg?"

"Yes, Dr. Bentley called five minutes ago," Grandma said as she reached for her fork. "Nutmeg is expected to make a full recovery. We can pick her up in a few hours. He just wants to give her some extra fluids. Then, when she's home, we need to give her some antibiotics on a schedule."

"Okay, good to know. That's a relief. Well, enjoy your breakfast. I'm off to see Henry now."

"Tell him I said hello," Grandma said with a smile. "What did you make him?"

"My special happy cookies," I said, placing them in a transparent container. "To properly thank him."

"Yes—good idea. Thank him for me too. You know, I've said this before, but...it really is a shame that he's married. He's so kind and thoughtful. And you two would make such a lovely couple."

I looked down, sadly. "Yeah, I know. Anyway, I'll see you later and let you know how it went. Hope Henry doesn't mind me dropping by unannounced."

"From the way he looks at you, I don't think he will," Grandma said with a wink. "See you later, dear."

I waved goodbye, then grabbed my keys and headed outside to my truck. Placing the cookies on the passenger seat, I hopped behind the wheel, then sped off down the street. At a red light, my phone buzzed. I pulled it out immediately in case it was Grandma texting something important.

Can't wait to see you after dinner, Jack had texted. *It'll be fun!*

Right—my second date with Jack. Honestly, I'd almost completely forgotten about it with everything going on with Nutmeg and Henry. Would Jack or Ty have helped pay off the vet bill, I wondered?

When the light turned green, I stepped on the gas, then looked around at the street signs. I was searching for the address that Chief Teller had given me for Henry. After turning down a long, residential street, passing dozens of homes, I finally came across Henry's house. The numbers above it read 63 and the road sign said MAPLE RIDGE ROAD. It was simple and small with a garden out front, a one-car garage, and a big window overlooking a living room. Perfect for a small family—like Henry and his wife.

Just as I put on my signal to turn into his driveway, another sedan pulled in first. I frowned and wondered who was visiting Henry's house this early. Was it his wife? I really didn't want to see her again.

I pulled in beside the sedan, grabbing my container of cookies and stepping out. The driver's door to the sedan opened and an older lady in her sixties got out of the car. She was wearing plain clothes with a purse, then turned to lock her sedan. She turned to me with a smile and looked to be too old to be his wife. The more I stared at her, the more I found her familiar. But from where?

"Hello there," she began, peering in through my window. "Here to visit Henry?"

"Uh, that's right," I replied, stepping out. "I'm Angie. Angie Linden. Who are you?"

"Oh, you're Angie? Henry's told me a lot about you. We chat on the phone every night. You run that bakery with your grandma, right?"

How did she know that? And how often did Henry talk about me?

"Yeah, that's me. I met Henry a few days ago when he moved to town."

"Aw, that's nice—I'm glad he's making friends." She

held out a hand. "Oh, sorry—I'm being rude. I'm Lynette Brant, Henry's mother. It's so nice to meet you."

Then it clicked. I had seen her in the picture with Henry back at the fire station. No wonder she looked familiar.

"Likewise," I said, shaking her hand. "I'm just here to drop off some cookies and check on Henry. You know, properly welcome him to town. Are you doing the same?"

Lynette glanced at the house, sighing. "Yes, somewhat. I'm here to check on him too. Drove all the way here from Boston. I'm worried about my boy these days."

"Oh. Why is that?"

Before Lynette could respond, the front door opened. Henry—in his pajama bottoms with no shirt—bent down to grab the newspaper at his doorstep, then noticed us standing in his driveway. I had to admit, he was very handsome without a shirt on. His abs were sculpted like one of those ancient Greek statues. I tried not to drool in front of his mother.

"Oh, hey, Mom," he began. "And...Angie? What are you two doing here?"

"Seems we both had the idea to check on you today," Lynette said with a laugh. "Come on, let's head inside. And put on a shirt, will you, Henry? You've got company."

Henry opened the door wider, letting his mother enter the house first. He seemed puzzled when he glanced at me. "You came to check on me too?"

"I did. Hope you don't mind," I said, handing the container of cookies to Henry. "Chief Teller gave me your address. I baked these for you—partly to welcome you to New Harbor, partly to thank you for helping us pay Nutmeg's vet bills. Which we're totally going to pay you back for, by the way."

Henry took the cookies, then shook his head. "That's nice, but not necessary. The five grand I had...well, I didn't want it anyway. I was glad to get rid of it."

I blinked, wondering why he didn't want the money. Why would anyone turn down five grand?

"Anyway, come on in. These cookies look amazing, by the way," he said, glancing at the container. "I'm just going to put on a shirt. Make yourself at home—grab whatever drink or food you'd like from the fridge."

I nodded, entering his house and closing the front door. Henry set the cookies down on the table as he rushed up the nearby stairs. His mother was already looking around, grabbing a bottle of water out of the fridge.

"Would you like some water, Angie?" his mom asked. "Henry's got plenty."

"Sure," I said with a nod, entering the kitchen. "That would be nice, thank you."

"Here you go," Lynette said, handing me the bottle. "This is my first time visiting Henry in his new house. I'm glad he was able to find something so quickly. Do you think he's fitting in well around New Harbor?"

"I'd say yes," I replied, sipping my water. "He's already made friends. And got a job and a house. I'd say he's doing better than well."

"Oh, that's good. Like I said, I've been worried about him. I'm sure he's hoping New Harbor will be a fresh start. He really needs it."

A fresh start from what? I didn't know what his mother was talking about. She walked around the house, checking out the rooms and looking at the paintings on the wall. Henry had a lot of firefighter memorabilia scattered around. He also had medals and trophies for all the people he had saved back in Boston, proudly displaying them in the living room.

"My son's got quite the medals, hmm?" Lynette asked, gesturing at one on the wall. "He's made me so proud. I always knew he was special."

"That he is," I said with a nod, pointing at a picture of Henry in full firefighter gear. "That's a nice one."

"Doesn't he look so handsome in his uniform?" his mom asked, smiling. "It's just a shame he had to leave Boston. He'd built up a good life there, then it all fell apart. It's just...so hard to watch as a parent, you know?"

Before I could respond, wondering how Henry's life had fallen apart when he seemed fine, the staircase creaked. He came down in a blue T-shirt and a pair of jeans. I couldn't see his abs anymore. What a shame.

"Sorry to keep you two waiting," he began. "Mom, it's nice of you to come visit, but you really didn't have to. I'm fine."

"Are you?" his mother asked, raising an eyebrow. "What you've been through would be hard on anyone. I just wanted to drop by and make sure."

Henry glanced at me before turning back to his mom, looking embarrassed. "Really, everything's okay. I'm settling in well around here. Now, I'm eager to try out those cookies Angie bought."

Henry walked over to the table, opening the container. He reached in and grabbed a happy cookie before biting off a piece. As he chewed, he nodded, glancing at the cookie.

"This is delicious," he began. "The best cookie I've ever had."

I grinned. "Glad to hear it—it was the least I could do. Would you like one, Lynette?"

"Yes, please," his mother replied. I leaned forward,

grabbing a cookie out of the container to hand to her. "Thank you. I heard you mention something at the door about paying Henry back?"

"Yes, but he refused," I said, glancing at Henry as he continued eating his cookie. "My and my grandma's cat was really sick yesterday. We took her to the emergency vet in Boston, the closest one, and realized she had a blockage. Henry happened to be in the area, driving around."

"Back in Boston?" his mom asked, eyeing him. "And you didn't tell me?"

Henry sighed. "Sorry, Mom. Just wanted to be alone. Clear my head."

"Uh-huh. Please, keep going, Angie. I hope this story has a happy ending. I can't bear to see any animal injured."

"Me neither—and it does, don't worry. The vet told us it was going to be five grand to remove the blockage, but we couldn't afford it. My grandma started talking about putting our bakery up for sale to pay it off, and when Henry found out, he dropped off an envelope at the front desk with five grand inside. Saved the day." I turned to Henry with a smile. "Thank you, Henry. I can't say that enough."

He shrugged, finishing his cookie. His eyes were twinkling though. "Eh, it was nothing. Don't mention it."

"Well, we thought it was big. My grandma said you'll get free desserts for life."

Henry snorted. "Sounds perfect. Thank you, Angie."

"You just gave away five grand?" his mother asked, looking shocked. "To a girl you just met? My, she must be special to you."

His cheeks turned red. "Mom, please. I just wanted to help. I didn't need or want the money anyway. It was... tainted."

"Ah," his mother said, patting his back. "So, you and Lauren finally settled the divorce?"

"What divorce?" I asked.

My head was spinning. I thought Henry had been married this whole time—he even wore a ring. What was going on?

Henry looked uncomfortable, rubbing his neck. "It's...not something I like to talk about, but my wife and I—ex-wife now—recently got divorced. Had to go back to Boston to get some of my things. The money I gave you was from our shared bank accounts. I started saving for the future. Except...there's no future anymore."

"Oh," I said, softly. "Henry, I'm so sorry."

"Don't. It's all right," he said, clearing his throat. "I'm fine. Look, not that I'm not happy you two are here, but I have to get ready for work. It's my first official day on the job. So...talk later?"

I nodded. "Of course, I should head to the bakery anyway. See you later, Henry."

He watched me go, heading toward the door. The reason he still wore a wedding ring was puzzling, but at least I had my answer now. Henry wasn't married—he wasn't taken after all. That woman at the restaurant wasn't his wife.

Instead, he was a divorcé. I had so many questions. And one lingered in my mind...did that mean he was open to dating?

As I opened Henry's front door, heading to my truck, I heard his mom talking to him as she left. I lingered near my vehicle so I could eavesdrop and pretended to struggle with my keys. "Call me when you can, okay? I think you should talk to someone about this. Get it all out."

"Mom, really—I'm fine, like I said," Henry replied. "There's nothing to talk about."

His mom hesitated but still stepped outside, nodding. "All right, sweetie. If you say so. Good luck at work."

He thanked her and shut the door, vanishing inside. His mom shook her head and walked toward her sedan. As she put her purse on the passenger seat, she turned to me.

"He can be real stubborn sometimes. It's like...he shuts down when he's upset," his mom muttered. "It's always driven me crazy. But thanks for bringing my son some cookies—that was kind of you. And he needs that right now. Kindness from a friend."

A friend. Of course, that was what he needed. There he was, going through something challenging and I was already thinking about asking him out. That wasn't right.

I swallowed the lump in my throat. "Of course. Anytime. Nice meeting you, Lynette."

"You too, Angie. And best of luck with your bakery. You're as sweet as Henry made you out to be," she said with a smile. "Be gentle with him. He's been through a lot."

"I will." I glanced toward the house, then back at his mom. "Do you know what happened? What ended the marriage, I mean?"

"I really don't. Like I said, Henry tends to shut down when he's upset. I still call him every day but he's so reluctant to talk about the divorce. I'm not sure why they didn't work out—he and Lauren were madly in love. Oh, wait...I think I have a picture."

I waited beside my truck as Lynette reached into her pocket, pulling out a smartphone. She waded through her photo album before bringing up a picture. It was Henry and a beautiful brunette woman, smiling at the beach in their bathing suits. They looked happy.

"That was from the Fourth of July last year. Weren't they such a gorgeous couple?" his mom asked, and I nodded in agreement. "I don't know what happened to sour their marriage this fast. They were only married two years ago."

"Wow. That's short-lived," I said, as she put her phone away. "Poor Henry."

"Yes, definitely. He really wanted them to work out. I don't know all the details, but whatever happened really destroyed him. He quit the job he loved, left Boston and all his friends behind, and moved to this small town. Whatever happened must've been devastating."

I paused for a moment, thinking. What could cause a rift like that between a married couple? They looked so in love in the photo from last summer.

"Anyway, don't tell Henry I told you that. He's very private. In fact, I'm surprised he even told me about you," Lynette said, reaching for her door. "You must've made a good impression for him to speak so openly about you. And giving you money for your cat...my son has never done that for anyone before."

I blushed. "Well, I'm honored. Henry's made a good impression on me too. Anyway, I hope we'll see each other again soon, Lynette. Have a good day."

She smiled, getting into her sedan and backing out of Henry's driveway. I got into my truck and felt like someone was watching me. When I looked up, it was Henry, dressed in his firefighter tee and staring at me through the window. He gave me a slight smile before pulling the curtains closed.

As I backed out of his driveway, my dreams had come true—Henry was available. But I didn't think he was ready to date after going through such an awful divorce. If a friend was what he needed, then that was what I was going to be. The best damn friend ever.

And if he wanted to be more...then maybe that was okay with me too. If he wasn't still in love with his ex. And if only I could decide to let Ty and Jack go.

Decisions, decisions. Life was full of them—and they were all messy.

Chapter Sixteen

I headed back to the bakery, parking on the street and entering through the door with the chime of the bell. Grandma and Mackenzie were already there, serving customers bagels, muffins, and other delicious treats for breakfast. The whole place smelled heavenly—like cinnamon and vanilla. My favorite scents.

Grandma smiled when she noticed me. I put my purse down and reached for an apron. "There she is! Just in time too—the interviewer will be here soon. How did it go with Henry? Did you give him the smile cookies?"

"I did—he loved them." I waited for the last customer to leave the bakery, then leaned over the counter. "And you two need to hear what I found out."

"What's going on?" Mackenzie asked, poking her head inside from the kitchen.

"Well, Henry isn't married at all like I thought. He just went through a messy divorce, actually."

"But...you said he had a wedding ring on," Grandma said, pointing at hers on her hand. "I wear mine because I still love your grandpa very much. If he's still wearing the ring, maybe he can't let go."

I shrugged. "Yeah, I guess. Or maybe it's out of habit. And the money he gave us to save Nutmeg? That was money he saved up with his wife for the future. Money, he said was pointless now. That's why he was in Boston—settling the divorce."

"Damn," Mackenzie said. "He must really like you to give you that money."

"Or he was just being kind," I said. "He clearly didn't want the money—he said it reminded him of his ex. I don't know what happened between them, but whatever it was, he's been really distraught about it. I ran into his mom, who was checking on him, who said the divorce destroyed him."

Grandma nodded, placing cupcakes in a box. "I bet—it's an awful, awful thing to go through. Poor Henry."

"But this is good, isn't it?" Mackenzie asked, wiping her floury hands on her apron. "Henry's single. You can date him now."

"Mackenzie has a good point," Grandma said. "I'm sure he could use some love after his disastrous divorce."

I sighed, pulling back from the counter. "I don't know—seems he's still getting over his ex. And I really don't want to be the rebound. I should just be his friend, comfort him through this. It's the least I can do."

Grandma smiled. "That's nice of you, dear. Did you tell him we'd pay him back in full? And thank him for saving our bakery?"

"I did—but he said don't worry about it. He doesn't want the money back."

"That man," Grandma said. "Truly a sweetheart.

Anyway, dear—can you help me set up before the interviewer gets here? Should be any minute now."

I nodded, still thinking about Henry as I helped Grandma move some chairs for our interview and set up decorations. Grandma was piddling around and making sure the bakery was spotless, but I thought it looked fine. Mackenzie was still in the kitchen, preparing orders for the day.

When we heard a knock on the door, we spun around, noticing a news reporter standing there. He was handsome —in his mid-sixties with salt and pepper hair, blue eyes, and a matching blue suit. He held a fluffy microphone and waved at us with a smile as a camerawoman held a massive camera on her shoulder behind him.

Grandma fixed her hair, then applied a little lipstick. "Ah, he's here. Come on, everyone—showtime!"

Mackenzie came out of the kitchen, drying her washed hands on a towel as Grandma opened the door. She let the news reporter and the camerawoman inside with a smile and gestured at the table.

"Hello, so nice to see you," she began. "Please, have a seat anywhere you'd like."

"Thank you," the reporter said with a grin. "I've heard a lot of good things about your bakery over the years. I'm glad you agreed to an interview."

"Well, thank you for offering. Times have been tough since my husband passed away, so we need all the exposure we can get."

The reporter frowned, sitting down across from Grandma. "I'm so sorry to hear that. Lou was quite popular around New Harbor, wasn't he?"

Grandma looked sad. "Yes—yes, he was. It was his idea to put fortunes in the desserts, actually, something our customers really love. Oh, where are my manners? This is my granddaughter, Angie, and our employee, Mackenzie Teller."

"Hi," Mackenzie said, then an oven dinged in the kitchen. "Be right back—gotta get the everything bagels."

Mackenzie vanished into the kitchen as I sat down, shaking the reporter's hand. "Hi, nice to meet you. And you are...?"

"Mitch. Mitch McCready," he replied, smiling a pearly-white grin. "I've worked with the local news for over forty years. Worked my way up the ladder to be their lead newscaster. And I've loved desserts and sweets since I was a little boy."

"Then we'll get along well," Grandma joked, putting the CLOSED sign on the door. "Let me just close the bakery for our interview so we aren't interrupted. And, oh, let me get you some desserts and coffee. On the house."

"Thank you, we'd love that."

Grandma scurried into the kitchen, then returned a moment later with a tray of scones, muffins, tea, and coffee. She set it down on the table, letting us help ourselves. Mitch bit into the lemon scone and smiled.

"This is amazing!" he cried. "So warm and delicious. And lemon is my favorite."

"Really? It's mine too," Grandma said, her eyes twinkling. "I'm glad you like it. Well, we're ready to begin the interview whenever you are."

"Wonderful. Linda, please hit record," Mitch said to his camerawoman, swallowing the rest of his scone. "But before we start, I just wanted to say...I lost a spouse too. My wife, Donna, in a car crash a few years ago. I know the pain. Again, I'm very sorry for your loss."

Grandma swallowed a lump in her throat. "Thank you, Mitch. And I'm sorry for yours as well."

"Yes—it's a terrible, terrible thing." Mitch shook his head. "Anyway, let's speak about more pleasant things. So, Esther, why don't you tell us a little bit of the history behind your bakery?"

Grandma ran through the shop's past, telling Mitch all about how it was Grandpa's dream to bake. She helped him save up enough money and they opened the bakery thirty years ago. When Grandpa had the idea to put fortunes in each dessert, the bakery exploded in popularity.

"And where did he get that idea from?" Mitch asked. "From fortune cookies?"

"Yes, partly. We loved getting Chinese takeout, especially on our anniversaries. But my husband was a kind man," Grandma said with a warm smile. "He always wanted the best for people. I think that's why he loved putting sweet messages in the desserts. He wanted people to smile, especially those struggling. It's a tradition we've carried on since his passing."

Mitch grinned. "That's a lovely tradition. And you, Angie? Growing up with bakers for grandparents must've been fun."

"Oh, yeah—I got to test out a lot of desserts. I was always hyper from the sugar overload," I joked, making Grandma laugh. "I couldn't imagine doing anything other than helping Grandma run this bakery and honor my grandpa's legacy."

"Yes, I'm so grateful for my granddaughter," Grandma said, reaching for my hand and squeezing it. "I'd be lost without her. And I've been trying to help her find a partner—as strong of a love as her grandpa and I had."

I blushed. "Grandma, please..."

Mitch laughed. "Oh, I think that's a nice idea. Love is a beautiful thing to have."

"Agreed." Grandma nodded. "My Angie deserves a man who is kind, loyal, and thoughtful. She hasn't had much luck in love, but hopefully, the tide is turning. And you know, she already has her sights on an incredible man, but I'm not sure he's completely over his ex-wife yet."

"Grandma," I whispered, embarrassed.

"It's all right, dear," she said, patting my shoulder. "No harm in having a little crush. Anyway, Angie is still looking for Mr. Right. If there are any men out there who would like to step up, we'd love to hear from them. Our bakery is open seven days a week."

"Of course—I'll add that to my news segment. 'A bakery owner's granddaughter's quest for love.' I like that headline," Mitch said, writing it down in his notepad. "Now, is there anything else you want the public to know?"

"Yes—we'll be taking part in the annual Sweet Treats Festival soon," Grandma said. "There will be different vendors selling desserts and merchandise. And there should be fun games for the kids too."

"Oh, wonderful! I'll have to stop by then," Mitch said, gesturing at the camerawoman. "Okay, you can shut it off now—"

When the door opened with a chime, all our heads shot up. Lucy stepped into the bakery and looked around with her nose in the air. Did she ever stop giving off her holier-than-thou energy?

We should've locked the door.

"This place smells funny," she grumbled to herself. "Too much sugar in the air. Gross."

Grandma rose to her feet. "I'm sorry, but we're closed right now. Didn't you see the sign on the window?"

"I saw it," Lucy said with a shrug. "And that news van outside. What's going on?'

"We're being interviewed for the local news," I replied. "Our bakery's going to feature tonight."

Lucy looked jealous, crossing her arms. "Really? This piece of crap bakery is getting a news segment?"

"I beg to differ," Mitch said, turning to Lucy. "I had their desserts and they're incredible. Definitely worth the hype."

"Agree to disagree," Lucy sneered. "How come I've never gotten a TV interview? I run a business too, you know. The Green Machine. It's much healthier—and better —than this place."

"Ah, I've heard of it," Mitch said with a nod. "I'm sorry, but I'm not into health food. Desserts have a special place in my heart."

Lucy looked like she would explode. "I bet I could change your mind if you gave me the chance. I'm free later today. Why don't you drop by for an interview, and I'll let you sample the menu?"

Mitch shifted in his seat, looking uncomfortable. "Actually, I'm quite busy today. Lots to do. I'll let you know if I have an available spot."

Lucy narrowed her eyes, saying nothing. It didn't look like she believed him.

"Anyway," I said, clearing my throat, "we're in the middle of an interview here. And the sign does say closed. So, if you wouldn't mind..."

Lucy walked over, tapping on the camera. "Is this thing on?"

The camerawoman nodded. "Yep, that's right."

"Good. I have a complaint to make about this place," Lucy said, bending down to look into the camera. "I found a hair in my cupcake last time. And you know what? I've heard rumors they have rats in the kitchen!"

"That's a lie!" I cried, rising to my feet. "We've never had rats. And you've never come in here. So how could you find a hair in a cupcake you didn't even eat?"

"Well, I did. Doesn't seem very professional, if you ask me," Lucy said, glancing between Mitch and the camerawoman. "Maybe you might want to rethink featuring this bakery on your show. I wouldn't spend a dime at this place."

"Thank you, but I'm a big fan of the bakery," Mitch said, speaking up for us. "And I'd really like to get back to the interview now."

Lucy glanced around the table, her eyes landing on me. She gave me a hard glare. "Fine, I have things to do anyway. If you ever want that interview, my restaurant's just down the block. The Green Machine—you can't miss it."

Mitch faked a smile. "All right. Goodbye, Lucy."

She barely looked back at us as she fled the bakery, slamming the door behind her. Everything turned quiet for a few seconds.

"I'm so sorry about that," Grandma said. "Lucy...well, we don't really get along. She's our biggest competitor."

"And rudest," I added. "I can't stand her. We didn't get along in high school, either, and she just won't leave us alone."

Maybe I shouldn't have been saying that stuff to a reporter, but honestly? Lucy was the worst–and I didn't care who knew. Besides, she was probably saying worse about me behind my back.

"I knew it. I had her type pegged as soon as she walked in. I know a mean girl when I see one," Mitch said, shaking his head in disgust. "I'll cut her out of the interview and forget all that nonsense. I don't believe for a second that you would have rats. It was clearly an attempt to make you look bad after noticing the news van outside."

Grandma sighed in relief. "Thank you, Mitch. We appreciate your support."

"Of course. Anyway, we have everything we need. Esther, Angie, it was truly love to meet you two. I wish you the best of luck with your bakery."

We rose to our feet and shook his hand. Grandma smiled. "Thank you for coming. Looking forward to seeing our bakery on TV."

"I'm going back to the news station to edit the footage right away. Should air tonight with the regular news," Mitch said with a smile. "And Esther, I hope this isn't inappropriate for me to say, but...I think you're an amazing lady. The town is lucky to have you."

"Why, thank you, Mitch," Grandma said, walking him to the door. "I try my best."

"I'm sure you do. Maybe we could grab coffee sometime? Discuss your plans for the bakery?"

Grandma hesitated. "Well, I am terribly busy, but...I'll let you know. Have a great day, Mitch."

He nodded, waving goodbye as he left with his camerawoman. They got into their news van outside the bakery and sped off. I walked over to Grandma, watching them fade down the street.

"Okay, am I crazy...or was he totally flirting with you?" I asked.

"Hmm?" Grandma asked, turning to me. "Oh, I'm sure he was just being polite. It's his job as a reporter to get to know people in town."

"No, I'm pretty sure he was flirting with you. You know, in an old man way," I joked. "Would it be so bad if he was?"

Grandma put the OPEN sign on the door, pausing. "I...I don't know. I can't imagine being with anyone but your grandfather."

"But I'm sure he wouldn't want you to be alone for the rest of your life. That's not fair," I said, walking toward her. "If you had died instead, would you have wanted that for Grandpa?"

Grandma thought for a moment. "No...no, I wouldn't have. I'd want him to be happy. And if that included falling in love again, then I would be thrilled for him."

"Exactly. You know, you've been trying to find me a partner so badly that you haven't even stopped to think about yourself. Maybe you should try dating again. Doesn't have to be today, but someday. Take another chance at love."

Grandma sighed, picking up the empty tray of scones. "I'm not so sure about that, dear. I've made peace with the fact that I'll be a widow until I die. I'm more interested in ensuring your happiness."

"I know—you always were, Grandma. But it isn't selfish to think about your own happiness too. Maybe you could have something special with someone else. Like Mitch for example."

"But...he isn't your grandfather."

"And he never will be. You're not replacing him. Think of it this way," I said, leaning against the table. "Lots of people lose pets, then go on to adopt another. It doesn't mean they're replacing the old pet or forgetting about them. It just means they want to open their hearts again and love someone else. Is that so wrong?"

Grandma smiled. "Dear, you're beginning to sound like me. Tell you what? I'll think about it."

"Good, that's all I ask. Okay, need me to help with anything?"

"Yes—you can put icing on some cookies in the kitchen. Tomorrow, you can pick up Nutmeg. And then you can also get ready for your date with Jack."

Crap, I'd almost forgotten. "Right. Let's hope he doesn't watch the interview tonight and see you telling Mitch all about my crush on Henry."

"I never mentioned him by name, darling," Grandma said, vanishing into the kitchen. She emerged a second later. "I just thought that maybe, if he was willing to get over his ex, it would encourage him to ask you out. Like you said to me, perhaps he'll want another shot at love."

Maybe he would. I crossed my fingers, hoping it would all work out. With our bakery, with Grandma's love life, with Henry.

We needed some good news these days.

Chapter Seventeen

After helping Grandma with what she needed around the bakery, I got in my truck and drove to Boston to pick up Nutmeg. She was glad to see a familiar face and practically jumped in my arms. Dr. Bentley confirmed she was doing better, then I thanked him as we left.

When I brought Nutmeg home, she was back to her usual self—sleeping around the house, licking herself, and eating large amounts of kibble. All thanks to Henry. I wasn't sure baking cookies was enough of a thank you, but it would have to do for now.

I tidied up the house, sweeping and dusting before my date later. Sure, the chores needed to get done, but I was also nervous about the date and wanted to keep my hands busy. Then I took a relaxing bath, washed my hair, and picked out an outfit. When all of that was done, I started cooking pork chops for Grandma for dinner, then she was unlocking the door.

"Nutmeg?" she called out. "Are you here, darling?"

Despite Nutmeg being half-blind and half-deaf, she still managed to hear Grandma. She slowly made her way over to her, rubbing against her leg and purring. Grandma smiled and reached down to pet her.

I watched them with a grin, relieved we didn't have to lose that old cat. "She seems fine to me. Dr. Bentley even said she was doing much better."

"Good. Let's hope she stays that way," Grandma said, giving Nutmeg one final pet. Then she sniffed the air. "My, that smells incredible. What are you cooking?"

"Pork chops," I said, gesturing at the pan on the stove. "We have some time to kill before my date. Hey, do you think you could get your special recipe book from the basement? I want to impress Jack."

"Of course—but don't let him see any of my secret ingredients. If he marries you, perhaps I'll consider letting him take a peek."

I laughed. "It's only what, our third date? It's a bit too soon for marriage. But don't worry—I won't let him see it."

Grandma nodded, heading into the basement to grab her old recipe book. It was one that she and Grandpa had crafted together after hours of hard work in the kitchen to find out what tasted the best. She dusted it off, then left the large book of recipes on the counter.

"Dinner's almost ready," I said, flipping the pork chops. "Can you set the table?"

"Actually, I hope you don't mind, but I thought we could turn the news on while we eat," Grandma said, walking into the TV and reaching for the remote. "Our segment is supposed to air tonight. I'll grab the dinner trays, and we can eat in front of the TV."

"Okay, sure. That was fast. Let's hope Mitch kept his promise, and edited out Lucy's comments, and made us look good."

"I'm sure he did," Grandma said, turning on the TV.

"Ooh, there he is. You know, I think Mitch is quite handsome. The silver hair looks nice on him."

I laughed from the kitchen. "And he's single. Just saying."

Grandma shook her head, though I thought I saw a hint of a smile when I poked my head into the living room. "Quickly, dear—it's starting."

As fast as I could, I plated the pork chops, apple sauce, and salad, then brought out two plates for Grandma and me. She had assembled the TV trays in front of the couch and we quickly sat down. Grandma reached for the TV remote, turning it up as she handed me a fork.

Mitch was sitting behind his news desk, chatting with another anchor. "...and I went on a special assignment today to Lucky's Baked Goods, a popular bakery in town."

The other news anchor grinned. "Oh, I've had their pie! It was amazing."

"Yes, very tasty," Mitch agreed. "And the owner, Esther Linden, is a lovely, lovely woman."

When I noticed Grandma blushing, I playfully nudged her arm. "Seems you aren't the only one who thinks the other is attractive."

Grandma just laughed, then Mitch continued. "...and without further ado, here's the interview I did with the family. I think you'll enjoy it as much as I did."

The interview played on the TV, the rude parts with Lucy taken out. I sighed in relief as I ate my pork chops. We came across as kind and outgoing, answering Mitch's questions and showing off our desserts. Then Grandma mentioned I had a crush on someone in town who was getting over a divorce.

I closed my eyes. "Oh, man...I hope Henry doesn't see this."

"Why?" Grandma asked, sipping her soda. "I hope he does. Maybe it'll give him the kick in the rump to finally ask you out."

Then the camera cut back to Mitch sitting behind the news desk. A picture of my face was on the screen.

"You heard it straight from the horse's mouth," Mitch said with a smile. "Esther is looking for a good man for her granddaughter, Angie. Could that man be you?"

How embarrassing.

"And here I thought the matchmaking had ended after the speed dating thing," I grumbled. "Now you've got Mitch helping out your little plan."

Grandma laughed. "This is a good thing, dear. You deserve to find someone special. Even Mitch himself thinks so."

I shook my head as Mitch continued. "I had a great time at their bakery today. It was an honor and a privilege to interview them. So, New Harbor—what are you waiting for? Head over to Lucky's Baked Goods ASAP and try out their amazing desserts. You won't be disappointed by their food *or* their warmth."

When the news story changed, I nodded. "That went well. Well, despite you meddling in my love life again."

Grandma winked.

I rolled my eyes, then continued. "Anyway, I have no doubt more people will be tempted to come into our bakery now."

Grandma nodded, taking a bite of her pork chop. "Yes, I'm relieved it went over so well. Amazing work on the pork chops, by the way."

I smiled, thanking Grandma for her kind words before getting back to our meal. We chatted before cleaning up. I did the dishes, then wiped down the kitchen so the area was ready for Jack and me.

"I should get out of your hair," Grandma said, checking her watch. "Almost time for Jack to arrive. I think I'll head to the coffee shop—keep thinking over Sonya's engagement party desserts."

"Good idea. I'll let you know when the date is over. And thanks for giving us some privacy, Grandma."

She kissed my cheek. "Of course, dear—it's the least I can do. I've never told you this, but…I'm so grateful to have your support at the bakery. I'm not sure I could keep going if not for you. If I was all alone, well…I think I would've fallen into a deep depression without your grandpa. You saved me from that."

"And you saved me too, Grandma," I said, trying not to cry. "I'm glad to have you."

Grandma smiled. "Okay, I should go now—before I have you tearing up before your date. Let me know how it goes. Bye, sweetie!"

I waved as Grandma left the house, getting into her sedan and driving off down the darkening street. I cleaned up a bit more and set out the baking ingredients on the table before feeding Nutmeg for dinner. She was eating her bowl of cat food when the doorbell rang.

"Showtime," I murmured to myself.

I walked over to the door, smoothing out my dress shirt and jeans and hoped I looked presentable. After peeking at myself in the hanging mirror, I opened the door. Jack stood there, holding a bouquet of roses.

He grinned. "Hi, Angie. You look as beautiful as ever."

"Aw, thank you, Jack. Are those for me?"

"Yes—picked them up on my way here," he said, handing over the roses. "May I come in?"

"Of course!" I said as I took the roses. "Make yourself at home. I'm going to find a place for these flowers. And you'll probably meet our cat, Nutmeg, too. She's just eating dinner."

Jack walked into our house, closing the door before he noticed Nutmeg. "Aw, what a cute cat. Looks pretty old."

"Yeah, she's sixteen," I said, grabbing an empty vase off the counter. I placed the roses inside and filled it up with water. "Still hanging on to her nine lives."

"That's impressive." Jack moved toward Nutmeg, bending down to pet her. "Hey, little kitty."

Nutmeg smelled Jack, then backed away with a hiss. I had never seen her behave that way before. Jack looked a little afraid, standing up and moving away.

"Oh, I'm so sorry," I said, rushing over. "Bad kitty. We don't hiss at guests, all right?"

Nutmeg looked at me and then back at Jack before walking toward the staircase, vanishing upstairs. Jack was still staring at her as she disappeared.

"It's all right. Guess she didn't like me very much," he began. "I've never been a cat person, though."

"That's fair. It's probably not you—she's still recovering from surgery. Had to take her to an emergency vet in Boston. Cost us five grand for the operation."

"Oof," Jack said, shaking his head. "All that over a cat? That's kind of a waste of money."

That rubbed me the wrong way. It almost sounded heartless. "Well, maybe to you, but we love Nutmeg. We'd do anything for her. She was my grandpa's cat. So she's extra special."

Jack turned to me. "Hmm. Well, agree to disagree."

I cleared my throat. "Right. Anyway, have a seat. I can take your coat. Would you like coffee or tea?"

"Coffee would be great, thanks," Jack said, handing me his coat. "You have a beautiful house."

"Thank you," I said, walking to the front door to hang his coat on a hook. "My grandparents have owned it for over thirty years."

"Nice," Jack said, sitting at the island and glancing around. "They must've come up with so many recipes in this place. I'm eager to learn a few—really step up my baking game."

I smiled, gesturing at the baking ingredients on the table. "Then tonight's your lucky night. So, we're going to make my grandma's famous chocolate cake. With some secret ingredients."

Jack looked intrigued. "I don't suppose you could share them, could you?"

"Sorry—my lips are sealed. It's a family recipe."

"Too bad. But at least I get to have a taste," he said, glancing around as I began to combine flour and baking powder in a big bowl. "Hey, is that the Linden family recipe book?"

He gestured at the book sitting on the counter, then I nodded. "The one and only. There are decades worth of recipes in there, all perfected by my grandparents. For family eyes only, of course."

"Of course," Jack said, stepping back with a smile. "So, is there anything I can do to help? Anything that's not top-secret?"

"Yep—you can stir the flour, please and thank you. I just need to review the recipe book to make sure I'm making it right."

Jack nodded, stirring the flour and baking powder together as I read over the recipe. Without him seeing—and making him turn around for the secret ingredients—I followed it to the letter, patiently waiting for the cake to bake in the oven. Jack and I drank coffee at the table while it baked.

"So, how did you get so interested in baking?" I asked.

Jack shrugged. "It's kind of a new hobby, to be honest. I wanted to try something different. And my stepsister is really eager for me to learn so I can teach her. She owns a restaurant too, always wanting to try out different recipes."

"Aw, that's nice. I guess you're close to your stepsister?"

"Very." Jack sipped his coffee. "I'd do anything for her. You don't have any siblings, do you?"

"Nope—it's just me. Which meant my grandparents gave me all their attention. Still, sometimes I wish I had a little sister or something."

When the oven bell dinged, I rose to my feet and walked over. I picked up my oven mitts and removed the cake from the oven. It was glistening in the light—looking delicious, hot, and smelling fantastic.

"Dear Lord," Jack said, rising to his feet and walking over. "That smells incredible!"

I smiled. "I know—I wouldn't expect any less from my grandma's tried and true recipe. Here, you can have the first bite."

I grabbed a big knife, cutting into the cake. I gave Jack a big piece on a plate with a fork. As he bit into it, he nodded.

"Oh, yeah—this is fantastic. Whatever secret ingredients you put inside made it incredible."

"Thank you," I said, grabbing my own piece. "It's easy to see why it's my grandma's favorite. Anyway, I had a great time with you, Jack. I hope you learned a few tricks of the trade tonight."

"I did. Very eager to put it all to good use," he said, quickly finishing his piece of cake. "Seriously, tell your grandma that's fantastic. She should be proud. No wonder your bakery is so popular."

"Aw, thank you. I'm sure she'll be happy to hear that. I'll be right back—just need to use the bathroom. But feel free to help yourself to another slice."

Jack nodded, eyeing the delicious cake as I walked down the hall to use the bathroom. I washed my hands when I was finished, walked out, and found Jack waiting near the door.

"I should probably go. I have to get up early tomorrow," Jack began, holding his jacket. "As much as I wish I could stay. I'm really enjoying our time together, Angie."

Putting his comment about Nutmeg aside, I agreed. "Same here. Get home safely, all right? Thanks for coming over."

He nodded, opening the door and walking outside. He waved as he got into his sedan and drove off into the dark. I shut the door, feeling pretty good about the date. It had gone well—and it was easy talking to Jack. Something that I thought was very important in a relationship.

I pulled out my smartphone, texting Grandma. *Jack just left*, I wrote. *We had a great time baking. He's a fast learner.*

Grandma texted back quickly. *Wonderful! I'm just finishing up my tea and then I'll be home. You can tell me all about it in person.*

I promised I would, putting my phone away and doing all the dishes in the kitchen. Fifteen minutes later, the door unlocked, then Grandma walked inside with a grin.

"There you are," she began. "Mmm, you must've baked my chocolate cake. I could smell that heavenly dessert from a mile away."

I laughed. "I did—and it was a crowd-pleaser. Jack loved it."

Grandma put her purse down, taking off her coat. "That's good to hear, darling. And you didn't tell him any of the secret ingredients?"

"Nope—I even made him turn around when I added them to the cake. He was a perfect gentleman. Didn't even peek."

"That's what I like to hear," Grandma said, sitting at the island. "So, tell me everything. I live for romantic gossip these days."

I shook my head with a chuckle, telling Grandma all about the date and how close Jack was with his stepsister. Then we started talking about all the recipes I could show Jack next time since this date had gone so well.

"Perhaps you could bake him a heart-shaped cake. Or strawberry strudel," Grandma said, rising to her feet. "Those are good. Let me see if I have something special you could show Jack. Where did you put my recipe book?"

"Oh, it's over there," I said, pointing at the counter. It was empty. "Or it was. I left it right there."

Grandma walked to the empty counter. "There's nothing here, sweetie. Are you sure you didn't move it when Jack came over?"

"No—I kept it there so I wouldn't lose it. It has to be here somewhere. Right? Oh my God, I think I'm going to have a panic attack."

"Deep breaths, dear. We'll find it."

"Okay, okay." I ran a hand through my hair. "I'll check the kitchen and living room, just in case. You can try the upstairs and basement. Maybe...maybe I moved it and don't remember."

Grandma nodded, heading downstairs to start her search. I turned the entire kitchen and living room upside down—searching through old drawers and cupboards—but

I didn't see the recipe book. It was large and heavy so there was no missing it. Where could it have gone?

Grandma went upstairs, then came back down a few minutes later. "It's not upstairs either. How could a recipe book vanish?"

I pulled out my phone, finding Jack's number. "Here, let me text Jack. Maybe he saw me move it."

Hey Jack, it's Angie, I wrote. *Me and my grandma are having a hard time finding her recipe book, the one I showed you tonight. Do you remember me putting it somewhere?*

Once I sent the text, Grandma and I sat on the couch, waiting. Then we waited and waited some more. I noticed Jack had seen my message—as proven by the READ timestamp under it—but didn't respond. The minutes ticked by and there was still no response.

Just what was going on?

Chapter Eighteen

Grandma and I sat in silence for a few minutes, thinking about the missing recipe book. There was only one solution. Since Grandma was too polite to say it, it was going to have to be me.

"I think...I think Jack stole the recipe book," I finally said. "That explains why he left in such a hurry. And why he won't answer his phone. I think he stole it when I went to the bathroom, then hid it behind his coat."

"Hmm," Grandma said, shaking her head sadly. "But why? What does he have to gain from that?"

"I don't know. That's the worst part," I said, glancing out the window and wondering what Jack had planned. "Maybe he'll sell the recipes. Try to put us out of business."

"This is absurd," Grandma said, rising to her feet. "What did we ever do to him? Why would he do such an awful thing?"

"I have no clue. Maybe...maybe he planned this all along. Maybe that's why he wanted to come to my house on the second date—to see what he could take. In hindsight, it's a little strange how much he talked about baking. He was always asking if we had tips or secrets to share. Seems like he had a goal in mind."

Grandma ran a hand through her white hair, looking frazzled. "I just can't believe it. When we spoke on Bumble, he seemed like such a nice man. Polite and respectful. Perhaps I misjudged him."

"Or maybe that's what he wanted you to think. What he wanted everything to think," I said, approaching Grandma and reaching for her hand. "Don't blame yourself. If anyone's to blame here, it's him. And me for being so stupid to leave the recipe book out. I was practically asking for him to steal it."

Grandma shook her head. "No, dear—it's not your fault either. I blame Jack and Jack alone. Has he answered any of your texts?"

I checked my phone. "Nope, nothing. I'll try calling him. One sec."

I pressed his contact on my phone, then waited for it to ring. But it went straight to voicemail. And his voicemail was full so I couldn't leave a message.

I sighed, hanging up. "I think he might've blocked my number. It goes straight to voicemail when I call."

"Then what are we going to do?" Grandma asked, on the verge of tears. "The recipe book your grandpa and I worked so hard on for decades…gone!"

I felt so bad for Grandma. And guilty. This was my fault—and I was going to fix it. Either by hunting Jack down like a criminal or rewriting the recipe book. I could do the latter right now.

"Come on," I said, walking into the kitchen. I fetched some blank paper and a pen out of the bottom drawer. "I'm sure we can recreate the recipe book. You still remember a lot of the recipes, right?"

"Like the back of my hand," Grandma said, sniffling. "Your grandpa and I made them over and over again and I eventually memorized them. But...there are some I'm sure I can't recreate even if I tried."

"Well, we have to give it a shot," I said, sitting at the table with the pen and paper. "Come on—we'll start in alphabetical order. It was probably time to update that old recipe book, anyway. Let's go with...apple pie. What do you need for that?"

Grandma sat beside me, then we spent hours at the kitchen table, rewriting all the recipes she perfected with Grandpa. There were a few she couldn't remember but we got most of it down. When I looked up at the clock, it was four a.m.

"Oh my gosh," I said, yawning. "We've been sitting here longer than I thought. But we did well."

"Yes, we did—not perfect, but it's a start. And we both need our rest." Grandma rose to her feet, sighing. "I'm so sorry, Angie. About Jack. I'm the one who encouraged you to see him. I feel like it's partly my fault."

I rose to my feet, setting the papers aside with the recipes on them. "No, Grandma. It's just like you said—I blame Jack and Jack alone. He made the choice to steal from us. And I intend to find him and find out why. Too bad I don't know where he lives..."

Grandma nodded, sadly. "Too bad, indeed. Just be careful, Angie. We don't know what his grand plan is. Don't get hurt just to get our recipes back—it isn't worth it. And Grandpa wouldn't want that. Anyway, thank you for trying to recreate the recipes with me. We'll start up again tomorrow. Try to get some sleep, hmm?"

I said goodnight to Grandma, watching her walk up the stairs to head to her bedroom. It broke my heart to see her so upset. Then it turned to rage. How could Jack do this? And why?

When I yawned again, I realized my plan for revenge could wait. I left the papers and pen on the table behind me and headed upstairs to my own room. I passed out quickly, waking up to my alarm at eight a.m. A second later, someone was texting my smartphone, making it buzz on the nightstand. I got up quickly to check it and hoped it would be Jack, growing a conscience.

But it was only Mackenzie. *Where are you and your grandma?* she texted. *I'm at the bakery but it's closed. Super weird.*

Sorry, I texted back. *We stayed up late. I'll wake up Grandma and we'll be on our way. Tell you all the drama when we arrive.*

Mackenzie sent an emoji of two eyeballs, wondering what was going on. I quickly dressed, brushed my teeth, and grabbed my purse before heading down the hall. As quietly as I could, I inched the door open to Grandma's room.

"Grandma?" I whispered. "Are you awake?"

She was lying in bed on her side, looking dejected. "Yes, I'm awake, dear. And I'm afraid I don't feel like opening the bakery today. You go ahead without me."

"Oh, Grandma," I said, walking over and sitting on her bed. Nutmeg was lying an inch away and meowed before going back to sleep. "I know you're upset about Jack stealing our recipe book, but we have to keep going. If only for Grandpa."

Grandma sighed. "I just...I don't see the point, dear. If we don't get that recipe book back, we'll lose some of those recipes forever. The only part of your grandpa I have left.

For today, at least, I don't want to see the bakery. I just want to lie here. Let me rest, dear. Please."

I rose to my feet. "Okay, Grandma. Call me if you need anything, all right?"

She promised she would, then I left her bedroom. I prepared Nutmeg's food for her—which she came scampering down the stairs to eat—and made some eggs and toast for Grandma. I put a lid over the plate, trying to keep it warm as long as I could, then left it on the island counter where she would see it. I knew she probably didn't feel like eating but she had to.

I left the house, locking the door behind me and getting into my truck. I tried texting and calling Jack again, but it wouldn't go through. Scowling, I turned the key in my ignition and took off down the street, heading to the bakery. When I made it to the main street, I noticed a new sign in the window of Lucy's restaurant.

It read: TRY OUR NEW CHOCOLATE CAKE TODAY! MADE IN-HOUSE WITH SECRET, DELICIOUS INGREDIENTS.

I pressed on the brakes, causing a car behind me to honk and swerve around. They swore at me as they passed but I didn't care. I had my answers now—I knew why Jack had gone out with me and stolen the recipe book.

He was working with Lucy, my enemy since high school. But how did they know each other?

I pulled over, parking on the street before stepping out. I approached the door to The Green Machine—shaped like a green juice—before opening it, stepping inside with the chime of a bell. More people than ever were in the restaurant, ordering green juices and the new chocolate cake. I saw Jack at one of the tables, wearing an apron and passing out free samples.

"It's delicious, if I do say so myself," he was telling a customer. "Made with secret ingredients. I can't tell you what they are, unfortunately."

Lucy stood behind the counter, selling more of the chocolate cake. They were selling fast—of course they were. Our desserts were amazing. I stood in line, waiting until I was next. Lucy smirked when she saw me.

"Well, well, well," she began. "Look who it is. Ms. Bakery Girl. Are you here to finally taste our superior food?"

"Superior? Hardly. And I wouldn't buy something from you if you were the last restaurant on Earth," I spat, making her smile fade. "I know what you did, Lucy. You told Jack to date me, didn't you? You two were in on it. You wanted him to steal my recipes. Why? Are you that immature and petty that you would try to ruin us like this? Over some stupid feud from high school?"

I noticed some of the customers staring at us, murmuring. Lucy laughed nervously and shook her head. "I really don't know what you're talking about, Angie. This recipe has been in my family for generations."

"Come to think of it," an older man said behind me, "the dessert does remind us of the cake you can get at Lucky's..."

"Purely coincidental, I promise you," Lucy said with a sweet smile. "The recipe is ours, fair and square."

I wasn't done exposing her in front of her customers. "But I thought you didn't serve dessert? That sugar gives you wrinkles and you were all about eating healthy?"

Lucy shrugged. "We decided to try something new—and it's brought in so many customers. By the way, have you met my new stepbrother, Jack?"

Jack walked over, smiling and waving. But it wasn't the

friendly smile he wore when we went out. No, this one was devious—he knew what he had done. Now their whispering at town hall made sense. They knew each other and planned this. Him telling her off on our date at the coffee shop and pretending to be strangers was all an act.

"You," I gritted. "You stole my recipe book when I went to the bathroom. And then you brought it here, gave it to Lucy, and recreated the desserts to steal our clientele."

Jack laughed. "That's quite the imagination you have. You can't prove that—and if you try, we've got lawyers waiting. So be very, very careful. Oh, did I mention my day job involves working as a paralegal?"

Of course it did. And I hated to admit it, but Jack was right. We had no proof they had stolen from us—it was our word against theirs. And they still had the recipe book hidden somewhere. Unless I could find it and show everyone they had taken it from us, it was a lost cause.

"So childish," I grumbled. "You really haven't matured past high school, Lucy. And it seems you're bringing your new stepbrother down to your level."

"All is fair in love and war and business," Lucy gloated. "Now, if you wouldn't mind, you're holding up the line. Next!"

A man in line pushed past me, approaching the desk. Lucy took his order as Jack continued to smirk my way. He had used me to get to the recipe book—all for his new stepsister's success. It was a sick and twisted plan, one that had worked. I was so ashamed I had fallen for it.

Trying to find love never worked out for me. Why did I even bother?

Shaking my head, I turned, leaving The Green Machine. I spotted Lucy's husband, Dan, serving coffee at a table. He noticed me, looking down. Was he ashamed? Did someone in Lucy's family actually have a conscience?

Hmm. Maybe there was a way to use him to expose Lucy. But how, I wondered?

While thinking, I walked down the street to the bakery where Mackenzie was waiting outside. When she saw me, she sighed, looking relieved.

"Finally! What took you so long?" she asked. "Usually, you and your grandma beat me here."

I reached into my pocket, getting out my key and unlocking the front door. "You remember Jack, that guy my grandma conspired with to meet me? Well, you'll never believe what he's done..."

After I let Mackenzie into the restaurant, I told her everything—all about Jack and Lucy's devious plan. Mackenzie couldn't believe it.

"This...this has to be illegal!" she cried. "Stealing your recipe book? You should call the sheriff. Or the mayor. I could get my dad involved too!"

I shook my head, putting the OPEN sign on the door. "No, Jack was right—we have no proof. If we start making wild accusations, we could get in trouble. The legal kind."

Mackenzie leaned on the counter, looking upset. "This sucks. We can't just let them steal your grandparents' recipes!"

"I know, I know. I'm trying to think of what to do. In the meantime, let's just carry on with business and pretend Lousy Lucy doesn't exist."

"If you say so," Mackenzie said, putting her apron on. "We've got a few orders to fill. How's your grandma taking all this?"

"Not good. She won't get out of bed."

Mackenzie sneered. "Man, that pisses me off! Esther's

such a nice woman. You think of a plan, let me know. I'll be involved one hundred percent to steal back that recipe book and humiliate Lucy and her stupid stepbrother. Any day of the week."

I smiled. "Thanks, Mackenzie. We're grateful for you."

"Hey, you, your grandma, and your grandpa have been angels to me. If anything, I'm grateful for *you.* Holler if you need anything, okay? I'll be in the kitchen, icing the cupcakes. And practicing for my big baking test."

"Okay. Don't worry—you got this."

"Fingers crossed. Oh, look—a customer. I think you'll like who it is."

Mackenzie giggled, then headed into the kitchen. I spun around when I heard the chime of the door and noticed Henry walking in. He had on his full firefighter uniform and looked handsome.

"Hey, Angie," he began. "How's business?"

I shrugged. "Could be better. We've...run into a little problem."

He frowned. "Uh-oh. What's going on?"

"You remember Jack, that guy you met at the firefighter event? Well, we had a date at my house last night. It was going well...until I stepped out of the kitchen for a couple of minutes and he stole my grandma's recipe book."

"What?" Henry's eyes widened. "Why would he do that?"

I gestured out the window. "Because he's the stepbrother of Lucy Rhett, the mean girl from high school and our biggest competitor. He stole our recipes to give to her. They're already selling my grandma's secret chocolate cake as their own. To get back at us, I guess."

Henry was already turning toward the door. "Then I'm

going to march down to her restaurant and demand she give you back the book—"

"No, stop," I said, reaching for his arm. His bicep was big and strong, and I tried not to blush. "Let's not do anything hasty. I need a good plan to expose them—and getting into a fight isn't going to solve anything."

Henry relaxed. "All right, I see your point. Do you know what you're going to do?"

"No, not yet. And my grandma's pretty devastated. But thanks for listening, Henry. I appreciate it."

"Of course, anytime. And when you think of a way to get back at them, just let me know. I'll be around to help."

I blushed again. "Thanks, that's generous. You've been so good to my grandma and me. First with Nutmeg, now this."

"You seem like good people. I like good people," Henry said, simply. Then he looked awkward as he fidgeted with his uniform. "I, uh, came here to tell you something. Can we talk? In private?"

His eyes glanced toward the kitchen, making me look back. Mackenzie was peering out at us through the slit in the door. I snorted at her obvious spying. When she saw us looking, she ducked below the door.

"Of course," I said, gesturing down the hall. "My grandma's office is this way. Come on."

With my heart pounding, I led Henry to Grandma's office, wondering what he had to say to me. And the thought of being alone with Henry sent a tingle up my spine.

Chapter Nineteen

I led Henry into Grandma's office, shutting the door behind us. Grandma had decorated everything—a clock shaped like a cupcake, an air freshener that smelled like cotton candy, and a muffin-shaped garbage can. She had gone a little overboard.

"Wow," Henry said, glancing around. "This office is every dessert lover's dream."

I laughed. "Yeah, Grandma went all out. So...what did you want to talk about?"

Henry cleared his throat. "First off, Chief Teller apologized for yelling at me. Said he was sure I had done the right thing by punching Jim. He completely changed his tune. You didn't have anything to do with that, did you?"

"I might have," I said, cracking a small smile. "I'm sorry —I know you told me not to talk to him. But I couldn't let him be mad at you, not when you were only trying to do the right thing."

Henry nodded. "I appreciate that. At least Chief Teller thinks I'm less of a brute now."

"Of course, I'm glad it worked out. And I saw Jim

poking around once, but other than that, he's left us alone. Let's hope that's it for good."

"Yeah, me too. But that wasn't what I wanted to talk to you about." Henry took a deep breath. "I saw your TV interview last night."

"You watched that, did you?" I asked, cringing. "My grandma was pretty embarrassing. But I think it went well."

"It did, no doubt. You two were naturals. I'm sure it'll draw a lot more customers to your bakery."

"Good—that'll show Lucy."

"Yeah, definitely. I, uh...I heard what your grandma said. That you had a crush on someone who used to be married?"

"That's my grandma," I stammered, laughing nervously. "Always saying crazy things. Believe me, she's gotten even worse since my grandpa died."

"Was it true? Do you have feelings for someone?"

I didn't know what to say. "Well, I, um..."

Henry stepped closer. "Because, you know, maybe hypothetically...someone else has feelings for you too. And they're scared of those feelings."

"Really?" I asked, raising an eyebrow. "Why? Hypothetically, of course."

"Right, hypothetically. Let's just say...they were badly hurt in a past relationship. Betrayed, even. And although they have feelings for someone—strong feelings, because their crush is an amazing person—they're afraid of making the same mistakes. And they're afraid it's too soon."

"I don't blame them. That sounds reasonable," I said with a nod. "But, you know...I'm going to sound a lot like my grandma here, but I have to say it. Every relationship is different, and I'm sure this person isn't like people in the past. Sometimes, you just have to do the thing that scares you and take a chance. Or you'll regret it."

Henry searched my eyes. "Maybe you're right. Hypothetically speaking."

I laughed. "I don't think I've ever heard the word hypothetically used so much in one conversation."

"It is getting a bit ridiculous, isn't it?" Henry asked, cracking a smile. His big dimples made my heart swoon. Then he shrugged. "Just found it easier to say, that's all. Do you understand what I mean?"

"I do. And I think it's brave of you to come here and tell me that."

"Thanks, I was a bit nervous. I've run into burning buildings to save kids no problem. But when it comes to love? I'm a nervous wreck."

"Aren't we all?" I joked.

Henry nodded, the room turning silent. We stared at each other wordlessly for a few seconds. I felt a blush creeping across my face. I couldn't believe it—Henry actually had feelings for me, and he was standing so close that I could reach out and touch him. All the drama with Lucy and Jack just melted away.

Was it too soon to kiss him, I wondered? Because I really wanted to. I found myself leaning in, and for a second, I swore he was doing the same.

There was a knock on the door, and we both jumped. I opened the door and found Mackenzie standing there. She peered in at us. "Oh, sorry—hope I didn't interrupt."

I shook my head. "It's fine. What's going on?"

"Your grandma's here. Thought you might want to break the news about Lucy yourself. Couldn't bring myself to do it. You tell Henry about the whole recipe stealing situation?"

"She did," Henry said with a nod. "It's so...juvenile. So high school of them. Like I said, if you need me for anything, just let me know."

"I'll keep that in mind. Still wondering what to do." I turned to Henry. "I should get out there. But we should talk again later."

Henry nodded. "Yeah, I have to get to work. But I'd like that. Think I could get a cupcake for the road? I came here hoping for a good luck fortune."

"Of course—follow me. Mackenzie was just baking them fresh."

I stepped out of the office, following Mackenzie down the hall with Henry in tow. Grandma had arrived and was already sweeping the floors. She still looked a little sad as she kept her head down, cleaning. Mackenzie shook her head and entered the kitchen behind us.

"Here you are," I said, reaching into the display counter and grabbing a cupcake. "Red velvet—my favorite. Hope you enjoy."

"Thanks. How much do I owe you?"

"It's on the house—the super cute firefighter special. And it's a thank you for saving Nutmeg."

Henry smiled, taking the cupcake. "That's thoughtful. Thank you. Now, let's see what the fortune has in store for me..."

Henry opened the cupcake, reaching for the fortune inside. He read it over silently.

"Oh, come on—don't leave me in suspense! What does it say?" I asked.

Henry held up the paper. "It says, 'better things are coming'. It's funny—I think they already have. See you later, Angie."

I smiled. "Bye, Henry. And good luck today."

He nodded, biting into the cupcake as he left. Grandma watched him go and glanced over at me. "Henry came by again? What for?"

I blushed. "Just for a cupcake—he needed some extra good luck for work. So, you decided to come in after all?"

Grandma sighed, setting aside her broom. "Yes, I did. I figured moping in bed all day wouldn't do me any good. Even though Nutmeg wanted me to nap with her. Is everything good around here?"

"Uh, it is. But Grandma...we have some news. Did you see the sign in Lucy's window on the way here?"

"No, I didn't. I took the back roads to enjoy the scenery. Why? What's going on?"

Mackenzie came out of the kitchen, adding more cupcakes to the display counter. "Oof, I can't say it. You tell her, Angie."

I cleared my throat. "We know why Jack stole the recipe book. He was working for Lucy—he's her new stepbrother. It was their plan all along to steal our desserts to sell at The Green Machine. To get more customers *and* get back at us."

Grandma's jaw dropped. "But...that's awful! How could they do such a despicable thing?"

"That's Lucy. She's been evil since high school," I said, shaking my head in disgust. "They threatened to sue us if we retaliated. So we have to think of what to do very, very carefully."

Grandma looked out the window, glaring at The Green Machine down the block. I'd never seen her so angry. "Surely there must be something we can do. Until we figure out, let's just say...karma will not be kind to those people. Lucy will get what's coming to her."

I agreed, but I hoped it would be sooner rather than later.

We joined Mackenzie in the kitchen, helping her bake desserts for another busy day. We were covered in flour as we sold dozens of cupcakes. I glanced out the window, noticing the long lines at Lucy's shop. No doubt due to our stolen recipe. Without us, she still would've been selling her unpopular green juices and losing profits.

As I thought of ways to get back at her, my phone buzzed. I pulled it out and hoped it would be Henry, but it was Ty instead.

Today's a P.D. day, he texted. *I've got some time off. Would you like to grab lunch? Estelle's is a nice place.*

I almost shuddered. My past two experiences at Estelle's hadn't gone over well. I stared at the text for a moment, wondering what I should do. If there was a chance to be with Henry, then he was the one I wanted. I figured I should break the news to Ty in person.

Sure, sounds good, I wrote back. *See you at noon?*

He sent a thumbs up, then I turned to Grandma. "Are you two okay here for a bit?"

"Of course. I was just going to teach Mackenzie some more baking tricks," Grandma said, turning to me. "Why?"

"Well, Ty wants to have lunch. Is it okay if I slip away?"

Grandma smiled. "Of course, dear. Best of luck on your date. Tell Ty I said hello."

I promised I would, removing my apron and hanging it up. I headed home first—showering and dressing casual before heading to *Estelle's*. When I entered through the front doors, I found Ty sitting near the kitchen, waving me over. I smiled and headed toward him.

"Hey, there you are," he said with a grin, gesturing at two glasses of water on the table. "Got us both water. Glad you could come on such short notice. It's nice to see you, Angie."

"You too, Ty," I said as I sat down, placing my purse beside me.

I wondered when I should drop the bomb that I had feelings for Henry. How would Ty take it? I didn't want to break his heart.

"So, what are you going to order?" he asked, looking over his menu.

I shrugged. "Something with a lot of carbs—they're my greatest love. Probably the pasta. You?"

"Good choice. I'm thinking salmon." The table vibrated, then he turned to his pocket. "Oh, sorry. Getting a text."

I nodded, sipping my water as Ty pulled his phone out of his pocket. I watched as he grinned at the screen and texted back. Whoever it was, he seemed to really like them.

Ty looked up, noticing me staring at him. "Sorry—didn't mean to be rude. That was just my principal. He was sending me some funny memes about teachers."

"You have his number? You two must be close."

Ty nodded, reaching for his water. "We've become good friends, yeah. He's a wonderful person. Oh, no..."

"What?"

Ty gestured behind me. "My parents are here. They must've followed me. I mentioned I was coming here for a date tonight, and they must've planned this."

I spun around, noticing two older people entering the restaurant. The man wore slacks and a sweater vest while the woman was wearing a purple dress and a black blazer. They scanned the restaurant, then noticed our table and rushed over.

"Hello!" the woman said, beaming at me. "You must be Angie. Ty told us you two had a lunch date today."

"That's me," I said with a smile. "And you are?"

"Ty's parents, Seymour and Gloria," the man replied,

shaking my hand. "We didn't mean to interrupt. We're just so excited for Ty—that he's finally found someone."

His mother nodded, squeezing his cheeks. "Yes, we're so proud of you, dear."

Ty blushed. "Mom, Dad—please. We're trying to have a quiet lunch here. Do you mind?"

"You're right, we're sorry." His mother stepped back. "I hope you don't think we're strange for following Ty here. We just wanted to meet you in person. Have a lovely lunch!"

They waved, heading out of the restaurant as Ty shook his head. "Sorry about that. As I mentioned before, my parents can be...overbearing. They're obsessed with me getting married and having kids."

"I thought my grandma was bad, but she's never crashed a date like that," I said with a little laugh. "Your parents are determined, that's for sure."

"I just call them nosy," Ty said, then his phone buzzed again. "Let me just check that..."

He pulled out his phone and read the text, then started laughing. I cleared my throat. "Let me guess. Your principal again?"

"Yeah—he's incredibly funny. Sorry, I know it's rude," Ty said, putting his phone back in his pocket as it continued to buzz. "I won't look at it again—I swear."

I hoped I wasn't out of line as I leaned forward. "Ty, I need to ask you something...and I'd like you to be honest. There won't be any judgement from me, okay?"

He looked worried. "All right. What's going on?"

"Do you have feelings for your principal?"

Ty froze for a second, looking like a deer caught in the headlines. He shifted uncomfortably in his seat. "What? Why...why would you think that?"

"Well, you keep smiling at your phone. And I saw the way you were looking at him at school. Maybe I'm wrong, but...you have romantic feelings for him, don't you?"

Ty looked toward the door. "I...okay, fine. But you can't tell my parents."

"Tell them what?"

"That I'm actually gay," Ty said, avoiding my eyes. "They have no idea. I'm too scared to tell them. They're conservative, you see, and I'm not sure they'd approve."

"Then why are you going out with women?"

"To please my parents. To get them off my back about getting married," Ty said, shaking his head. "They were so happy when I told them about you. Their faces lit up like a damn Christmas tree. They think I've never had a girlfriend, and it's true. I haven't. But I've had a few boyfriends. I broke up with my last one in the summer. Then I started working at the school and met Principal Sutter. It was love at first sight. It grew stronger when we started to talk and hang out more. And...maybe I'm delusional, but I think he feels the same."

I smiled. "That's nice. Have you told him?"

"No, not yet. I know, I know—I'm a coward. I'm just too afraid to be wrong and lose my job. I'm not even sure Principal Sutter is gay."

I leaned across the table, reaching for Ty's hand. "You can't be afraid when it comes to love, Ty. That's one thing I've learned from my grandmother. You should tell him how you feel."

Ty grimaced. "But...he's my boss. Wouldn't that be, I don't know, inappropriate?"

"Sometimes, you need to take a chance. Who knows? Maybe everything will work out for the best."

Ty breathed out. "Okay, maybe you're right. I'll think about it, at least. You aren't mad that I led you on?"

"No, of course not. I sympathize with your position. And I hope you can tell your parents one day who you really are. You deserve to be happy and live free. If they don't approve of that, then it's their loss. If they love you, they'll accept it. Point blank."

Ty smiled. "That's good advice, Angie. Thank you. Really."

"No problem. Guess my grandma really is rubbing off on me." I laughed. "I actually came here to tell you I had feelings for someone else, so this works out."

Ty reached for his glass of water. "Really? Who is it? Someone I know?"

"Maybe—he's new to town. Henry Brant. The firefighter?"

Ty sipped his water, nodding. "I've seen him around. He's handsome. Have you told him how you feel?"

"I have—and he feels the same. But he just got divorced. I'm not sure how it ended, but it sounds bad. Henry mentioned he was betrayed. As much as I like him, and now I know he likes me, I don't want to push him if he's not ready."

"Hmm. What advice did you just give me? That you can't be afraid when it comes to love? That applies to both you *and* Henry."

I laughed. "Hitting me with my own advice, are you? Touché, my friend. Touché."

"Well, it's good advice. Like I said, maybe it'll all work out and you'll be the second chance he's been hoping for. And then I can come to your wedding and you'll come to mine."

I clinked our glasses together. "Deal!"

Ty smiled. “I feel a thousand times better now. I’m glad I met you, Angie. I’d like us to stay friends.”

“Yeah, me too. We vibe well together.”

“Definitely. And I want to hear more about Henry while we eat. I figure I owe you a meal for dragging you out here. Now, start at the beginning and tell me everything about that hunk…”

Chapter Twenty

After having lunch with Ty, it was starting to feel like we were old friends. I told him all about Henry, my drama with Jack and Lucy, and how hard looking for love had been. In return, Ty told me about his ex-boyfriends, his crush on the principal, and more about his conservative parents. Ty was apologetic about leading me on but encouraged me to go for Henry.

"You never know—it could lead to something that lasts forever," Ty said, drinking his wine. "Henry might be the one."

"And if he isn't ready to date, I'm back to square one. Why is dating so complicated?"

Ty didn't have any answers but assured me he had bad luck with love too. It made me feel less alone. True to his word, he paid for lunch and we promised to keep in touch as friends. As I left the restaurant, walking down the street to my truck, someone came walking up behind me.

When I spun around, I came face-to-face with Adrian. And he was giving me his usual charming smile.

"Hey, Angie," he began. "We haven't talked in a while."

"Well, yeah. That's typically what happens when you break up with someone."

"Right. Anyway, I wanted you to know...I've been thinking about you. Thinking about *us*."

I crossed my arms. "You have?"

He nodded. "Yeah—a lot lately, actually. I think breaking up with you was a mistake. A really, really stupid one."

"Oh, it was. But for you, not for me."

He sighed. "Angie, come on—don't be that way. We were good together, weren't we?"

"It was fun for a while. But I'm looking for a real relationship, Adrian. Which includes loyalty. I don't want to worry about you flirting with waitresses behind my back."

Adrian turned red. "I...I didn't know you knew about that. I'm sorry, Angie. But please—give me another chance."

I reached into my pocket for my key, shaking my head. "I don't think so. Besides, what happened to that pretty blonde woman you were with?"

"She, uh...she dumped me. For another man at the office. And then I saw you on TV, being interviewed at your bakery, and it made me miss you."

Fortunately, I saw right through Adrian's lies. "See, I don't think that's true. I think you're the kind of person who can't handle being alone. And now that you don't have anyone, you've come crawling back to me when you see I'm doing just fine without you. Isn't that right?"

Adrian was lost for words. "That's...come on, that's not fair."

I turned, heading to my truck in the parking lot. "Sorry, Adrian—but we're done and I've moved on. I suggest you do the same."

I left him behind me, getting into my truck and pulling away. He was still sulking and looking disappointed in my rear-view mirror. But how naïve and desperate did he think I was? To just take him back after all his cheating?

Even if Henry wasn't ready to date and I never found another man again, I still wouldn't go back to Adrian. Not even if he was the last guy on Earth.

I drove back to the bakery, parking on the street before heading inside. Grandma and Mackenzie were still baking up a storm and serving cupcakes to customers. As one customer passed me, grinning with their cupcake in hand, Grandma noticed me walking inside.

"Ah, Angie! There you are," she said with a smile. "How did the date go?"

"Oh, just wonderful," I said, setting down my purse. "Turns out I'm not Ty's type. Like, at all."

Mackenzie came out of the kitchen with a fresh rack of muffins. "What's his type then?"

"Men," I said. "Turns out he's just not into me. He has feelings for someone else, actually."

Grandma rushed over, patting my shoulder. "Oh, sweetie, I'm so sorry. But at least you found out now rather than down the line."

I sighed. "Yeah, that's a good thing. We promised to stay friends though. And I encouraged him to ask out his principal who he has a crush on."

Grandma smiled. "I'm glad you did—I hope he listens. Everyone should have a chance at love."

"Agreed. So, both Ty and Jack are out of the game," Mackenzie said, adding the muffins to the display table. "Who does that leave?"

"Henry—if he could be persuaded to go on a date," I said, putting on my apron. "And you know what else happened? Adrian came back, begging for a second chance."

Mackenzie gasped. "No way! You told him to take a hike, right?"

"Of course. What do you take me for?"

"Thank goodness," Grandma said, placing a hand over her heart. "Never let the same man break your heart twice, darling. Once is enough. Now, could you help me with some apple turnovers?"

I nodded, heading into the kitchen with Grandma to help her with her latest recipe. Mackenzie joined us and Grandma took the opportunity to teach her some more about baking. Mackenzie was slowly getting the hang of it, though she still looked stressed.

"I'm really worried about my baking test tomorrow," she said. "If I don't pass, I'll be kicked out. And this is my dream! My parents spent a lot of money to send me to college. I don't want to screw it up."

I shook my head. "You won't—you're smart and you've practiced a lot. Plus, we believe in you."

Grandma nodded, removing her oven mitts. "Angie's right. We wouldn't have hired you if we didn't see something special."

"Well, thanks. But I'm still nervous. Can you two come with me to the test tomorrow? It's open to the public. Anyone can watch and taste test."

"Free food? I'm there," I joked. "We'll do whatever you need to feel more comfortable."

Grandma nodded. "We have complete faith in you, dear."

Mackenzie grinned, leaning in to hug us. "Thank you, thank you! I'll feel so much better with you guys there. You have a way of calming me down. Okay, what's next on the agenda?"

As Grandma showed her the list of orders, my cell phone rang. I pulled it out and realized it was Sonya calling. "Hello?"

"Hey, Angie. I've got a situation I need your help with."

Behind me, Grandma and Mackenzie were laughing about something, clanging mixing bowls around. I stepped out of the kitchen to hear her better. "Okay, sure. What's going on?"

"The venue where we're having the engagement party accidentally booked us for tonight. They just called and confirmed. We don't want to lose our space—it could take forever to get another hall rented. Do you think you and your grandma could make the desserts in time for tonight?"

I paused. "How much do you need?"

"Whatever you can make on such short notice."

"What about your guests?"

"Fortunately, all my guests are local and are able to make it. It's a relief. Anyway, I'm sorry—I hate rushing you like this."

"It's okay, Sonya—it's not your fault. Let me talk to my grandma and see what we can do. I'll text you what she says."

"Thanks, Angie. You really are the best. Talk soon."

Hanging up, I walked into the kitchen. Grandma and Mackenzie were still going over all the orders that needed to be filled. I cleared my throat, hoping we'd have enough time to make Sonya's desserts.

"So, we've got a baking emergency," I began. "Turns out Sonya's engagement party is tonight. Mishap on the venue's part. Anyway, she wants to know if we can make enough desserts in time."

Grandma turned, glancing at the clock. "It'll be a close call...but I think we can do it. Mackenzie, call everyone on the order list and tell them their desserts will be a day late. We've got an emergency catering event to do."

"Isn't that bad for business?" I asked.

"In a big city, most likely. In this small town? Our clients are sweethearts. They'll understand." Grandma smiled, glancing at Mackenzie. "Then I'll need both you and Angie's help in the kitchen."

Mackenzie gave Grandma a high-five, taking the list and rushing to her office to make the calls. I joined Grandma in the kitchen as we began baking Sonya's favorite desserts—lots of cherry pies and carrot muffins. I texted Sonya and told her we'd be ready for tonight. She was thrilled, just as I knew she'd be.

"For anyone else, I would've said no. But Sonya's special," Grandma said, rolling dough on the counter. "We'll have to bake through dinner, but I think we can make it."

"I hope so—I don't want to let Sonya down. Okay, what's next?"

Grandma guided me through the dessert list for Sonya's engagement party, and Mackenzie returned after successfully calling everyone. We were making progress. We already had dozens of cupcakes, muffins, and pies done in the span of a few hours. We stepped back to take a breather while looking at all the desserts on the table.

"I think we nailed it," Mackenzie said, grinning. "Her engagement party is going to have the best-tasting desserts ever."

"Totally," I said. "Thanks for your help. Sonya's going to be so happy."

"Then it's all worth it," Grandma replied, checking her

watch. "Almost time for the engagement party. Quickly—let's take all our desserts to the van and get going. Don't want to be late. Angie, do you have the address for the venue?"

"Yep, it's in my phone. I'll text it to you. It isn't far."

I texted them both the address, then we all grabbed the freshly made desserts. Grandma borrowed a friend's white delivery van for tonight. She had stuck the logo of our bakery on the side. After we loaded the back with desserts, Grandma and Mackenzie decided to ride together in the van, while I took my truck and followed them down the street. I scoffed in disgust as I drove past Lucy's restaurant, the chocolate cake sign still in the window.

What kind of a jealous loser steals someone's recipe? I was still having a hard time wrapping my head around that.

I followed Grandma's van, driving fifteen minutes into the outskirts of town. The venue for the engagement party was a small building, perfect for entertaining with a large barn in the distance. I pulled my truck onto the dirt, parking next to Grandma. I ran over to help her and Mackenzie fetch all the desserts from the back.

"Not bad if I do say so myself," Grandma said with a smile. "We did it, girls. We make a fabulous team."

"And that's one thing Lucy can't take from us," Mackenzie said. "She can steal our recipes, but this? How close we are? She'll never have that. She'll always be an evil, two-faced bitch. Oh, sorry for swearing, Mrs. Linden."

Grandma laughed. "No apology necessary, dear. I've called her much worse in my head. Now, where should we put all this?"

"Let's head into the venue and find Sonya," I said, picking up a tray of muffins. "She can tell us what to do."

Grandma nodded, then we divided all the desserts

amongst the three of us. We carried everything over the gravel parking lot toward the venue's front doors. Other people were starting to arrive—some I recognized as acquaintances from high school, some were Sonya's extended family, and I assumed some strangers were James' friends.

We pushed the door open to the venue, entering with a gasp. The place was beautiful—decorated with red balloons, large tables for people to sit at, and soft music playing on the overhead speakers. A door led outside to the farm where people could pet the animals. Sonya stood at the door, as beautiful as always, with a handsome, dark-haired man in his late thirties.

She finished greeting a guest, then turned to us. "Angie, you came! And you have the desserts. Thank you so much."

I smiled. "It was our pleasure. Where should we put them?"

"On the table back there, please. With the other finger foods. I just know people are going to love your desserts." She turned to Grandma and Mackenzie. "Nice to see you, Mrs. Linden. And you must be their new employee?"

"That's me," Mackenzie said with a smile. Then she turned to me. "You can stay here and chat—me and Mrs. Linden will bring all the desserts to the table."

"Okay, thanks," I said, handing what I was carrying to Mackenzie. "Careful, don't drop all our hard work."

Mackenzie and Grandma promised they wouldn't, pushing through people and rows of tables to put the desserts down. More people began to trickle in behind us as Sonya turned to me.

"So, this is James," she began, placing a hand on his shoulder. She was giggly and smiling like she'd just won the lottery. "My fiancé."

"Nice to meet you," I said, holding out my hand. "You two look nice together."

"Thank you," James said, shaking my hand and grinning. "I've heard a lot about you, you know. How close you and Sonya used to be as kids."

Used to be. That stung.

"I'm glad we reconnected," I replied. "Anyway, I won't keep you two—I'm sure you have more people to greet. I'll help Grandma and Mackenzie set up the desserts and stay out of your way."

"Of course—and thanks again," Sonya said, leaning in to hug me. "I'm so glad you could be here, Angie."

I smiled as I pulled away, walking toward the table. But I froze when I heard a familiar name.

"Ah, Henry!" James cried. "Nice to see you again."

I spun around, finding Henry standing there. He was embracing James in a side hug, as Sonya glanced between them with a smile. I stepped back, clearing my throat.

"Henry?" I asked. "How do you know James?"

Henry noticed me and pulled back from James. His eyes lit up as he looked at me. "Oh, James and I used to go to school together back in Boston. Feels like a lifetime ago now. How do you know James?"

"We actually just met. Sonya and I went to school together."

"Small world, I guess," Henry said, still staring at me.

James nodded. "Definitely. Well, enjoy yourselves. Eat some snacks. We'll be playing games, making speeches, and dancing later on."

I glanced at Henry, nodding politely before I scurried over to Grandma and Mackenzie. They were still setting up the desserts on the table. I kept my back turned, though I could feel Henry's gaze on me.

“Henry’s here,” I whispered to Grandma. “He knows Sonya’s fiancé, funny enough.”

“Hmm,” Grandma said, eyeing Henry. I turned around and watched as he took a seat by himself. “Are you going to spend some time with him? Now would be a great opportunity.”

“Maybe. For now, I’m more focused on making sure everyone likes the desserts. Want me to start handing them out?”

“Sure—that would be great. Make sure to take one to Henry. We won’t mind if Angie hangs out with him instead of us, will we?”

Grandma glanced at Mackenzie.

Mackenzie shook her head with a smile. “Not at all—go have fun. Get your man, girl.”

I laughed and rolled my eyes as I picked up a red velvet cupcake. I walked toward Henry’s table and sat down, sliding the cupcake toward him.

“Here you go,” I said. “Wanted you to be the first to try the party’s desserts.”

“Two cupcakes in one day? You’re going to make me gain weight,” Henry joked, taking a bite of the cupcake. Then he nodded. “Amazing, as always.”

I blushed. “Thank you. So, how’s work going?”

“Pretty good, actually. Mostly quiet. The most I did was play cards with the other firefighters and rescue a cat from a tree. Nothing serious going on. So, did you figure out what to do about Lucy yet?”

I sighed. “No, not yet. Hopefully soon…”

“What about Lucy?” Sonya asked, walking over. “Sorry, couldn’t help but overhear. Even her name gets me angry.”

“Then you’ll have to hear this,” I said as I spun around and told her the story.

Once I was finished, Sonya shook her head. "This is crazy! You have to get that recipe book back, Angie. Break into her restaurant or something."

"I'd rather not be arrested for breaking and entering, thanks. That would look really bad."

Sonya sighed. "All right, all right. I see your point. Why...why don't you wear a wire or something? Try to get Lucy to admit what she did on camera? Might be worth a try."

"I agree," Henry said.

I nodded. "That's a good idea, Sonya. But for now, let's not focus on someone like Lucy. I just want to celebrate your engagement and have a good time."

Chapter Twenty-One

The engagement party went on with delicious food—including our desserts which everyone loved—plus games and heartfelt speeches. I found Rachel, Sonya's sister, and chatted with her, congratulating her on her marriage and pregnancy. I even got to meet her husband who seemed like a nice guy. She was glowing and looked so happy as she rubbed her pregnant belly. As I smiled at her, catching up over drinks and good food, I hoped that would be me one day.

Sonya and James squared off against each other in beer pong and Sonya won, the entire crowd cheering her on. I sat with Grandma, Mackenzie, and Henry, enjoying the party. Then James stood up with a glass of champagne and toasted in Sonya's honor.

"I'm truly lucky to have found my soulmate," he said, glancing around at everyone. "And I wish you all the same. To Sonya—my best friend, my beloved, my future wife."

"To Sonya!" everyone shouted, raising their glasses in solidarity.

James sat back down, kissing Sonya on her blushing cheek. They were a perfect couple, and I was happy for them. I glanced over at Henry, noticing he looked a bit sad. Was he thinking about his failed marriage? I couldn't imagine how much that must've hurt—to find a spouse and then lose them. He deserved better.

"James is amazing, isn't he?" Sonya loudly asked the crowd, rising to her feet. "And, if you didn't know, he also has some killer dance moves. On that note, the dance floor is now open!"

Everyone cheered, finishing their drinks and getting up to dance. Sonya and James were the first ones out on the dance floor. Sonya's aunt was in charge of the music, putting on something fast. To my surprise, Mitch asked Grandma to dance, and they shimmied next to each other while chatting and laughing.

"I didn't know your grandmother could move like that," Henry said, watching them as he turned to me. "That's incredible for her age."

"Grandma will surprise you," I said with a little laugh. "She's my hero. And I hope she'll find love again. She deserves it."

"Agreed," Mackenzie said. Too young to drink, she was sipping a soda. "Say…why don't you two get up and dance?"

I turned to Henry, shrugging. "I wouldn't mind that. Henry?"

Henry awkwardly scratched his neck. "Well, I'm not that good of a dancer…but all right. I'll follow your lead, Angie."

I smiled, rising to my feet and holding out a hand. "Perfect. Follow me."

He stood up with a grin and took my hand. "Why, of course."

I felt a rush of butterflies creep up in my stomach as we held hands. I led him to the dance floor, pushing through everyone else. Grandma spotted us while still dancing with Mitch and gave me a wink. I blushed, turning to Henry.

"Dancing isn't that hard, really," I yelled over the music. "Just move your body a little—your hips and shoulders. Like this!"

As I shimmied, Henry copied my moves, though he looked a little embarrassed. "Like that?"

"Yep! You're doing great," I said with a smile. "You're going to give James a run for his money!"

Henry snorted. "Hardly, but thanks for your support. Are you enjoying the party so far?"

"I am," I replied, still dancing. "Me and my grandma can get really busy with work so it's nice to take a load off."

"Same here—being a firefighter can be a heavy profession. It gets intense sometimes. I really need to learn how to be less serious."

I smiled. "Well, it seems like you're on your way. Nice moves!"

He smiled back, continuing to dance before Sonya's aunt stopped the music. She turned to the crowd as they paused. "I thought we could switch it up—put on a slow song. I hope everyone has a partner!"

Everyone paired up, beginning to slow dance. Henry awkwardly scratched his neck and avoided eye contact.

"Um, did you...did you want to slow dance?" I asked. "Funny enough, I've never done it."

"Yeah, me either."

I raised an eyebrow. "Not even at your own wedding?"

Henry shook his head. "Nah, my ex didn't like to dance. We skipped it. But...if you're willing to put up with my mistakes, then sure, I'd like to dance with you."

I smiled. "Only if you promise to do the same. All right, put your hand here. I think this is how you do it..."

I looked at everyone else, watching how their feet and arms moved. I placed Henry's hands on my waist—trying not to blush—as mine went around his shoulders. As the slow song played, we swayed back and forth, looking anywhere beside each other's eyes. I was mostly staring at Henry's shoes to make sure I didn't step on his toes.

"Well, this is nice," I said, finally working up the courage to look at him. "Not bad for your first slow dance, huh?"

Henry nodded. "Yeah, it's going well so far. I'm surprised I haven't stepped on your foot yet."

I laughed. "The night is still young. Hey, Henry...can I tell you something?"

"Of course."

We turned lightly, slow dancing next to everyone else. I spotted Grandma and Mitch slow dancing a few feet away. "I...I've been thinking about what you said at the bakery. About liking me but being afraid."

Henry swallowed. "Yeah, I have too."

"Well, I wanted you to know you're not the only one. I've been burned in love, too—badly. But I want to try this with you."

Henry finally looked into my eyes. His eyes were a beautiful shade of blue, as deep as the ocean. I could see myself drowning in them forever. "So...what are you saying?"

"If you'd be okay with it," I stammered, "I'd like to take

you out on a date. Maybe...to get ice cream. Or the movies. You know, take it slow? I'm in no rush."

Henry hesitated, then nodded. "I think I'd like that. Why don't we go out tomorrow night? There's a new superhero movie playing at the theater downtown."

I smiled. "I'll be there. I know how scary it can be—getting back into dating after heartbreak. So thanks for taking a chance on me."

"I like what I've seen so far," Henry said, smiling. "You're an amazing woman."

I smiled back. "I feel the same way about you. Except, you know, the genders reversed."

As he laughed, the music stopped. We awkwardly stepped back as Sonya's aunt moved toward the music player. "All right, the slow dance is over. Back to tearing up the dance floor!"

She put on another fast song, then I noticed James and Sonya shimmying our way. James was the first to speak. "Angie, Henry! There you are. Enjoying the party?"

"Absolutely," I replied. "And the venue looks amazing. You did a great job, Sonya."

She smiled. "Thanks, Angie. Say, why don't we switch partners? I'll dance with Henry and James can dance with you?"

I shrugged. "Sure, why not?"

"Perfect!" James cried, grabbing my arm. "Sonya speaks very highly of you, Angie. I want to see if you've got the moves too!"

I laughed, letting him twirl me around. "I'll give it my best shot!"

We kept dancing, then I noticed Sonya and Henry having a good time. Even my grandma and Mitch were still laughing and dancing. I hoped and prayed that would be our future—no heartbreak, just good times, laughter, and love. A girl could dream.

"I actually had an ulterior motive for wanting to dance with you," James whispered, shimmying next to me. "It's about Henry."

I perked up. "Oh? I'm all ears."

"I've seen the way you look at him. And he looks at you the same," he said, making me blush. "You like him, don't you?"

I nodded. "I do. And he likes me too. I know he's guarded—been hurt before. So I'm trying to take it slow and convince him I won't hurt him."

"Smart. Be careful with him," James said, sneaking a glance at Henry. "He's one of my oldest friends, so I care about his well-being. And he might look all tough and strong on the outside, but on the inside? He's a big softie. Sensitive and thoughtful. And he's been hurt badly."

"So I've heard. I know he was married. Do you know what happened?"

James sighed. "I do—Henry confided in me a while back. But...I'm not sure I should tell you. It isn't my story to tell. Hopefully he'll open up to you, maybe as you get to know each other a bit better. I really hope you two get a happy ending."

I did too. When the music ended, James smiled at me, then walked back over to Sonya. Grandma and Mitch hugged and looked like they were exchanging phone numbers. I glanced at Henry who stood by himself near the far wall, already staring at me. I blushed and walked toward Grandma as Mitch left to get more drinks.

"What you got there?" I asked.

Grandma blushed. "Mitch's number. You know, just in case he has more questions about our bakery."

"Right, the bakery. Or a certain baker in particular."

Grandma only blushed harder, then changed the subject. "I saw you dancing with Henry. How did it go?"

"Great, actually. We're going on a date tomorrow night. To the movies. I told him I want to take it slow—not rush things. You know, because we've both been hurt before."

Grandma smiled. "Oh, I'm so glad. I'm sure you two will have a good time. Now, I do believe the engagement party is ending soon. Can you help me gather up all our containers?"

I nodded, following Grandma to the table of desserts. Mackenzie walked over and helped us clean up and organize our containers. Once we had everything, James and Sonya addressed the crowd one last time.

"Thank you all for coming and celebrating our love," Sonya said, grinning at James. "We hope you had a great time. We'll see you in a month for our wedding. Can't wait!"

James nodded. "It's going to be amazing—I finally get to marry the love of my life. Get home safely, everyone. Take care!"

Everyone said goodbye, leaving the venue to head to their cars. Henry found my eyes in the crowd and nodded at me before leaving. I followed Grandma and Mackenzie to her van, putting the containers in the back.

"I'll drive you home, Mackenzie. It's getting late," Grandma said, turning to me. "Meet you at home, darling?"

I nodded. "Sounds good. See you tomorrow for your baking test, Mackenzie. Hope you can get some good rest tonight."

She took a deep breath. "Right, the test. Thanks again for coming. I'll need all the moral support I can get. See you then!"

Grandma and Mackenzie got into the van, speeding off. I wasn't heading home as planned. I pulled out my smartphone, making sure my audio and video were working before an idea flashed across my mind.

I was going to expose a thief tonight.

I got into my truck, pulling away from the gravel parking lot as everyone left the venue. Henry had quickly vanished. Butterflies tingled in my stomach again when I thought of our date tomorrow, hoping it would go well. I didn't want to mess up my dream date with my dream guy. I had finally convinced him to drop his guard and go out with me, and I didn't want to ruin it.

I followed the heavy traffic, heading downtown to The Green Machine which was closing soon. People were still coming in and out with chocolate cake. Those should've been our customers, not Lucy's. It still made my blood boil.

I parked around the back, then paused. What if Lucy wouldn't admit her theft on camera? What if she knew what I was doing? I was going to have to be sneakier than that.

When I saw her walk out of the back door, carrying a bag of trash, I quietly got out of my truck and closed the door. I watched her enter the bakery and vanish inside. I tip-toed toward the back door, tugging on the handle. Lousy Lucy hadn't locked it—which was perfect for me. I turned on my phone camera with the volume turned up and slid it into my pocket.

I snuck in through the back door, ending up in the kitchen. When I heard talking getting louder, I dove behind a nearby wall, trying to hide. Lucy's voice followed.

"...and you should see how much money we've made," she said, and I could hear the grin in her voice. "That chocolate cake is going to make us famous. You lock the doors?"

"Yep, all taken care of," Jack said. "And I better be getting my cut. It wasn't easy pretending to like Angie, you know. She's just as annoying as you said."

I fought every urge to jump out and scare them, then curse them out. But I didn't. I had to remember I was doing this for Grandma—exposing Lucy and getting our clients back.

"Yeah, yeah—you'll get what I promised you," Lucy grumbled. "Stop being so damn greedy."

"I learned from you," Jack joked. "Has Angie tried to tell anyone we stole her grandma's recipe book? She doesn't have any proof, does she?"

"Nope—and no one would believe her," Lucy said, smirking again. "The story sounds pretty crazy."

I peeked around the corner, noticing Jack nodding. I held up my camera toward them as Jack spoke. "Good. You know, I can see why my father married your mother. If she's as smart and cunning as you, he's hit the jackpot. Your idea to steal Angie's recipe book was genius."

"I know," Lucy said with a grin. "I just wish my husband would see it that way. He still thinks we did something wrong."

"Screw him," Jack said. "Nothing wrong with getting a leg up on the competition."

"Exactly. Anyway, I need to clean before heading home. Since you brought me the recipe book, I'll reward you by letting you leave early."

"Sweet. Thanks, Lucy. See you tomorrow."

I held my breath as Jack walked by, heading out the back door. Lucy just chuckled to herself and walked into the dining area to clean. I lowered my camera, pausing the video and sneaking out the back door. Jack was gone as I rushed to my truck.

I got into the driver's seat, watching the video I had just recorded. It was all there—you could hear Lucy and Jack's conspiracy outright and see their faces. I grinned. Sneaking around had been a good choice.

I found Mitch's number in my contacts, then sent him the video. I texted him: *You'll want to check this out.* If anyone could help spread the news of what Lucy and Jack had done, it was him.

I put my truck in drive, then pulled out of the parking lot and headed home. Grandma's van had already beaten me there. As I pulled in, Mitch had texted back already.

What a story! he texted. *I'm so sorry Lucy and Jack stole your grandma's recipe book. Esther's a sweet woman and doesn't deserve that. I'll prepare a segment right away and air it tomorrow morning.*

I stepped out of my truck, grinning. Sonya's idea to wear a wire had worked—people were finally going to learn how evil Lucy and Jack were. I was hoping it would get them off our backs forever.

When I heard an engine roaring, I turned around. I saw a sedan sitting at the edge of our driveway. I squinted through the dark, realizing it was Jim sitting in the driver's seat. I hadn't seen or heard from him in a while. When he noticed me staring, he took off, his tires squealing down the road.

I shook my head as I entered the house, worrying about Jim. There was never a shortage of drama around town. Nutmeg came up to rub against my legs as Grandma was already sitting in front of the TV while watching a romantic comedy.

"There you are, dear," Grandma said, rising to her feet.

"Took you a while to get home. I was getting worried. Where were you?"

I finished petting Nutmeg, and grinned. "Let's just say... you'll definitely want to watch the news tomorrow morning, Grandma. Mitch's segment is going to be very, very interesting."

Chapter Twenty-Two

Although Grandma begged me for answers, I didn't tell her what was going on, wanting her to see it for herself. I knew she was going to be relieved. We went to bed shortly after that, then I woke up and found Grandma making pancakes and bacon in the kitchen. She threw a small piece of bacon on the floor for Nutmeg who quickly gobbled it up.

"Good morning, dear," Grandma said, plating the pancakes. "Almost time for the news. Are you sure you can't give me any hints?"

I shook my head, bending down to pet Nutmeg. "Nope—but trust me, it'll be worth the wait."

We ate breakfast at the table, going over what needed to be done at the bakery for the day, and I realized it was almost time for the news. I grabbed the TV remote, turning on the news station and sitting in front of the screen. Grandma walked over and stood beside me as the news started and Mitch's face appeared.

"Good morning, residents of New Harbor. I hope your day is fantastic," he began, sitting in front of a news desk with papers stacked neatly in front of him. "Last night, I received a very interesting video about members of our community. I trust you'll want to see this."

When the screen changed to my smartphone video, a bit grainy but still audible, I smiled. We finally had proof of what Lucy and Jack had done. The video played from where I had hidden near the back door, their words as clear as day.

"Oh my gosh," Grandma said, turning to me. "You got them to admit it!"

I shrugged. "It was dumb luck, really. I was going to head in and confront them, but I feared they'd know I was recording them. Using the back door was a better plan—and they did the rest."

Grandma hesitated as Jack and Lucy went on about their sinister plan. "But won't you get in legal trouble for recording them without their consent?"

"Hey, next time they should lock the door when they want to brag about their crimes. I had every right to take that video."

The video finished, then the screen returned to Mitch sitting behind his news desk. "How scandalous for Lucy Rhett at The Green Machine. I hope she apologizes to the Linden family for stealing their recipe book. Now, on to sports and the weather..."

As Mitch returned to the normal news, I rose to my feet, turning off the TV. "Hopefully, everyone in town will have seen it and know what happened. Lucy only has herself to blame for any flack that comes her way."

Grandma grinned. "I agree. And thank you, Angie. I'm so glad the truth was finally able to come out. Your grandpa would be very happy too."

"I'm sure he would be. I miss him. A lot."

Grandma leaned forward, reaching for my hand. "I do too, dear. I do too."

After cleaning up all the dishes, we got dressed and took our vehicles out for another day at the bakery. As I drove past The Green Machine, I noticed it was closed, something odd for an early morning. Was it possible Lucy was too cowardly to show her face?

I pulled into the parking lot behind the bakery, then followed Grandma inside. We opened the doors and served a few customers while baking new treats. Every customer that came inside asked us about Lucy and Jack.

"...and he only dated you to steal the recipe book? And then pass it off as their own dessert?" a customer asked, shaking her head. "That's truly despicable. I won't be buying anything from that place again."

I smiled. "Thank you, we appreciate your support. And I agree—it really is despicable."

As the customer nodded, taking her muffin and leaving, Grandma turned to me. "I must send Mitch a thank you card in the mail. Without his help, no one in New Harbor would know."

I winked. "Why don't you ask him out to dinner—your treat? That sounds like a proper way to thank him."

"Maybe you're right. I...have been thinking about him. About what it would be like to date again." Grandma paused. "I just wish it would stop feeling like I'm cheating on your grandpa."

"Hey, we both know you're not," I said, turning to her and reaching for her hand. "As much as I hate to say it, Grandpa's gone—he's never coming back. If you have another chance at love, another chance at happiness, why shouldn't you take it?"

Grandma smiled. "I'm glad you're starting to believe

that too, Angie. All right, I'll call him right now and ask him out on a date. As much as I miss your grandfather... I'm excited. I really like Mitch."

"As you should be. Go ahead—I'll stay here and serve any customers that come in."

Grandma nodded, heading into her office at the end of the hall to call Mitch on the phone. I heard laughing a second later and smiled, glad Grandma had found someone. Mitch seemed like a good person—and he had helped me spread the word of what Lucy and Jack had done. He definitely deserved free desserts.

As I wiped down the counter, the door opened with a chime. I looked up, expecting it to be another customer, when my smile faded. It was Lucy and Jack—and they both looked miserable with frowns on their faces.

"Sorry, but we don't serve lying snakes," I said, crossing my arms. "Get out."

"Not so fast," Lucy said with a huff. "Ever since your little morning segment aired, we've been getting threatening phone calls and texts. People are calling us thieves!"

"And? That's what you are."

"You had no right to record us," Jack snarled. "That's illegal!"

"Hardly. You deserve all the heat you're getting," I said, leaning forward. "No one messes with my grandparent's recipes and gets away with it. I hope you get all the karma that's coming to you."

"This isn't over," Lucy spat. "Trust me."

I rolled my eyes at her hollow threats, then Jack and Lucy left the bakery. I wasn't sad to see them go. Shaking my head, I got back to work cleaning the bakery as Grandma walked into the dining area with a smile on her face.

"Mitch and I have a dinner date Friday night," Grandma said. "I'm going to personally thank him for airing the story on Lucy and Jack."

"That's nice—I hope you have a good time."

"Thank you, dear. I wouldn't have been able to ask him out without your support." She paused, studying my face. "Are you all right? You look upset."

I sighed. "Yeah, I'm fine. Lucy and Jack just stopped by. Said they were getting threatening calls since the video aired. Lucy said it wasn't over. Our feud, I guess."

Grandma shook her head. "You think they would've learned their lesson after all this. Why can't they just leave us alone? Why can't Lucy just play nice?"

"That's who Lucy is—me and Sonya have known that since high school. I guess some people never grow up. And opposites attract. I didn't realize Jack was just like her."

Grandma grabbed her broom, sighing. "I pity people like that. No matter what they do, let's try to take the high road, dear. It's not worth stooping to their level."

I agreed, though I wasn't going to let them walk all over us. They had done that enough already.

After working the bakery for a few hours—serving customers who apologized for the whole Lucy incident—it was time to close up and head to Mackenzie's class. We put the CLOSED sign on the door, then hopped in my truck and drove to Trinity College. It was just outside New Harbor, closer to Boston.

"So, darling," Grandma began in the passenger seat, "are you excited about your date tonight with Henry? It's finally happening."

I beamed. "I know, I can't believe it. I'm going to pick up a new dress on the way home. I want to look nice."

"My, he must be special. You never went all out for Adrian."

I shrugged, stopping at a red light. "Things with Adrian...well, they never felt right. Something about Henry does."

"I felt that way about your grandfather," Grandma said with a smile. "Always go with your heart, darling. It'll never lead you astray."

As I pulled into the parking lot of Trinity College, parking near the doors, I hoped Grandma was right. We entered the small community college and asked the front desk where we could find the baking test. The secretary pointed down the hall, then we noticed some people had gathered there to watch.

"Oh my gosh," a man said, looking to be in his early twenties. "You're Angie and Esther Linden, the owners of Lucky's Baked Goods, right?"

"That's us," Grandma said with a smile. "You've heard of us?"

"Duh! You've got the best desserts in Massachusetts," another girl said with a smile. "And hey, we're sorry to hear about all the drama with The Green Machine. You deserve better."

"Thank you," I said with a nod. "We're just glad the truth is out. So, are you all here to watch the baking test?"

Everyone agreed, most of them aspiring bakers themselves. They asked Grandma tons of questions before the baking instructor opened the door to her classroom. We entered, finding empty seats as Mackenzie and the other students in the class stood at their kitchen workstations. Mackenzie smiled and waved when she saw us, visibly relaxing. I took a seat next to Grandma and hoped we could ease her nerves.

The teacher cleared her throat, turning to the audience. She was wearing an apron that was covered in flour from the previous class. "Welcome, everyone, and thank you for coming. My name is Professor Lois Goodwin. I'm sure my students are glad to have you here to cheer them on. This is the final baking test of the program—it's required to pass in order to be fully accredited as a baker. I hope all my students are ready for this."

I gave Mackenzie a thumbs-up, making her smile. She was setting up all her ingredients for the test as Grandma and I watched, along with the people in the seats around us.

"And I understand we have two talented bakers from Lucky's Baked Goods here," Professor Goodwin said, smiling at us. "Welcome. I just love your desserts—I tell my students about them all the time."

"Why, thank you," Grandma replied. "It wouldn't be possible without Mackenzie Teller. Who we know will pass with flying colors."

That made Mackenzie blush, hiding her face behind her bag of flour. Professor Goodwin nodded. "I believe that too. Now, without further ado, let's begin. I'll start the timer and then the students may reach for their baking supplies. The final test includes baking one of the hardest recipes—a baked Alaska—to prove these students are ready for the real world. On your marks, get set...bake!"

The professor placed an hourglass on the table that started to dribble sand down to start the test. All the students scrambled to reach for their ingredients, mixing and pouring and measuring. Mackenzie looked even more nervous as she reached for the ice cream in the freezer behind her. She dropped it on the floor, the loud slam echoing around the classroom. People began murmuring and staring at her as she picked it up. She set it down, then grabbed another, but it looked like she was about to cry out of either embarrassment or frustration. I knew I had to do something, clearing my throat.

"You got this, Mackenzie!" I yelled, hoping we were allowed to cheer people on like it was a soccer match. "Keep going!"

Mackenzie took a deep breath, turning back to her table of ingredients. She followed all of Grandma's tips and took it one step at a time. She put all the ingredients together from the pound cake to the ice cream and meringue and baked it in the oven for ten minutes. Then the students lit their desserts on fire. We held our breath, hoping it would all turn out as the hourglass stopped.

"And that's all we have time for!" Professor Goodwin said, grabbing the hourglass. "Please, remove your Baked Alaskas from the oven and place them on the counter. I'll try them myself before we let the audience try a bite."

Mackenzie and the other students placed the desserts on their tables, then stepped back. I noticed Mackenzie holding her breath. The professor tried each dessert one by one, some of them flat or melting. But Mackenzie's was holding together. Professor Goodwin got to her dessert, taking a bite. Her eyes widened.

"It's awful, isn't it?" Mackenzie asked, wincing. "I totally failed, didn't I?"

We leaned forward to hear the professor's response. "Are you kidding? This is amazing! The best one here, I think. You've been practicing, have you?"

"A lot," Mackenzie said, gesturing at us. "And I had the best teachers."

Professor Goodwin smiled. "It paid off, then. Well done, Mackenzie. You passed the program."

We cheered for Mackenzie, rising to our feet and walking over to congratulate her. Professor Goodwin was busy grading the other students as we chatted near Mackenzie's table.

"Phew, I'm glad that's over," Mackenzie said. "Thanks for coming to support me. When I dropped the ice cream... I'm not sure I would've kept going if you hadn't cheered me on. It was pretty embarrassing."

"Oh, nonsense, darling. I drop things all the time," Grandma said with a smile. "We're very proud of you—we knew you could do it. And your parents will be thrilled."

Mackenzie smiled. "Thank you, Mrs. Linden. I can't wait to tell Dad. He was really rooting for me."

"I bet. I'll help you clean up your station, then we can head to the bakery," Grandma said, turning to me. "You can head home and get ready for your date, dear. Tell Henry I said hi."

I nodded, congratulating Mackenzie once more before I left the college. I drove to the nearest clothing store, finding a little black dress with stockings. I picked out a new perfume—a gentle vanilla scent—before heading home to shower, get dressed, and do my make-up.

I wanted tonight to be special. Because Henry was special and deserved nothing less.

Grandma and Mackenzie texted me that they were at the bakery, baking new desserts for people who were apologizing for Lucy and Jack's behavior. I just wanted all the drama to be over between us and them. Lucy had tormented me enough in school.

I took a deep breath, checked my make-up in the mirror, then walked out to my truck. I drove to the small movie theater in town and looked around the parking lot for Henry. He hadn't arrived yet—but I was early. There was a small diner across the street where we could grab food after the film.

I waited, then waited some more, checking my phone for the time. It was getting later and later, and Henry still hadn't shown up. I knew we had agreed to meet up about ten minutes ago. Where was Henry?

"Relax," I told myself, taking a deep breath. "Maybe he's stuck in traffic. Maybe he had an emergency at the fire station. Or had to settle more paperwork with his divorce lawyer. It's probably nothing."

But a bad feeling nagged at me. I knew something wasn't right. I pulled out my smartphone, finding his contact. *Hey, I'm at the movie theater*, I texted. *Sitting in my red truck. Are you here yet? No rush—I understand if something came up! Just let me know. :)*

I stared at my phone for five minutes, waiting for a response, but nothing came. Then I saw the three little dots, indicating that Henry was typing. They kept disappearing and re-appearing.

"What's going on?" I muttered to myself.

Finally, his text came through a second later that made my stomach drop.

I'm sorry, I can't do this, he texted me. *This was a mistake.*

I sat in shock for a few seconds. Then I put my hands on the steering wheel and began to cry, my loud sobs filling the silence.

Chapter Twenty-Three

I sat in my truck for a while, bawling my eyes out. I knew Henry and I weren't together—and it wasn't like he'd left me at the altar or anything—but it still hurt. I thought I had finally found a decent person, someone who wouldn't get my hopes up and then bail. I had thought wrong.

Man, I really *was* unlucky in love.

I grabbed my smartphone, turning on the camera to look at myself. I was a wreck—red eyes, tear-stained cheeks, my mascara smudged and running. That was what love had done to me. Given me too many days of tears instead of laughter.

I was done with the dating scene. Forever, I decided. What was the point when it never worked out?

I turned my truck on, pulling out of the parking lot before anyone could see me. The last thing I wanted was for Lucy and Jack to make an appearance when I was already feeling low. I drove to the bakery, searching for Grandma. I needed a shoulder to cry on.

I parked on the street, then opened the door to the bakery with a chime. Grandma was mopping the floor when I came in, while Mackenzie was baking desserts in the back. Grandma looked up at me, surprised.

"Oh, Angie—it's you," she began. "Shouldn't you be at the movies with Henry right now? My, dear...you're crying. Is something wrong?"

I tried to keep it together and calmly explain what had happened. But with Grandma staring at me, looking sympathetic, I burst into tears again. Grandma set her mop aside and rushed over to hug me. I cried onto her shoulder, hearing the door to the kitchen opening.

"What's going on?" Mackenzie asked, leaning over the counter. "Angie, you're back. And crying. What happened? Did Lucy and Jack do something?"

"I can't stand those two," Grandma muttered. "They really need to learn their lesson."

I wiped my eyes, stepping back. "No, no...it's not Lucy and Jack. It's Henry. He didn't show up for our date. He sent me this text instead."

I showed Grandma the text Henry had sent me, then Mackenzie walked over and looked over my shoulder. Both their eyes widened.

"Henry...sent you that?" Grandma asked, shocked. "My goodness. I can't believe it! Why on Earth would he stand you up like that?"

"Yeah, that sounds pretty cowardly," Mackenzie added. "I thought he was better than that."

"I did too," I said with a sigh, slipping my phone in my pocket. "But I guess not. I guess he's too afraid to date after his divorce."

The bakery fell quiet. It looked like Grandma and Mackenzie didn't know what to say. What *could* they say? Nothing would make this right. The situation sucked—there was no sugar-coating it.

"Oh, darling," Grandma said, rubbing my back. "I'm so very sorry. You deserve better."

"Much, much better," Mackenzie added. "Just because Henry's afraid of commitment doesn't mean he has the right to break your heart. You're not his ex-wife. I mean, I don't know what happened between them, but he's gotta move on and let go eventually."

"Apparently, he can't," I said, shaking my head. "It was my fault for pursuing him when I knew he'd just gotten divorced. I should've kept my distance—shouldn't have listened when he said he had feelings for me."

"No, dear. It's not your fault," Grandma said, softly. "This is all on Henry. He led you on and hurt you—and he'll realize what he threw away one day. I promise you that."

I looked down. "I hope so. Grandma, I know you're busy, but...can you come home with me? Can we just sit on the couch and watch movies? I really don't want to be alone right now."

Grandma gave me a sympathetic smile. "Of course, dear. You don't even have to ask. Mackenzie, can you handle things while we're gone?"

"Absolutely. Especially now that I've graduated from baking school," Mackenzie said, proudly grinning. Then she turned to me. "Get some rest, Angie. Vent, scream, cry. Do whatever you have to. We're here for you."

I sniffled. "Okay—thanks, Mac. I'll do just that."

Grandma grabbed her coat, then gave Mackenzie some instructions before leaving the bakery with me. We headed to our cars and noticed The Green Machine was still closed. But I had a feeling Lucy and Jack weren't done with us just yet. I hoped that was drama for another day. Right now, I was too overwhelmed to deal with anything else.

I followed Grandma's sedan in my truck, heading home. I sighed when I entered and shut the door behind us. I told Grandma I was going to take a bath. Kicking off my shoes, I rushed upstairs to remove my dress, fancy make-up, and expensive perfume. I didn't need it anymore.

I then got into the bath, relaxing for a little while. I let the tears flow when they wanted to and didn't stop myself. But really, I shouldn't have been the one crying. I hadn't done anything wrong. Henry had. I hadn't lost something great—once again, Henry had. He would have to face that eventually, not me.

I got out of the bathtub, wrapping a towel around my body before heading into my room. I changed into the comfiest, coziest pajamas I could find—ones with polka dots and cats on them. Then I walked downstairs to find Grandma whispering on the phone.

"...yes, we can definitely reschedule for another time," Grandma was saying. "Thanks for being so understanding, Mitch. Bye-bye."

When she hung up, I frowned. "Were you talking to Mitch?"

"Oh, Angie! You scared me," Grandma said, turning to me and putting her smartphone away. "I didn't hear you come down the stairs. And yes, I was. I canceled our date on Friday."

I frowned. "But...what?"

"Because you need me more, dear. You'll always be number one to me. And Mitch understood—he gave his sympathies about Henry as well."

I stepped forward, shaking my head. "That's nice of you, Grandma, but please—go on that date with Mitch. Call him back and tell him it's all right. Don't hold back on finding love because of me."

"Are you sure? Because I can stay with you if you need me—"

"I'll be fine," I interrupted. "Don't worry. If anything, seeing you with Mitch will make me feel better. It'll remind me that love still exists."

"All right, darling—I'll call him tomorrow and tell him. For now, let's find a movie. Nothing romantic, of course. There's a recent horror movie that people are saying is just ghastly..."

As Grandma searched Netflix for horror movies—anything that didn't have happy couples in it—the doorbell rang. I frowned, rising to my feet and walking toward the door. For a second, I hoped it might be Henry, coming to admit he was wrong. But it wasn't.

When I opened the door, Sonya stood there, carrying a large grocery bag. She gave me a sympathetic smile. "Hey, Angie."

I leaned outside. "Sonya, hi. What are you doing here?"

"Well, don't be mad that she told me, but...your grandma called. Said Henry stood you up. I'm so, so sorry."

I sighed. "Yeah. And thanks. With how small this town is, I'm sure news will spread soon."

"True. You know, James told me about Henry. That he's got some trauma from his divorce. He didn't go into detail, but maybe Henry isn't the right person for a relationship. Just saying."

"I realize that now. Just wish I could go back in time and warn myself."

"You live and learn, right?" Sonya asked. "But hey, at least you exposed Lucy and Jack. I saw the news this morning. Nice going."

I smiled. "You were the one who suggested I secretly record them. I should be thanking you."

"Don't mention it. I just hope they'll go away—permanently. Maybe even close their shop," Sonya said, rolling her eyes. "Anyway, I didn't come here to talk about Lucy. Even just saying her name gives me a bad taste in my mouth. I'm here for a sleepover. You know, like the old days."

"A sleepover?" I asked, peeking into the bag. "That sounds fun. What did you bring?"

Sonya smiled, holding up the bag. "Everything you need to get over heartbreak. Ice cream, chips, candy. We're going to eat our feelings."

I laughed. "Sounds good to me. Come on inside—I'll get you a drink."

Sonya nodded, stepping inside the house and taking off her shoes. She still remembered her way around from when we were kids. Despite how sad the situation was, I was glad she had come over. It reminded me of the good old days. Grandma smiled, welcoming her inside as she took the bag of goodies.

Then the doorbell rang again and Grandma got up to answer it this time. Mackenzie walked inside, having closed the bakery after also receiving a call from Grandma. She wanted to join us and it felt like a fun girl's night.

We all got drinks and snacks, sitting on the couch to watch a few horror movies. Grandma turned off the lights and closed her eyes through some of it. It distracted me from Henry for a little while, laughing and joking with the girls. We left Henry and men completely out of our vocabulary—and it felt damn good.

We must've fallen asleep because the next thing I knew, I was waking up to sunlight poking through the curtains. Sonya, Grandma, and Mackenzie had passed out on the couch around me. I smiled as I woke up and stretched, grateful to have their support. I didn't know how else I would've survived if not for them.

Grandma stirred awake next, sitting up. "Oh, my…I must've fallen asleep. I'll get started on breakfast."

"I'll help," I said, rising to my feet. "Waffles should be good for everyone."

"Mmm, waffles," Mackenzie said, still half-asleep, making us laugh.

I headed into the kitchen with Grandma, helping her make the waffles, bacon, and fruit for breakfast. I was just pouring the juice as Sonya and Mackenzie woke up and joined us at the table. Then Grandma brought the food over and we all dug in.

"So, is everyone coming to the Sweet Treats Festival tomorrow?" Grandma asked. "Everything should be arriving today. The mayor is going to help us set up, as well as Mitch."

"I'll be there for sure," Mackenzie said, biting a piece off her waffle. "Wouldn't miss all the amazing desserts you're making for the world. And I'll help in the kitchen with whatever you need."

"Thank you, Mackenzie. We'll definitely need it. The mayor estimates thousands of people will come out. And not just citizens of New Harbor but tourists too. Sonya, will you join us?"

Sonya nodded, sipping her juice. "James and I will be there. The perk of owning your own business is taking whatever days off that you want."

Grandma smiled. "Perfect! I'm so happy we'll all be there. And you too, right, Angie?"

I sighed. "Well, I don't really feel like celebrating…but all right, I'll be there. Only to support the bakery."

"Good. There's just one problem," Grandma said,

awkwardly. "The firefighters rented a booth at the festival. They'll be there, trying to raise money for their fire station. Which means...you'll most likely run into Henry."

The table turned quiet. I shrugged, taking a bite of my bacon. "I guess that's unavoidable. I should get used to seeing him around—it's a small town. I'll have to get over what happened eventually."

"That's a good idea," Mackenzie said. "Don't give that idiot another thought. Live your life, be happy, and forget all about him. And maybe you'll find someone great in the process."

I thought I had—that was the problem. And Henry had stomped all over my hopes and dreams with those big firefighter boots of his.

Sonya checked her watch, rising to her feet. "Well, I should get going—have to open my shop. Lots of weddings on the horizon. And since James has the day off, he's coming to help me. Isn't that sweet of him?"

I nodded and smiled, though I felt that familiar pang of jealousy again. Why were some people luckier in love than others? For some, love was easy as pie. For others—like me—it was like decoding Shakespeare while reciting Latin and jumping on one foot. I'd never understand how it all worked.

"But this was fun," Sonya continued, putting on her coat. "I'm glad I came over. We should do sleepovers more often."

"Agreed. I felt like a kid again," I said, leading Sonya to the door. "Have fun at work. See you again soon."

She nodded, leaving the house and getting into her BMW outside. She sped off as I closed the door. Grandma had risen to her feet, grabbing the dirty plates to bring them to the kitchen.

"Mackenzie, do you think you could run the bakery again?" Grandma asked from the kitchen. "Good experience for when you want to open your own. I think Angie and I should stay home today. We have some last-minute notes to go over with the festival."

I whistled. "Sounds like a busy day."

Grandma laughed. "Always, dear. That's the life of an entrepreneur. Mackenzie?"

"Of course, Mrs. Linden," she said, grabbing her jacket off the wall. "I'll keep you posted if anything exciting happens. Take care, Angie—it was fun hanging out with you. Hope you don't let Henry get you down forever."

I sighed, leading her to the door. "Yeah, I hope so too. Out of curiosity...how are things going with Melissa, that cute girl at the coffee shop?"

Mackenzie hesitated. "Things...aren't going at all. I'm still too nervous to talk to her."

I grabbed my coat off the wall. "Well, today, things are going to change."

Mackenzie raised an eyebrow. "Huh? What are you talking about?"

"I'm going to help you talk to her," I said, turning toward the kitchen. "Grandma, I'm running to the coffee shop with Mac. I'll bring you back a coffee!"

"Okay—thank you, dear!" Grandma shouted as she started the dishes.

I turned to Mackenzie. "Come on, let's go. Your lady is waiting."

Mackenzie reached for my arm, stopping me. "Whoa, whoa, whoa...wait a second. I'm not sure I'm ready to talk to her yet. To ask her out. What if she says no?"

"Then she says no. Better to find out than wonder forever, right?" I asked, noticing how skeptical Mackenzie looked. "All right, I'm going to level with you. Love didn't work out for me—it never has. But you have a chance with Melissa. So does Grandma with Mitch and Sonya with James. And I want to see it work out for all of you."

"Wow," Mackenzie said with a smile. "That's kind of you. Some people—like Lucy—might've felt vindictive if Henry had done to her what he did to you. She might've even tried to sabotage other people's relationships."

I shook my head, reaching for my keys in my pocket. "Well, it's a good thing I'm not Lucy. Just because I can't find love doesn't mean other people shouldn't. Now, are you coming or not?"

Mackenzie took a deep breath. "Yeah, I'm coming. It's past time I talked to her. I mean, I passed my bakery test yesterday and that was freaking hard. If I can do that, I can do anything—including talking to a girl I've had a massive crush on for a year."

I led her to my truck, smiling. "For a year?"

"Yeah," Mackenzie said, shyly. "I've been watching her for a while. And not in, like, a creepy stalker way, but more like, me trying to figure out the perfect opening line. And then agonizing over it at night."

"I was a lot like you at your age," I said, unlocking the doors and getting into my truck. "But sometimes, you just need to take a chance. Who knows? Maybe Melissa will feel the same way."

As Mackenzie got in the truck, and I backed out, I decided to take my own advice. Although Henry hadn't worked out, I was glad I had taken a chance. That was brave of me after everything I'd been through with Adrian.

One day, I hoped my bravery would pay off and lead me to an amazing man. The perfect match. It had to.

Right?

Chapter Twenty-Four

I drove Mackenzie to the Cool Beans Coffee Shop, parking near the front doors. She took a deep breath before getting out of my truck. As we approached the front doors, I turned to her.

"Are you ready?" I asked.

She nodded. "I think so. Ugh, my hands are shaking..."

"It's all right," I said, placing my hand on her shoulder. "Falling in love is brave. It takes a lot of courage. For what it's worth, I'm proud of you for doing this."

Mackenzie smiled. "Thanks, Angie. Seriously—I'm really lucky to have you and Mrs. Linden. You just know how to make everything better."

"That's what we're here for. Okay, I see Melissa working at the register. Do you know what you'll say?"

We looked through the window, watching as Melissa served coffee to dozens of customers in line. Mackenzie stared at her for a while before turning to me.

"I was just going to walk up and say...um..."

"Maybe it would be more helpful if you had a plan," I said. "Go up to her and ask her how she is. Introduce yourself. Then, say you think she's super cute and that you want to get to know her. Maybe ask for her number. If she's creeped out, apologize and leave."

Mackenzie nodded. "Okay, that sounds like a good idea. Will you come in with me? Maybe sit down? It'd make me feel better if you were there."

"Of course," I said with a smile. "Lead the way."

Mackenzie opened the door to the coffee shop, entering and looking nervous. I patted her shoulder to encourage her before finding an empty table to sit at. I gave Mackenzie a thumbs-up before she went over and stood in line. When it was her turn, Melissa glanced at her. I leaned closer to hear their conversation.

"Next!" Melissa said with a smile. "What can I get for you?"

"Uh, a latte please. With soy milk," Mackenzie said, nervously playing with her hands.

Melissa punched it into the cash register. "Great! Anything else?"

"Um, yeah, there was something," Mackenzie stammered. "My name...my name is Mackenzie. Mackenzie Teller. I come in here a lot."

"Yeah, I've seen you in here," Melissa said. "You work at that bakery down the street, right? Wasn't it on the news because some restaurant stole their recipe or something?"

"Yeah, it was. Long story," Mackenzie said, looking awkward. "Anyway, I was just wondering if...if maybe you..."

"Come on!" a guy waiting in line behind Mackenzie said. "I'm already late for work. What's the damn hold up?"

Melissa gave Mackenzie a sympathetic smile. "Sorry about that—people get antsy when they don't get their coffee. Anything else?"

"Uh, no," Mackenzie said, sighing. "That'll be all."

"Great—I'll bring your coffee out when it's ready. Next!"

Mackenzie stood off to the side, waiting for her latte near the counter as the angry man behind her stepped toward the cash register to pay. Mackenzie looked back at me with a grimace. That hadn't gone to plan.

After Melissa took the man's order, she made Mackenzie's latte, bringing it to her with a smile. "Here you are—hope you enjoy. Have a great day!"

"You too," Mackenzie said, taking the latte and walking over to me. "Well...that didn't go over well."

"Tell me about it," I grumbled. "You were just about to ask her out before that guy ruined everything."

Mackenzie shook her head. "I knew this was a bad idea. Come on—let's just go. It's clear I'm never going to be able to ask out Melissa."

I hated seeing Mackenzie so upset. I rose to my feet, gesturing at the cash register. "Wait a second. You have a really big crush on Melissa, right? And you'd love to take her out?"

"Well, duh," Mackenzie said. "It just...I don't know, never works out for me. Maybe I'm cursed."

"Nah, I'm pretty sure I'm the unlucky one here," I joked. "I'll help you. Stay here, Mackenzie."

Mackenzie raised an eyebrow. "Why? What are you up to? Angie, come back!"

But I had already walked away, heading toward the line. I waited as each customer placed their order. The woman ahead of me placed her coffee order and then it was my turn. I approached the register where Melissa was smiling at me.

"Hello there," she began. "What can I get you?"

"Nothing, actually. I already had coffee today," I replied, glancing back at Mackenzie. "Look, you see my friend over there? Mackenzie Teller? You've met her before, right?"

"Of course. She comes in here for coffee all the time," Melissa said, glancing at Mackenzie. She was beet red. "Every day, actually."

"Right. Well, your coffee is delicious, but that's not the only reason she comes in here," I explained. "She thinks you're super cute and would love to take you out on a date sometime. She was trying to ask for your number before that guy in line got impatient. What do you say? She's pretty cute, right?"

Melissa glanced over at Mackenzie. "Really? She has a crush...on me?"

"That's right. She's a really nice girl—polite, kind, hard-working. Just earned her baking certification. But you can ask her all about that on a date. Say, to the movies tomorrow night? I can give her your phone number if you'd like."

Melissa smiled. "That would be great, thank you. I thought she'd never ask me out. I've been waiting for weeks, but I was just as shy as her. Thanks for doing this."

"No problem. Playing matchmaker is pretty fun," I said with a laugh, reminding myself of my grandma. "So, you've had a crush on her for a while too?"

"Yeah, ever since I saw her working at the bakery," Melissa said, writing her phone number on a napkin. "I just thought she already had a partner or something. It's good to know she's single. Here—give her my number. Tell her to call anytime."

I took the napkin, nodding. "Will do. Thanks, Melissa. I hope you two have a great date."

As she smiled at me, I moved out of line, letting the

next customer order. I walked over to Mackenzie where she sat at the table while watching us. I slid the napkin with Melissa's phone number on it toward her.

"Voilà," I said. "Here it is—Melissa's highly-coveted phone number."

Mackenzie's jaw fell. "You...actually got it? And she knows it's for me, right?"

I laughed. "Of course, silly. She said she's had a crush on you for a while too. She was just waiting for you to make the first move. You can call her anytime, she said. She'd love to go on a date."

"Wow. I...I can't believe it," Mackenzie said, picking up the napkin and staring at it. "This is like my wildest dream come true. Thank you for going over there, Angie. Seriously, I owe you one."

"Oh, don't mention it. Just happy I could help. I didn't want you to leave empty-handed."

"Thanks to you, I won't," Mackenzie said, sliding the napkin into her pocket. "I'll call her after work. Thanks again."

"You're welcome. So, should I drive you to the bakery?"

Mackenzie beamed. "Yeah, please and thank you. I have a feeling I'm going to have the best day ever."

I laughed, leading Mackenzie to the door. She waved at Melissa with a blush. The barista was already looking at us with a smile, waving back. I had a feeling they were going to be a great couple.

As I opened the door to leave, Lucy walked in, banging into my shoulder. "Hey, watch it!"

"You walked into me," I argued.

Everyone in the coffee shop turned, staring at Lucy. Some began to murmur. News of how she and Jack had stolen Grandma's recipe book had definitely spread far and wide.

"What are you looking at?" Lucy huffed, scanning the coffee shop.

No one responded—they just shook their heads, returning to their coffee and donuts.

"Serves you right," Mackenzie muttered. "For what you did."

"And my grandma and I would like our recipe book back now, thanks," I added. "Since, you know, it does belong to us."

Lucy stepped closer to me, getting in my face. "You want it back? Fine. But it's not going to be easy. I think I have a way to settle the feud between us forever."

I crossed my arms. "All right, I'm listening."

"A cooking competition—just you and me. Your old granny can sit this one out," Lucy spat. "Tomorrow morning at the community center. Whoever wins gets to keep the recipe book and gets bragging rights. We'll see who's the best baker between us."

"Wait, let me get this straight," Mackenzie said. "Angie has to win back her own recipe book that you stole? It belongs to her! She shouldn't have to compete against you to win it."

Lucy shrugged. "Those are the rules. Jack and I came up with the plan last night—a way to settle things between us. Take it or leave it."

"Just one question," I began. "If I win, and you give me back the recipe book, will you finally leave us alone? No more coming into our bakery and harassing us?"

"That's right—you have my word. And if we win, you'll do the same for us. We'll keep the recipe book and get rid of you forever. No more of your little news segments."

"And you'll play fair? No sabotage or rigging the competition in your favor?"

"Yep." Lucy put up a hand. "I solemnly swear that I have no tricks up my sleeve. It'll just be the two of us, challenging each other to a bake-off. The town will decide who's better. And the winner takes all."

Mackenzie scoffed. "This is ridiculous. You should just return the recipe book where it belongs—"

I held out my hand at Lucy. "Deal. Let's shake on it."

"Perfect," Lucy said with a smirk, shaking my hand. "See you tomorrow at the community center. And be prepared to lose—hard."

As Lucy went to stand in line and order a coffee, Mackenzie turned to me. "Are you crazy? You can't do a bake-off against Lucy! She never plays fair. If you ask me, you should just get a lawyer involved to get your recipe book back and let her sit in the mess she created."

"Maybe I should have, but I couldn't pass up the opportunity to get Lucy off our backs. Grandma doesn't need her crap," I said, eyeing Lucy in line as she ordered a coffee. "I don't want any more drama after this. Now, all I have to do is beat Lucy at her own game."

"Good luck with that," Mackenzie grumbled. "Because I have my doubts she'll play fair. I hope you have some tricks up your sleeve."

I opened the door, leaving the coffee shop with Mackenzie. "Oh, I always do. Grandma taught me everything I needed to know."

We headed to my truck, then I drove Mackenzie to the bakery. She promised to hold down the fort as I headed home to relax with Grandma. But now I was preoccupied with the bake-off—and how I was going to win.

And more importantly, how to convince Grandma this was a good idea.

I pulled into our driveway, then headed inside. Nutmeg was waiting for me by the door as usual. As I kicked off my boots and shrugged out of my coat, I spotted Grandma sitting on the couch, writing out a list. She looked up when she saw me.

"Ah, dear—there you are," she said with a smile. "How did it go with Mackenzie?"

"She got Melissa's number and they're planning a date. In fact, Melissa's had a crush on her this whole time too. She was as shy as Mackenzie and waiting for her to make the first move."

"Well, would you look at that? It all worked out for the best. I'm just sorry you didn't have the same luck with Henry."

I looked down. "Yeah, same here. What are you working on?"

"I told you—our recipes for the Sweet Treats Festival and the bake sale at the senior home. I was just about to start baking if you'd like to help."

"Of course. But Grandma...there's something you need to know."

Grandma looked up from her list. "Oh? Is everything all right?"

"I...sort of got myself into a bake-off against Lucy," I said. Grandma's eyes widened. "But hear me out! She said if I win, she'll give us back the recipe book *and* leave us alone. For good. Doesn't that sound great?"

"It does—if you win. What happens if you lose?"

"Then we say goodbye to the recipe book forever. I know—it sucks, but I don't see any other way to get her off our backs. She was the one who proposed the idea. I think this is the only way to get rid of her."

Grandma sighed, rising to her feet. "Okay, dear. If you think it's a good idea, I believe in you. I know you're an excellent baker. When is it taking place?"

"Tomorrow morning at the community center. I'd better start practicing."

"Of course. I'll help," Grandma said, walking into the kitchen. "Do you...do you really think you'll win?"

"I hope so," I said, as I grabbed a cookie sheet out of a bottom drawer. "I have to—for you and Grandpa. You deserve to have that recipe book back. I'll do whatever it takes to win it for you."

Grandma smiled. "I know you will, dear. Fingers crossed it works out."

Something had to. As I practiced a few recipes, gearing up for the bake-off tomorrow, Grandma was making brownies and cupcakes for the senior home. After a few hours, we had everything ready and the kitchen smelled delicious.

"Ah, freshly-baked desserts," I said, sniffing the air. "Nothing compares."

"It's always a comforting smell to me too. Are we ready to go? I promised the mayor I'd bring the senior home some baked goodies today. You know, to improve morale. It can get lonely living in a retirement home."

"Yep, I'm ready. Let me just grab my keys."

Grandma nodded, placing all the desserts in containers for the bake sale. "Okay, sweetie. You know...I'm very glad you've decided to keep living with me. I realize I could be just like those seniors in that retirement home. Aging, alone, and grieving. Having a strong support system is so necessary while you've lost someone."

I leaned in, hugging Grandma. “And I feel the same about you. You’ll always have me, Grandma.”

“And I will always be with you, dear. Never forget that,” Grandma said, beaming. “Despite everything, we’re lucky to still have each other.”

Grandma was right. Despite all the drama with Lucy and Jack, my failed romance with Henry, and Grandpa passing away, Grandma had been my rock through it all. The one constant I could depend on.

Even if I lost the bake-off and never found love, as long as I still had her, I would be okay.

Chapter Twenty-Five

We drove to Queenswood Villa, the retirement home just outside of New Harbor. After I pulled into the parking lot, I got out with Grandma, helping her carry the desserts into the facility. It was a large building—a pretty garden growing outside, hundreds of rooms for the senior citizens, a bingo hall, and a pool around the back. It didn't look like a bad place to grow old.

As we entered, the seniors looked up, hoping we were there to see them. They sat around the foyer with their wheelchairs and walkers. Some of them were trying to escape—confused and dazed—so the nurses had to gently guide them back to their rooms.

Grandma approached the secretary sitting at the front desk. "Hello there—I'm Esther Linden and this is my granddaughter, Angela. Mayor Cartier asked us to host the bake sale today?"

"Yes—of course. The seniors here have been looking forward to it all week," the secretary said, rising to her feet. "Please, follow me to the hall. There will be plenty of tables to set up your desserts."

We nodded, following the woman down the corridor, passing dozens of senior citizens. She led us to a convention hall where Mayor Cartier was busy setting up tables for everyone. Some other people from town had arrived, bringing their own homemade goodies to the bake sale.

"Thanks again for agreeing to this," the secretary said. "You've really brightened up our residents' days."

Grandma smiled. "That's what we like to hear. Thank you for showing us the way—we'll set up now. Dear, if you could follow me?"

I went with Grandma, waving goodbye to the secretary who returned to the front desk. We found a long table and began assembling it with brownies, cupcakes, muffins, and more for the senior citizens. Mayor Cartier walked over and began chatting with Grandma.

"...and the retirement home is close to my heart," Mayor Cartier was saying. "All four of my grandparents stayed here and received excellent care. So I'm always willing to give back. I'm glad you agreed as well."

"Oh, of course. I have some old friends who are staying here," Grandma said, looking into the crowd as the senior citizens began to pour in. "Anything we can do to help."

They continued chatting for a little bit, then Mayor Cartier made her rounds, most likely canvassing for the upcoming election. Grandma began serving a group of elderly ladies who had limped over with their canes and asked for cookies. As she took their money, handing them the cookies they wanted, I felt someone tap me on my shoulder.

When I spun around, it was an elderly man, full of wrinkles. He wore overalls, used a cane to get around, and was holding a daffodil from the garden outside in his hand. He smoothed down his grey hair before speaking.

"Hello there, gorgeous," he began. "This is for you."

When he handed me the flower, I took it, surprised. "Oh, wow...thank you."

"My pleasure. My name is Roy," he said, shaking my hand. "And what a lovely lady you are."

I couldn't believe it—this old guy was flirting with me. If only men my age were as interested.

"Roy, stop bothering that poor young girl," an elderly woman said, wheeling over to us. She wore a blue dress and had grey hair that she tucked behind a wrinkled ear. "I'm sorry, young lady. Roy still thinks he's in his twenties."

"One day, it'll work, Edna," Roy shot back. "One day."

"Yeah, yeah," Edna said, waving him off. "Go check out the bake sale and stop harassing women. Oh, Esther—is that you? My, I haven't seen you in a while."

Grandma turned around, smiling as the man named Roy walked away. "Hi, Edna. So nice to see you again. What has it been? Twenty, twenty-five years?"

"Something like that. How's your husband?"

Grandma paused. "I'm afraid Lou passed away last year. My granddaughter and I have been running his bakery since then."

"Oh, dear. I'm so very sorry," Edna said, softly. "He was truly a kind man. And I take it this must be your granddaughter?"

"That's me," I said, shaking her hand. "Nice to meet you. How do you know my grandma?"

"We used to go to school together—back in our younger days," Grandma said with a smile. "What's new with you, Edna? Doing anything fun these days?"

Edna gestured at an elderly man in the crowd who was wearing a suit. "Well, I just started dating Darren. He's such a gentleman. He's definitely my reason for getting up in the morning."

Even seniors had found love. I felt totally and completely alone.

Grandma smiled. "That's so lovely. I hope you two are very happy. Can I interest you in one of our desserts?"

As Edna glanced around the table, inspecting her options, I left Grandma alone to mingle. I politely said hello to all the seniors and nurses and promoted our bakery. When I heard a familiar voice down the hallway, I paused.

Henry. He was here—and wearing his firefighter uniform.

"I'm just glad you and your cat are doing well, Mrs. Holmes," he was saying to a small elderly woman. She was carrying a little orange kitty. "Try to make sure he doesn't escape again, okay?"

"I'll try my best," the old woman replied, stroking her cat. "Thank you again for saving him from that tree. I don't know what I would've done without you. You're my hero, Henry."

He smiled. "Happy to be of service, ma'am. Enjoy the bake sale."

The lady nodded, bringing her cat with her as she entered the hall to survey the desserts. Henry scanned the room before his eyes fell on me. But he didn't smile and wave as usual. He swallowed hard as I made my way over to him.

"Hey, Henry," I began. "What are you doing here?"

"Oh, I came to check on an old woman whose cat I rescued from a tree," he said, pointing at Mrs. Holmes in the crowd. "Both of them are doing much better. What are you doing here?"

"The mayor asked my grandma to bring desserts for the bake sale. Apparently, the seniors have been looking forward to it all week."

"Well, that's good." He noticed the flower in my hand. "Who's that from?"

Why did Henry even care? He made it clear he didn't want me—and he didn't get to have his cake and eat it too.

"An admirer," I said, leaving out the details. "So...we haven't talked since you stood me up the other night."

Henry sighed. "I know. I've been meaning to text or call, but...I haven't had the guts. I'm so sorry, Angie. Really."

I looked him dead in the eyes. "Don't apologize—just tell me this. Why did you do it? Why did you tell me you had feelings for me, get my hopes up, and then crush me like that? What did I ever do to you?"

Some people in the hall started to stare at us and murmur, hearing my raised voice. I spotted Grandma looking over with concern.

Henry looked down. "You're right—you didn't deserve that. I let my own fears get in the way of being with you. What happened between me and my ex-wife...it really messed me up. Badly."

"So you hurt me first," I said, crossing my arms. "You're fine with pain as long as you're not the one hurting, right? Typical. Look, I'm not your ex, Henry. Whatever happened between you two is just that—between you. I shouldn't have been punished for something I've never done. I never would've wanted to hurt you."

"That's what my ex said too," Henry said, softly. "And that didn't end well."

I shook my head. "Stubborn. Here I thought we might

have something—that you felt a connection too. I should've known you were just like all the rest."

Henry looked offended. "Angie, I'm really not. I want the same things you do. And yeah, we did have a connection. A very strong one. I've always wanted a happily-ever-after—"

"No, we don't want the same things," I interrupted. "I wanted you. I wanted you so much that I was willing to put my fears about dating aside. I guess you couldn't do the same. And I certainly wouldn't have stood you up and made you feel like an idiot."

He stepped closer. "You're not an idiot, Angie. Far from it. This is all me—it's all my fault. You did nothing wrong."

"At least we're in agreement, then," I said, sighing. "Goodbye, Henry. And good luck."

I turned away, heading back to Grandma's table while trying not to cry. I could feel Henry's eyes on my back, still watching me. Grandma patted my shoulder before she walked away. I watched as she approached Henry, said a few choice words to him, then he turned around and left. Grandma only shook her head and walked back to the table.

"I'm sorry you had to see him, darling," Grandma said. "I asked him to leave since it was upsetting you. And I told him that he lost a wonderful woman."

"Thanks, Grandma. You always have my back."

"Until the end of time," she said with a smile. "Come on—let's mingle some more. I want to hand out some free samples to the seniors with lower incomes. Everyone should get a dessert."

"What about our table? Who's going to watch it while we're gone?"

"Oh, I got a nice lady from another table to watch ours. It'll be okay, don't worry."

I nodded, picking up a tray of cookies and following Grandma. We introduced ourselves to all the seniors and handed out free samples. Once the desserts were gone, the mayor invited us into the great hall to enjoy some coffee with the senior citizens. Another large group was playing Bingo down the hall.

I sat next to Grandma, sipping my coffee as she, Edna, and the other senior citizens reminisced about the good old days. Record players, black and white televisions, and rotary phones came up but I couldn't relate. I sat there quietly, listening to them chat.

"...and my husband, Lou, was always writing down new baking recipes on his typewriter in the attic," Grandma told the group. "Sometimes, all I could hear at night was that damn dinging sound!"

Everyone laughed, sharing their own memories. I was glad we had brought some joy to the senior home.

Grandma gestured at me, placing a hand on my shoulder. "My granddaughter's Gen Z—only twenty-four. She has no idea what we're talking about."

"Yeah, old technology really isn't my forte," I joked. "I grew up with Internet and TV so it's all I've ever known."

"Lucky," one of the old ladies said. "My husband and I used to listen to the radio when we were young. It took us a long time to afford a black and white TV. Ah, I miss my Gerald so much."

The group nodded, then began sharing their experiences with love. Most of them were widowed like Grandma, their partners passing away from old age. Yet they still kept that love alive.

"Unbeknownst to my granddaughter, I go to my

husband's grave every Friday after work," Grandma said to the group. "To lay down flowers and take care of the headstone. Lou gave me fifty-two blissful years of marriage. It's the least I can do for him."

"I still write letters to my Gerald," the old lady named Bertha said. "Love...love sticks with you forever. Out of everything I've done in my life, nothing compares to marrying my Gerald. I'd do it all over again, any day of the week."

"I agree," Grandma said, glancing at me. "My Angie hasn't had the best luck when it comes to love. Can any of you offer her some advice?"

All the old people were eager to talk to me. And their advice was largely the same.

"Don't give up on looking for it," an older man named Ricardo said. "It's hard to find, but when you do, boy, is it worth it. Love will transform you."

"And keep you going," another old woman said. "It's simply the greatest thing in the whole world."

I wanted to believe that, but after everything that had happened with Jack, Ty, and Henry, I wasn't so sure of it anymore. All these women were lucky to have found great partners. But did that love even exist anymore?

"Yes—I keep telling my Angie that too. I hope one day, she'll believe me," Grandma said with a wink, rising to her feet. "Anyway, we should get going. We hope you all enjoyed the bake sale."

The seniors nodded, then begged us to come back. Grandma promised we would—and that we'd have new desserts next time. The senior's eyes lit up when they heard that.

Me and Grandma grabbed our empty dessert containers, then took them out to my truck. We drove back home and put them away before Grandma checked the time on the wall clock. Almost dinner.

"Now, are you sure you don't want me to stay with you?" she asked. "Because Mitch and I rescheduled our date for tonight. But if you'd rather have me stay in—"

"Grandma, really. It's fine," I urged. "Go out and have a great time. I'll be okay alone—I think I'm just going to order takeout and watch reality TV. And let me know how it goes, all right? Oh, man, I've turned into you."

Grandma laughed. "Good! The apple doesn't fall far from the tree, dear. All right, if you're sure. Have a great evening and I'll see you later."

Grandma kissed my cheek, then touched up her makeup and grabbed her purse. She waved goodbye as she headed outside to get into her sedan. I watched her leave before I shut the door, fed Nutmeg, and checked out the Chinese takeout menu that we kept in the fridge. I ordered General Tao's Chicken, egg rolls, chicken balls, fried rice, and of course, lots of dessert. They had a picture of egg tarts on their menu that looked amazing.

"Utensils for one, please," I told the lady on the phone. "I'm...uh, eating alone tonight."

The food arrived thirty minutes later. I paid the delivery guy at the door and took the food. They had thrown in some fortune cookies as a free gift. Maybe the cooks at the restaurant felt bad for me. I cracked one open, reading it in the kitchen light.

"Love will light the way," I read aloud. "Really? Because all it's ever done is make me miserable."

I sat down on the couch, eating my Chinese food and watching some reality TV. Nothing like TV drama to distract me from my own problems—like my heartbreak over Henry and the bake-off with Lucy tomorrow. I was really nervous about the latter.

As I downed another egg roll, dipping it in loads of plum sauce, the doorbell rang. I wiped the oil from my hands and got up to answer the door. When I opened it, my jaw dropped.

Mom and Dad stood there—and they were arguing. I hadn't seen them in years. Why had they come to visit? And why now?

I almost groaned. Just another problem to deal with.

Chapter Twenty-Six

I cleared my throat, trying to interrupt their bickering. It reminded me of all the times they argued when I was a kid. "Um, Mom, Dad? Sorry to interrupt, but what are you two doing here?"

Mom turned to me, then I noticed she was dragging a polka-dotted suitcase behind her. She looked like a mess—frizzy brown hair, smudged make-up, and a baggy sweater with tights. She was also carrying a half-drunk bottle of wine. Dad looked much better, tanned and relaxed. His balding head was smooth and shiny and he was wearing a Hawaiian shirt with shorts despite the chilly weather in New Harbor.

"Your grandma called," Mom said. "Told us we should come out and see you. I jumped on a train as fast as I could. The trip was long, but I made it. It's been a while, hasn't it?"

I nodded. "It has. Dad, Grandma called you too?"

"She did. I finally told Esther how sorry I was to hear about your grandfather," Dad said, dragging along his own black suitcase. "I thought it was a good idea to come see you. I just didn't know we would have...company."

Mom sneered. "And neither did I. Where's your new girlfriend? The one who's young enough to be Angie's sister?"

Dad crossed his arms. "And how do you know about that? Have you been stalking my Facebook again?"

"Hardly," Mom said, rolling her eyes. "It's just what I've heard through the grapevine."

"Well, if you must know, Jenny's at home. She's looking after our dogs," Dad explained. "She moved in a few months ago."

Mom looked disappointed. "Moved in? Oh. Then I guess things are serious."

Dad nodded. "They are. I can really see a future with Jenny—despite the age gap. But honestly, when we're together, it's never a problem. We have so much in common that everything else fades away."

"Yeah, right," Mom sneered. "I give it a year before it ends. You were never good at commitment, Greg."

"I wasn't good at commitment with *you*, Patricia," Dad shot back, glaring at her. "We were never right for each other. The only good thing that came out of our relationship was Angie. And I don't want to spend all our time here arguing in front of her. So, how's our little pumpkin doing?"

With Mom and Dad's eyes on me, I faked a smile. "Good. Things are...good. Anyway, do you two want to come in?"

"Yes, please," Mom said, pushing past me. "Now I remember why I never liked New Harbor. It's freaking freezing in this town!"

Dad rolled his eyes, following Mom inside. I took their

suitcases—one to the basement where Dad would stay on the pull-out couch, then one to the guest room upstairs where Mom would sleep. I thought it was best to keep them far away from each other.

When I came back down the stairs, Mom and Dad were arguing again in hushed whispers. The only thing worse than never finding love was ending up like that—bickering with my ex until the end of time. I was glad they had divorced.

I cleared my throat, hushing them. "Okay, everything's set up. Mom, you're upstairs, and Dad, you'll be in the basement. Let me know if you need anything. There are plenty of blankets and towels."

"Thank you, hun," Mom said, glancing around. "So, where's your grandmother? Working hard at the bakery?"

I shook my head. "Not exactly. She's on a date."

"A date?" Dad asked, raising an eyebrow. "Good for her."

"A date? At her age?" Mom rolled her eyes. "That's a bit ridiculous. Plus, I think it's too soon. It's only been a year since Dad died."

"Everyone needs love, Patricia," Dad said, turning to her. "You should try it sometime. Maybe then you won't be as bitter."

"I'm going to pretend you didn't just say that," Mom hissed. "You know, if I'd known my mother had invited you too, I wouldn't have come. You were always so condescending."

"Me?" Dad huffed. "You should try looking in the mirror. You were always such a Debbie Downer, finding fault in everything—"

"Enough!" I shouted, making them both jump. "If all you're going to do is argue, then you two can get back on the train and head home. I have enough to deal with. Now, are you going to act like mature adults or bicker like children?"

"I can be mature," Dad said. "Sorry, Angie."

"Yes, sorry, sweetie," Mom said, sighing. "We'll stop. For now."

They glared at each other but didn't say anything. It was a start, at least. I nodded. "Good. Now, you can make yourselves comfortable on the couch. There's leftover Chinese food in the fridge if you're hungry. We can watch a movie together if you two promise to be on your best behavior."

Mom and Dad promised, though I didn't know how long it would last. I'd have to take advantage of the peace while I still could.

"I'll take some of that Chinese food, honey," Mom said. "The food on the train was awful."

"Same here," Dad added. "I'd love some Chinese food. Eggrolls are my favorite."

"Mine too," Mom said, opening her bottle of wine.

Finally, something they agreed on. They sat down at the dining room table while I prepared two plates. A minute later, Nutmeg came down the stairs. She remembered them, letting both of them pet her.

"I can't believe Nutmeg is still alive," Mom said, scratching behind her ears. "Cats really must have nine lives."

"We almost lost her," I said, bringing two plates out to the dining room table. "We rushed her to the vet after threw up. Turns out she had a blockage. And it was super expensive to fix."

"I bet," Dad said, reaching for a fork. "Did you sort it out? Or did you need your mom and I to loan you some money?"

I shook my head. "No, it's all right—we paid the bill. A...friend of mine paid it in full."

Mom raised an eyebrow, biting into her egg roll. "What kind of friend?"

"No one," I said, sitting down with them. "It's...no one."

"Are you all right, Angie?" Dad asked. "You look upset."

I debated telling them about Henry, but I didn't want Mom to lecture me again on how love wasn't real. So I just shrugged.

"I'm fine," I said. "Really, there's nothing to worry about. So, what have you two been up to?"

To my surprise, Mom and Dad remained civil, getting me up to speed. They talked about their jobs, our extended family, and new hobbies they had picked up. I was just grateful to have a mature conversation with them.

"But tell us about you," Dad said. "Other than taking care of the bakery with your grandma, what have you been up to?"

I shrugged, leaving out all the dates I'd been on. "Oh, a little of this and that. Sonya's getting married. Me and Grandma just catered her engagement party."

"Really? Little Sonya?" Dad asked, wide-eyed. "Congrats to her! I'll have to send her a gift in the mail."

Mom scoffed. "Marriage is so...archaic. There's no need for it anymore. And fifty percent of marriages end in divorce, you know. Just look at ours for an example."

Dad rolled his eyes, finishing his Chinese food. "Oh, don't be such a buzzkill, Patricia. Just be happy for the girl."

"She and James look great together," I added. "They seem very excited about the wedding."

"We'll see how long it lasts," Mom grumbled, drinking straight from her wine bottle.

I shook my head, changing the subject. "I'm actually glad you two are here. I'll need some extra support tomorrow."

"Oh?" Dad asked. "What's going on?"

I was just about to tell them about the bake-off against Lucy when the front door opened. Grandma walked in, smiling and waving at someone in the driveway. I walked to the window and saw Mitch grinning, then driving away in a sports car.

She walked in, closing the door behind her and noticing Mom and Dad. "Aw, you two made it! I'm so glad."

"There you are," Mom said as she rose to her feet. "Angie said you were on a date? Seriously, Mother?"

"What's wrong with that, dear?" Grandma asked, putting her purse down. "I had a lovely time. Mitch is an amazing person—and a talented newscaster. We have another date next week."

I smiled. "I'm happy for you, Grandma."

"Yes, so am I," Dad said, rising to his feet and walking toward Grandma. "Nice to see you again, Esther."

"Ah, Greg. Nice to see you as well. Thank you both for coming. Anyway, make yourselves at home! I'm sure Angie is happy to have you here."

"As long as they keep the bickering to a minimum," I said, staring at Mom and Dad. "How long are you two planning to stay?"

"A few days, I suppose," Mom said. "Until I have to go back to work."

Dad nodded. "Yes, a few days sounds nice. I work from home now so my schedule is flexible."

"Well, good for you," Mom sneered. "Now, what were you going to tell us before your grandmother walked in?"

"Tomorrow morning, I have a bake-off against Lucy

Rhett at the community center. She's our competitor and a total mean girl."

"A bake-off sounds fun," Dad said.

I shook my head. "Not this one. You should hear what Lucy's done to us."

"That name sounds familiar," Mom said, frowning. "Is it the same Lucy you went to high school with? The mean girl you used to complain about?"

"Yep—and she's gotten a lot worse..."

After I told them everything, Dad scoffed. "Lucy can't get away with this! I'll head to her restaurant right now and tell her to stay away from you."

I shook my head. "No, Dad. That won't work. Like I told Mackenzie, sometimes you have to beat people at their own game. This is why I'm glad you two are here—I'll need your support in the bake-off. It'll help me win."

"You'll have our unconditional support, darling," Grandma said. "We'll be there to cheer you on."

"Yes, of course," Mom added. "That recipe book was Grandpa's greatest treasure. I can't believe that bitch stole it!"

"Well, with a little luck, I'll get it back," I said, yawning. "I'm getting tired. I need my rest for tomorrow."

"Sounds like a good idea," Grandma said. "I'm tired too. Did you find a place to sleep for both your parents?"

"Yep—Dad's in the basement and Mom will be upstairs."

"Good," Grandma said, glancing at them. "Let me know if you need anything. Goodnight, all."

Mom and Dad nodded, heading to their designated sleep areas. I cleaned up their plates while they were gone and wiped down the table. When I noticed Grandma watching me, I looked up with a frown.

"What?"

Grandma sighed. "I hope you don't let your parents convince you that love isn't real, darling. I know they can be a bit...difficult."

"You can say that again," I mumbled. "I was starting to believe in love again—I really was–until Henry ruined it. Maybe it's for the best. I'm happy you found Mitch, though."

Grandma gave me a sympathetic smile. "Thank you, dear. And I hope you find someone special too. Goodnight, sweetie."

I said goodnight to Grandma, then headed up to my room. I fell asleep as soon as my head hit the pillow, trying to ignore Mom and Dad's drama, and my fear that love didn't exist anymore. Mom and Dad weren't the best role models for commitment.

When I woke up the next morning, Grandma was downstairs with Mom and Dad, making breakfast for everyone. I sighed in relief when they seemed civil. We ate breakfast together, chatting about the town and the competition.

"Are you ready for today, sweetie?" Grandma asked.

I took a deep breath. "I think so. I just hope Lucy will play fair."

"She better," Dad said. "Or she'll have to deal with me. Come on, we don't want to be late."

I nodded, heading upstairs to get ready. I had years of baking knowledge from working with my grandparents. I should've been well-prepared, yet I still felt nervous. But I had to do this.

When I came back down the stairs, Mom and Dad were outside, waiting for us in the backseat of Grandma's sedan. I could see them arguing a little through the window as I shook my head. Grandma was waiting near the door, holding her purse.

"There you are," she began. "Angie...I wanted to thank you for doing this. I know you're only competing against Lucy to win the recipe book back."

"Someone has to," I replied. "That belonged to Grandpa, not some high school mean girl. And I think we need to stand up to bullies. Show them that their behavior isn't right."

Grandma smiled. "I'm proud of you, Angie. Whether or not you win the recipe book back, I want you to remember that."

I leaned in, hugging her tight. "Thanks, Grandma. Love you."

"And I love you more, dear." She pulled back, glancing out the window. "We should get a move on before your parents' bickering gets worse. Those two are like oil and water. Do you have everything you need?"

"Almost—one sec."

I walked into the kitchen, gathering some important ingredients. Flour, sugar, eggs, baking powder. All the baking essentials. As I carried them out to the car, I hoped it would be enough to win against Lucy.

Mom and Dad hushed when we both hopped in the front seat of Grandma's sedan. Grandma drove to the local New Harbor community center, decorated blue and white, searching for a place to park. It seemed like every spot was taken.

"My goodness, the community center is busy today," Grandma said. "I'll have to park on the street. That's the only place left."

After Grandma parked along the road, I stepped out, carrying my container of ingredients. We walked through the busy parking lot, heading inside through the double doors. I noticed hundreds of people murmuring in the entryway.

"Jeez, is there a sports game or something going on?" Mom asked as we glanced around. "This place is packed like sardines!"

As I pushed through the crowd, accidentally bumping into some people, Sonya came running up to us. "Angie, there you are!"

I frowned. "Sonya? What are you doing here?"

"You haven't heard? Lucy spread the word that you two are having a bake-off. Said it was the cooking contest of the decade or something."

I rolled my eyes. That sounded like Lucy, always such a drama queen.

"Ah, no wonder there are so many people here," Dad said. "They all came to watch you."

I swallowed hard, feeling nervous. "I should've known. Lucy did always love the attention."

"Yep, she hasn't changed," Sonya said, sighing. "Don't worry—I came to support you. I fully believe you'll kick that mean girl's ass."

I laughed. "Here's hoping. My parents are back in town, by the way."

When I gestured at them, Sonya's eyes lit up. "Patricia, Greg! I haven't seen you in years. How are you two doing?"

As they caught up, talking loudly over the crowd, people began to recognize Grandma and me. They murmured about us like we weren't even there. Before I could push through the crowd, Lucy walked over to us with Jack and her husband following like loyal puppies.

"There you are. Finally," Lucy hissed. "You ready for the bake-off?"

I held up my ingredients. "Yep, I am. I just didn't realize you were inviting everyone in town."

"I've always liked an audience," Lucy said with a smile. "I'm just glad they showed up. They're still mad at me after that little expose you filmed."

"I'm sorry to say it, Ms. Rhett, but you brought that on yourself," Grandma said, shooting a frown at Lucy and Jack. "I'm very disappointed in the two of you. That recipe book is one of the last things I have of my late husband."

"Yeah, it's a bit ridiculous Angie has to beat you to win back what's hers," Sonya added. "Why can't you just stop being such a huge bitch for one second and return it?"

Lucy sneered. "Sonya, I thought I recognized you. Your big nose tends to stick out in a crowd."

Jack snickered, making Sonya gasp in shock. I felt like I was transported right back to my high school days. Lucy's husband, Dan, just shook his head in disapproval.

"All right, stop," I said, glaring at Lucy. "We're going to be civil and play fair. That's what you promised, after all."

"Oh, of course," Lucy said, gesturing down the hall. "The kitchen I rented is this way. May the best baker win."

Chapter Twenty-Seven

I followed Lucy, heading to one of the convention halls in the community center. They had a kitchen that you could rent for cooking and baking classes. Grandma and I had given one a long time ago, but I never thought I'd be back here for this reason–to get back my recipe book and convince my old high school bully to leave us alone.

Life was funny that way.

I entered the kitchen, noticing there were two counters set up. Lucy had already arrived and set up her counter with the baking ingredients she'd need. Dozens of seats lined the class, then the crowd began to pour in. They looked eager as they took their seats.

I walked over to my counter, putting my container of ingredients down, having flashbacks to Mackenzie's exam. Lucy and Jack went to their counter and began whispering while staring at me. Lucy's husband kept his distance with a frown and his arms crossed. I tried not to focus on them, setting up all the ingredients I'd need.

Grandma, Sonya, Mom, and Dad took their seats in the front row, giving me a thumbs-up. I appreciated their support so much. It had helped Mackenzie pass her baking test, and I hoped it would have the same effect on me. Speaking of Mackenzie, she and Melissa pushed through the crowd a minute later, waving at us as they sat in the back. I smiled, glad they were together and here to show their support.

Then Mitch and James walked in, finding Grandma and Sonya and sitting next to them. They introduced themselves to Mom and Dad. Mom didn't seem too impressed with Mitch, but I didn't think she'd be happy about whoever Grandma was dating.

I wondered—was I destined to become like my mother? Scorned, bitter, and fed up with love? I hoped not, but with the way things were going, it seemed likely. I didn't want it to end up that way—I wanted to believe in love. I just wished love would start believing in *me* for a change.

When Henry walked through the doors, glancing around, I froze. What was he doing here? Once his eyes found me, he walked over, looking awkward.

"Hey, Angie," he began. "Heard about the bake-off today. Everyone in town's been talking about it."

I glanced over at Lucy who was still whispering about me to Jack. "Yeah, Lucy made sure of that. She always did have a big mouth. What are you doing here?"

Henry rubbed the back of his neck, nervously. "I just…I wanted to come and show my support. To cheer you on. Despite everything, I really do care about you, Angie. Even if you don't think I do."

"Well, you have a funny way of showing it," I said, continuing to assemble my ingredients. Then I sighed. "Look, I appreciate you coming, but you didn't have to. I'm more than capable of beating Lucy without you."

"I know. That's what I always liked about you. You're

strong, a damned good baker, and you really care about your grandmother. I know you're going to defeat Lucy and get your family's recipe book back."

If Henry had said that to me a week ago, I would've been over the moon. Weak in the knees. Tongue-tied. But now, after standing me up, I only shrugged.

"Thanks for that," I said with a nod. "Now, if you'll excuse me, I need to get ready for the bake-off."

"Right. Good luck, Angie. I'm rooting for you."

He walked away, finding a seat in the audience near the back. I hoped I'd be able to focus with him around. When I glanced over at Grandma, she was already looking at me as everyone else talked around her.

"Are you okay, dear?" she mouthed.

I nodded, giving her a thumbs-up. Though I felt the opposite. Just as I finished setting up, picking out the baking tools I needed from the drawer, Lucy walked to the front of the crowd.

"Thank you all for being here," she began, quieting the audience. "Now, I know you think I'm some recipe stealer—"

"Because you are!" Sonya shouted from the audience.

"Silence, please," Lucy huffed. "But today, it doesn't really matter. Angie and I are going to solve all our troubles with a good old-fashioned bake-off. Whoever wins gets bragging rights, the recipe book, and the town's support. Isn't that right, Angie?"

"That's right," I said, looking into the crowd. "This is the baking war to end all baking wars."

"Good," Lucy said with a smile. "Now, before we start, I thought we could share a little about our restaurants with the crowd..."

As Lucy rambled on about herself, taking the time to

brag about her degrees and background, I started to get nervous. What if I couldn't defeat Lucy? What if I came all this way just to lose Grandma's recipe book forever? I couldn't think of a worse fate.

"Angie? Is there something you want to tell the crowd about yourself?" Lucy asked, turning to me. She had on her soft and sweet voice which was a complete lie. "Other than the fact that you have the worst fashion sense I've ever seen..."

Jack snickered, from a seat in the front row. But Lucy's husband wasn't laughing. Did Jack really find Lucy's mean girl act cute?

I shook my head. "Yeah, sure—I've got something to say. Lucy, you've always been a jealous, petty, mean girl who peaked in high school. Because you have nothing better to do, you continue to harass us. And getting your stepbrother to date me to steal my recipe book was proof of how catty you are. So whether I win or lose this bake-off, I know I'll never be as cruel and pathetic as you. Which feels like I've already won."

Lucy glared at me, a vein popping out of her forehead that not even Botox could fix. The crowd began to murmur about Lucy again as she walked over to her counter.

"I'm going to make you eat those words, Angie," Lucy grumbled. "No more talk—we're going to settle this here. Get ready, get set...bake!"

As Lucy reached for her ingredients, hoping to bake something the crowd would vote for, I got to work. I had just picked up the flour and sugar and was about to combine them in a big bowl when Lucy's husband rose to his feet.

"Stop. Stop the bake-off!" he cried. "I have something to say."

"Oh, sit down," Jack snarled, trying to drag him down. "And be quiet."

"Yes, there won't be any interruptions," Lucy spat, as she glared at her husband. "If you can't be quiet, then go home."

"No, I have to say this," Dan said, turning around to stare at the audience. "Lucy rigged the competition. She's cheating!"

Everyone in the audience began murmuring. What on Earth was going on?

I stopped combining the flour and sugar, frowning. "What are you talking about? How did she rig this?"

Her husband turned around. "She drove to a bakery in Boston that makes the best cheesecake. Seriously, it's Heaven. We went there on our honeymoon. Anyway, she brought it back and is keeping it in one of the drawers in her counter. She's going to pass it off as her own when the competition's over. She'll pretend she made it and hopes everyone will crown her as the winner."

"Would you shut up?" Lucy snarled, then faked a laugh, turning to the audience. "I'm so sorry, everyone. It seems my husband is confused. I really have no idea what he's talking about."

I wiped the flour off my hands, walking toward her counter. "There's one way to prove that. Let me search your counter, Lucy."

Lucy crossed her arms. "That's...that's ridiculous! I'm not hiding anything."

"Then let us see it," Grandma said from the audience. "Prove to everyone your husband's lying."

Lucy hesitated, staring at Jack in the audience. He was speechless. I took advantage of her hesitation to reach into the drawer of her counter. And lo and behold, a fresh cheesecake was sitting in there. And smelling incredible.

I pulled out the cheesecake, holding it up. "Lucy's husband was right. What do you have to say for yourself, Lucy?"

Her face turned red. "I...I don't know how that got in there. Someone's setting me up!"

"The convention hall must have security cameras," Sonya said, rising to her feet. "Let's find them and play them back. We can find out who put that cheesecake in there once and for all."

When Lucy didn't respond, I turned to her. "What's wrong? Cat got your tongue?"

"I hate you," she snarled. "I have since the day I met you in high school."

"And I knew you were a mean girl the day I met you," I said, setting the cheesecake down. "I think I recognize where this came from. Hopeland Bakery, right?"

"Oh, they make amazing desserts!" Grandma cried. "Their family has been baking for a hundred years. I would never admit this lightly, but...they're much better than us."

"Which Lucy knew. She was hoping to cheat, passing off a cheesecake from a five-star bakery as her own." I shook my head. "I'd say I'm surprised, but honestly? That sounds right up your alley, Lucy."

"Well, what else was I supposed to do?" she hissed. "My reputation was on the line! I had to win this damn bake-off."

"Your reputation was on the line because of you, Lucy. You asked Jack to steal my recipe book. You caused all this," I said, looking into the crowd. "And Lucy promised me she would keep this competition fair and square. No tricks, no games. She broke that promise by buying this cheesecake in advance. If you ask me...I think this forfeits her spot. I should win by default."

"What? No!" Jack cried, rising to his feet. "That's not fair!"

"None of this has been fair," I said, shaking my head in disgust. "Thanks to the two of you. What does the crowd think? Everyone in favor of Lucy's disqualification say 'aye.'"

"Aye!" the crowd shouted, coming to my defense.

I turned to Lucy who was wide-eyed. "Well, I guess I won this baking competition. And I barely lifted a finger. I'd like that recipe book back now, thanks. You know, since it was ours in the first place."

"Fine," Lucy grumbled, turning to Jack. Then I saw a hint of a smile on her face. "Jack, you brought the recipe book, right? Initiate Operation Failsafe."

Jack nodded, pulling the recipe book out of his tote bag. Then he reached into his pocket, grabbing a lighter and holding it under the recipe book. Everyone watched in shock as Lucy turned to me.

"I was never giving you that recipe book back, Angie," she spat. "If I can't have it, neither can you. Say goodbye to all your grandfather's recipes. Do it, Jack!"

"No!" Grandma cried, rising to her feet.

I was just about to lunge forward when I realized I didn't have to. Henry leapt over the seats, jumping on Jack and wrestling him to the ground. The lighter and recipe book went flying out of his hands. Grandma quickly reached down, grabbing the recipe book while Sonya took the lighter away.

"I don't think so," Henry snarled, holding Jack under him. "There won't be any fires on my watch."

"Get off me, you brute!" Jack said, struggling underneath Henry.

When Lucy realized she had lost, she took off, running to the back door and vanishing outside. People in the audience looked surprised. But honestly, I had expected Lucy to do something like this. She had proven she was nasty and vicious years ago. And her new stepbrother fit into the family well.

"Just let him go, Henry," I said, walking over. "Lucy's gone, anyway."

"You sure?" Henry asked, looking up at me as he held Jack down. "Because we could call the police. You could press charges."

I glanced at my grandma who was still holding the recipe book, looking relieved to see it. She was nearly on the verge of tears.

"No, it's all right," I said, glancing back at Henry. "I'm just glad we got the recipe book back. And that everyone in town sees Lucy for what she really is. Let him up, please."

"You're lucky Angie's a kind woman," Henry growled down at Jack. "Because I would've knocked your lights out for that."

Henry rose to his feet, then Jack slowly stepped up. He was panting as he turned to me. "Really? You're...just going to let me go?"

I nodded. "Yep. But if you and Lucy ever come back and harass my family again, you'll regret it. So stay away—for good this time. And leave New Harbor."

"I'll tell Lucy that," Jack said, looking awkward. "And, uh, thanks for not pressing charges. I really don't want to go to jail."

"Now apologize for everything you put her through," Henry growled. "Don't make me hold you down again."

"Really, I'm sorry," Jack said, turning to me. "In hindsight, I realize I was an asshole. Dating you, leading you on, then stealing your recipe book. But I swear—I'll leave New Harbor and never come back. And I'll take Lucy with me. I can convince her, she'll listen to me."

"Good," I said with a nod. "That's all I want. Now, go—get out of here. Before I change my mind."

Jack ran to the door, disappearing outside. We all watched them go as the crowd murmured around us.

"You sure you really want to let him go?" Henry asked. "Because I'd be more than happy to jump on him again. Even though Chief Teller probably wouldn't like that."

I smiled. "Really, it's fine. But thank you, Henry. If you hadn't intervened, Jack would've set that recipe book on fire right in front of everyone."

"Yes, thank you," Grandma said, clutching the recipe book for dear life. "Despite what you did to my granddaughter...I do think you're a good man, Henry. And I wish you the best."

Mom and Dad looked confused, not understanding our history, but Henry nodded. "Thank you. Just glad I could help."

"For that, I'll forever be grateful. It's not just about the recipes in here, you know. It's about my husband. He held this book in his hands, made it something incredible. If I keep it, it's like...I'm keeping him. And I'm going to put it under lock and key now."

"Good idea," I said with a nod. "But hopefully, Lucy's recipe stealing days are over."

"What if she wrote down all those recipes already, though?" Sonya asked. "Or, like, photocopied the book?"

I shrugged. "Doesn't matter—everyone knows Lucy's reputation now. She can copycat the recipes all she wants but they'll never taste as good as the original. That I know for a fact."

Grandma smiled. "Well, I'm glad all that nonsense is over now. We should get home now, dear. We have some recipes to plan for the festival tomorrow."

"Right." I turned to Henry. "Are you going to see the Sweet Treats Festival?"

He nodded. "Yeah, the firefighters booked a table. We're trying to raise money for our yearly calendar. So...I guess I'll see you there."

"You will. Feel free to come get a cupcake. On the house, again, for your help."

Henry smiled. "Can't wait. See you then, Angie."

He nodded at everyone, then left the community center through the back doors. I watched him go with a sigh. When Sonya reached for my arm, I turned to look at her.

"You did it!" she cried. "You finally beat Lucy—and humiliated her. Our teenage selves would be so happy right now!"

I laughed. "Yeah, they'd definitely be celebrating. I'm just sad it took so long."

"Karma always comes around," James said. "That's something I've learned in life."

Grandma nodded. "Very true. All right, are we ready to leave?"

"You can all head out to the car, yeah," I said, turning to the audience. "I just need to do something first."

Grandma left first, taking Mom and Dad with her while carrying her beloved recipe book. Sonya, James, Mackenzie, and Melissa all gave me one final congratulations before following. People in the audience began to clear out, still murmuring about the bake-off. I knew rumors would be spreading about today for a long time.

I approached Lucy's husband who was still sitting in his seat, shaking his head. He looked deep in thought.

I cleared my throat. "Sorry to interrupt..."

"No worries," Dan said, looking up at me. "I was just getting ready to leave."

"I see. Well, I just wanted to thank you. If you hadn't told everyone what Lucy did, we never would've known and I would've lost the bake-off. As her husband, it must've been hard. But I'm really grateful to you for doing the right thing."

He rose to his feet. "It's no problem. I'm just sorry I didn't stop Lucy before—that it took me so long to see how awful of a person she is. I contacted my lawyer this morning. He's drawing up the divorce papers as we speak."

"Oh, wow. Best of luck with that."

"Thanks. And, you know, I think she has something going on with that stepbrother of hers. As messed up as that is." He shook his head in disgust. "Anyway, I need to get going, but I'm glad you got your recipe book back. I wish you and your grandmother the best."

I thanked him one last time, watching him leave the community center. I had done it—I had gotten the recipe book back to Grandma, even if it wasn't exactly the way I had pictured it.

I wasn't going to forget this victory any time soon.

Chapter Twenty-Eight

I went home with Grandma, Mom, and Dad after that, still riding high from beating Lucy. I felt like I was on cloud nine—that nothing could tear me down. Not even all of my failed relationships.

When we got home, we made dinner—ribs, rice, and salad—before watching movies together on the couch. Mom and Dad finally stopped bickering, and I couldn't help but feel as if this was the way things were supposed to be. No fighting, just love and harmony. The only missing piece was Grandpa. But honestly?

I felt his spirit all around us, holding us tight.

If I was lucky, maybe I'd have it all one day. A husband, kids. Maybe even grandkids. But that seemed like a pipe dream.

At nine p.m., Grandma yawned, rising to her feet. "Well, I should get to bed. It's been a long day. And we have a lot to do at the festival tomorrow."

I nodded. "Sounds good. Should I get up early to help with the desserts?"

"Yes, please, dear. Your parents can help us too if they don't mind."

Mom shrugged. "I've got nothing better to do. As long as we get to taste these desserts."

Grandma laughed. "Of course. I'll even have pumpkin pie—your favorite when you were a child. And for you, Greg, I'll have those holiday cookies you love so much."

Dad grinned. "You thought of everything, Esther. Thank you. We'd both love to help."

Mom shot Dad a glare, but this time, she didn't argue. Maybe things really were looking up.

"Splendid. See you all tomorrow," Grandma said, heading to the stairs. "Get some rest!"

Mom followed a moment later, heading to her room upstairs. I was just about to follow, when Dad cleared his throat. "Uh, sweetie, before you go to bed...can I talk to you?"

I shrugged, turning to him. "Sure. Everything okay?"

"Oh, yes—everything's fine. I wanted to talk to you about that Henry fellow. The man who came to see you at the community center."

I swallowed hard. "What about him?"

"I saw the way you were looking at him. And the way he was looking at you. Is there something between you two, or am I just imagining things?"

I opened my mouth to speak but suddenly, no words came out. I felt myself tearing up.

Dad gasped, reaching for my arm. "I'm sorry, Angie—I didn't realize it was a touchy subject. We don't have to talk about it if you don't want to."

"No, it's okay," I said, wiping away my tears. "We were supposed to go on a date. We had so much in common, so much chemistry. He's been so kind to me and Grandma. Then he stood me up."

"Why would he do that? Is he out of his mind?"

"No, he's just heartbroken. His last marriage ended in divorce. I'm still not entirely sure why, but apparently, it was nasty. Gave him massive trust issues."

"That's hogwash!" Dad cried. "It shouldn't matter how his last relationship ended. You're not his ex, you're you. Someone completely different. Doesn't he realize that?"

"I thought he did," I said, sitting on the couch with a sigh. "But I guess not."

Dad sat next to me. "Angie, I'm so sorry. I hope Henry wakes up and realizes what a wonderful young woman you are. Before he loses you forever."

I turned to Dad. "Do you think he'll ever change his mind?"

"I don't know, sweetie. You know my track record with love hasn't been great, either." Dad stared up toward Mom's room. "But I still believe in love. If two people are committed, it can work. I believe that."

"Mom might disagree with you."

Dad chortled. "I know—she was always a pessimist. She got worse after our marriage ended. But I'm telling you, we weren't meant to be together. True love does exist, sweetie. Sometimes it just takes a while to find it."

I took a deep breath. "Yeah, okay. Maybe you're right. And if not Henry, then...maybe someone better."

He rose to his feet, smiling. "That's the spirit. If you ever need to talk, you have my number. I'm never too busy for you."

"Thanks, Dad. I love you."

"Love you too, kiddo," he said, kissing the top of my head. "See you tomorrow for the festival."

I nodded as he walked away, heading to the basement to his makeshift bed. I sat in the living room for a while and thought about Henry. Could I forgive him for standing me up? And would he ever realize we had something special and he should take a chance? I couldn't force him to see that—he was going to have to come to that realization on his own.

After thinking about Henry for a while, driving myself insane with all the possibilities, I finally brushed my teeth and headed to bed.

I woke up the next morning, eagerly getting dressed for the festival. I heard Grandma making breakfast for the four of us in the kitchen. As I walked down the stairs, the TV was on and Mitch was talking about local news and the Sweet Treats Festival.

"...and Lucky's Baked Goods will be at the festival as well," Mitch was saying behind his news desk. "I know I'll be spending a lot of time there, eating their amazing desserts. Now, on to today's weather. It's going to be cool but sunny..."

Grandma smiled, making scrambled eggs. "Good morning, dear. Mitch is helping promote our table at the festival."

I laughed, walking toward the table to sit with Mom and Dad. "I see that. He's been a big help. Morning, everyone. How did you all sleep?"

I chatted with Mom and Dad, while Grandma served us breakfast, and then sat down to join us. Despite Mom's grumpiness, she still helped us bake a bunch of desserts.

Mackenzie texted Grandma that she was doing the same at the bakery.

"Mackenzie said The Green Machine closed its doors. Even the sign is missing," Grandma said, reading the text from her smartphone. "It seems Lucy and Jack are gone for good."

"Finally," I grumbled. "I'm just glad they won't be bothering us anymore."

"I am too, though I'm sad it had to come to this. New Harbor is big enough for the both of us," Grandma said, placing muffins in a container. "It would've been nice to co-exist."

"Yeah, but Lucy ruined that. She's the one who plotted to steal our recipe book and destroy us. I say good riddance." I picked up another container of mini pies. "Now, are we ready to go? We don't want to be late for the festival."

After grabbing all the desserts we'd made, we clamored into Grandma's van, heading downtown. The streets had been blocked off for the festival. The mayor and volunteers were busy setting up tables for all the vendors, then hanging lights and candy decorations everywhere. Some volunteers were getting last-minute games ready. I was surprised at how fast they had put it all together, but it looked like they had a lot of volunteers to make it happen.

"So, this festival happens every year?" Dad asked, glancing out the window.

I nodded. "Yep—all the restaurants and bakeries in town bring their food to share. And there are games too."

"Your mother used to love coming here as a child," Grandma said with a smile, parking on the street. "Don't you remember, Patricia? How your father won you that stuffed bear?"

"I do," Mom said, sighing. "Those were good times."

"Yes, they were. And I know he would want us to enjoy ourselves," Grandma said, opening her door. "So let's not disappoint. I think I see our table over there—let's head over and set up."

I nodded, then we all helped Grandma carry the containers of desserts we had made to a small table. Other restaurants were setting up around us and politely smiled. I spotted Henry arriving with his firefighters, selling their own baked goods at a special table to benefit the fire station. The mayor walked over to us, thanking us for coming. I let Mom, Dad, and Grandma chat with her while I walked over to Henry at his table.

"Hey," I began. "Those look good."

"Oh, thanks. We all helped Chief Teller bake them," Henry said, gesturing at a plate of peanut butter cookies. "All proceeds go to funding the fire station."

"Well, how can I refuse that?" I said with a smile, pulling a five-dollar bill out of my pocket. "Here you go. One cookie, please. Keep the change."

"Generous of you. Thanks," Henry said, handing me the cookie. "Enjoy. And Angie...it's nice to see you."

"You too." I bit into my cookie. "This is amazing."

Henry laughed. "Thanks—that's the batch I made. While not as good as your grandmother's, it's edible, at least."

"Don't sell yourself short. You're very talented," I said with a smile. Henry's firefighters walked over to the table, helping to sell the other cookies around us while we chatted. "So, are you going to take part in any of the games?"

Henry shrugged. "I don't know, probably not. Not really my thing."

Chief Teller walked over, hearing the end of our conversation. "Oh, you have to, Henry! It's to benefit the fire station. Why don't you and Angie walk around and check out the games? We can handle the table."

Chief Teller gave me a little wink. I appreciated what he was trying to do, but if Henry didn't want to be with me, all the meddling in the world couldn't force him.

Henry nodded. "All right—thanks, Chief. So, Angie, where do you want to start first?"

I glanced around the festival. "Ooh, I see something interesting. Come on!"

I grabbed Henry's hand, tugging him toward a tank full of water. A boy was tossing balls at the target, so we waited patiently for our turn. A man sat on a short diving board above the tank, staring at a board with a target. The boy's ball hit the target, the diving board collapsed, and the man dropped into the water with a splash.

"Winner!" the volunteer running the game cried. "Here you go, kid. A balloon just for you."

"Thanks!" the boy said, taking the balloon. He helped his dad out of the tank, soaking wet, and then they walked away."

I turned to Henry. "I bet I can dunk you."

The corners of his mouth turned upward. "Oh, yeah?"

"Yeah. Let's make a bet. If I dunk you, you owe my bakery ten bucks. If I can't dunk you, I'll donate to the fire station."

Henry laughed. "If it's for charity, why not? You've got a deal."

When Henry ripped his shirt off, showing his toned abs and biceps, I tried not to stare. He approached the volunteer and gestured at the tank.

"I'm ready," he said. "Let's do this."

The volunteer smiled, opening the door for him to get into the tank. "Good luck. Take a seat on the diving board."

Henry climbed into the tank from a side ladder, then sat on the diving board and looked at me. People began to stare and murmur, mostly women ogling his ripped abs. This was for my bakery—I needed to win. And okay, maybe I wanted to see Henry wet and shirtless.

"You'll get three tries," the volunteer said, handing me a rubber ball. "Good luck to you as well."

I nodded, taking a deep breath. The first ball I threw didn't even come close to the target. People murmured in disappointment behind me.

Henry rubbed his hands together. "Looks like I'm going to win this bet. Thanks for your support, Angie."

"Yeah, yeah. It's not over yet!" I said, taking another ball from the volunteer. "Let me try again."

When I threw the ball, it came close to the target but bounced off the side.

Henry yawned on the diving board. "Is that the best you can do?"

"Really? Are you trash-talking me?" I said with a laugh, taking another ball from the volunteer. I tried to give myself a quick pep talk. "Okay, last ball, Angie. No pressure..."

I decided to leave it up to chance, hoping luck would have my back for once. I closed my eyes and threw the ball. When I heard a slam and then a splash, I opened my eyes, watching Henry floating in the water, wiping droplets off his face. The volunteers and people watching clapped.

Henry rose above the water, jumping out of the tank. He was soaking wet from head to toe—and hot. I tried not to stare.

"Nice one," Henry said, walking over to me. "Guess your bakery's ten dollars richer."

"It was just luck, that's all," I said with a laugh. "Thanks for being such a great sport. Hang on, I'll get you a towel."

The volunteer had towels set up on a table for the participants. I grabbed one, handing it to Henry who took it from me and began drying himself off. His dark hair was slick and still wet when he finished.

"That was fun," he said, putting his shirt back on. Then he handed me a wet ten-dollar bill from his soaked pants. "Here, the donation I owe you. What should we do now?"

I smiled and took his hand again. Surprisingly, he didn't resist. "Come on, I see a claw machine. We can try to win a teddy bear!"

For the rest of the festival, we played all the games, having a great time together. Henry and I couldn't stop laughing. Grandma watched us, smiling and giving me a wink. It was fun to hang out with Henry—it reminded me of how much we had in common. It was just a shame it couldn't lead to anything more. Henry ended up winning me a koala bear, one that was cuddly and soft.

We purchased ice cream, supporting a local parlor, and continued walking around the festival. Henry and I both liked the same flavor—mint chocolate chip. What were the odds of that?

"You know, I'm glad I moved to New Harbor," Henry said. "It's such a nice town. So close-knit."

I nodded. "Yeah, it's a great place to live. I'm glad you moved here too."

Henry paused. "Angie...I know I've said it before, but I'm really sorry I stood you up. I shouldn't have done that. It was immature of me."

"It's okay, Henry."

"No, it's not," he said, firmly. "I do like you, Angie. You're a wonderful person. I'm sorry my own fears got in the way and screwed things up between us."

"I am too." I paused. "If you don't mind me asking... what happened between you and your ex-wife?"

Henry said nothing. I feared I had said something wrong, that I had pushed him away. Again.

"If you don't want to tell me, it's fine," I said, finishing my ice cream. "I don't want to make you uncomfortable or anything—"

"No, it's all right," Henry said, sitting on a nearby bench. It was decorated with fake pumpkins and hay for fall. "I really loved her. I...I thought we'd be together forever. But then I found out she was cheating on me. With someone I knew."

I sat next to him, wide-eyed. "Gosh, I'm so sorry. Being cheated on hurts. Who was it? An old friend?"

"My dad," Henry said, looking down. "My own father. He was at my wedding and watched us say our vows. And then he does this."

When he turned silent, I placed a hand on his back. "Wow, Henry...I don't know what to say. That's awful. You deserve better."

"But that wasn't all. She also got pregnant with his baby. Right before she told me, she cleared out all of our joint savings accounts and ran away with him. My divorce lawyer—the woman you saw at Estelle's—managed to track her down. That five grand I gave you was the most I could get. When I saw her in Boston, collecting my money, she didn't even apologize. She was smug about it. Not even my mom knows. They got divorced long before Dad did that, but still."

I didn't know what to say. "Sheesh...no wonder you're so slow to trust. I get it now."

He turned to me. "It rocked my world, that's for sure. And it changed everything. That was why I left Boston, why I left everything behind. So, trust me—it isn't you. You've done nothing wrong. You've been perfect, actually. A dream woman. I'm the one with the baggage, with the issues."

I rose to my feet. "But you can work through them, Henry. You don't have to be alone and cut yourself off from love forever. You can try again—with someone new. Don't you think you deserve a fresh start?"

Henry looked skeptical as he stood up. "I...I just don't know, Angie. I've never told anyone this, not even my mother, but...I'm afraid. I don't want the same thing to happen again. That's why I can't risk a relationship."

"But Henry, you'll never know if you never try—"

Henry shook his head. "I think I should head home. I'm not feeling too well. But I had a great time with you, Angie. Enjoy that bear. I'll see you around, okay?"

Before I could say anything else, Henry rushed to the parking lot, getting into his truck and driving off. I sighed and returned to Grandma's table to help Mom, Dad, and Mackenzie, who had just arrived, sell desserts.

There was nothing else I could do.

Chapter Twenty-Nine

Selling desserts all day at the Sweet Treats Festival was exhausting, but we were making a lot of money. We stayed all day until the sun went down. Sadly, Henry didn't return, leaving his firefighters wondering where he had gone.

I was surprised when Ty came over to our table, hand-in-hand with his school's principal, Mr. Sutter. "Hey, Angie. You got a minute to talk?"

"For you? Of course," I said with a smile. "What's going on?"

"I just wanted to thank you," Ty said, gesturing at Mr. Sutter, "for giving me the courage to speak up. We're dating now. Boyfriend and boyfriend. This is our first festival together—hopefully the first of many."

"Yes, thank you," Principal Sutter said with a smile. "I was just waiting for Ty to make the first move. I didn't want him to think I was abusing my position of power or anything."

I smiled. "Of course—I'm happy it worked out for you two. You deserve to be happy."

"Thanks, Angie," Ty said. "We're keeping it professional at school. There are rules against workplace fraternization, after all. But out here, we're free."

"That's great. Did you tell your parents?"

Ty sighed, glancing at Principal Sutter. "We did—just yesterday. My parents were disappointed, as I predicted, but I think they're slowly coming around. I hope they'll be completely onboard one day."

"My family already is," Principal Sutter said. "They welcomed Ty with open arms. Especially my mum."

"I'm glad to hear that. At least one family is supportive," I said, turning to Ty. "Really, I'm happy for you. I love to see love working out."

Ty and Principal Sutter, Grandma and Mitch, Mackenzie and Melissa, Sonya and James. Even Dad and his younger girlfriend. It seemed everyone had a partner but me. Well, and Mom, but she didn't seem too interested in dating anyway.

"Like I said, I owe it all to you. You're the one who convinced me to live my truth," Ty said with a grin. "Thanks for everything, Angie."

"Of course. And I hope you'll keep me in mind as your maid of honor if it comes to that."

Both Ty and Principal Sutter smiled. "Marriage is still far away, but definitely," Ty said. "Anyway, how are things with Henry?"

I sighed, leaning against my table. "Oh, crap—I haven't told you yet. We had a date planned, but...he stood me up. He just wasn't ready to date after his marriage ended badly."

Ty frowned. "Oh, Angie...I'm so sorry. That really sucks."

"I've been stood up. I know how bad it hurts," Principal

Sutter said. "And I've been disappointed by love before, but it's never stopped me from trying. I hope this Henry guy works up the courage and realizes you aren't his ex."

I appreciated the thought, but it didn't seem like it would happen. I nodded anyway. "Here's hoping. So, can I get you two anything?"

Ty and his boyfriend bought a few cookies, donating generously to our bakery. I thanked them but they said it was the least they could do since I had played matchmaker. After they walked away, Grandma came over to me with a pink cupcake.

"This is for you, dear. You look like you could use a pick-me-up," she said, handing me the cupcake. "Go on, read the fortune inside."

I picked the edible paper out of the cupcake, reading it aloud. "*There's always time for second chances.* It's a nice sentiment, Grandma, but...I don't know. Henry left again."

Grandma nodded, sadly. "I know, sweetie—I saw. And right after it seemed like you two were having such a good time. I'm so sorry things haven't gone the way you wanted."

"That's life," I said with a shrug, taking a bite of the cupcake. "Sometimes, it sucks."

Grandma tried to encourage me—even offered to host another round of speed dating—but I declined. I only seemed to attract broken men or guys like Jim and Jack. No deal.

We sold out of our desserts a little while later, then collected all of our containers and bid goodbye to the other vendors. The sun was starting to set, and people were packing up and heading home. The mayor stopped us on our way out and thanked us again for participating in the festival, then we headed home to have a nice salmon dinner.

After we ate, Grandma sat at the coffee table with her glasses, counting up the stack of bills from our booth, while Mom, Dad, and I relaxed.

"My goodness! So much money. Hopefully, I'll be able to keep some of this in savings so we won't have a situation like Nutmeg again. Maybe we can even afford to expand our business and hire new employees."

I smiled. "That sounds perfect. And Mom, Dad, thanks for your help. Now, I'd love to stay awake and watch a movie, but I'm beat. Think I'm going to head to bed."

"Goodnight, dear!" Grandma called out. "Thanks for all your help today."

"Yes, even I had a good time," Mom said, eyeing Dad, "despite the company. Goodnight, honey."

Dad just shook his head. "Goodnight, Angie. And I hope you remember what we talked about."

Mom and Grandma were puzzled, but I just nodded, then headed upstairs to bed. All I wanted to do was change into my pajamas and sleep. I passed out quickly, only waking when I heard a thump outside my bedroom window. I laid in bed for a moment, hearing only Mom and Grandma snoring loudly down the hall.

Another thump from outside. I climbed out of bed and walked to the window, looking out. After a moment of searching and squinting, I spotted Jim outside. The spark of a flame in his hand helped to illuminate him through the darkness. But what was he doing here?

A second later, I got my answer.

With wide eyes, I realized he was using a match to set fire to the side of our house near the kitchen. Frozen in disbelief, I watched as he grabbed a gasoline can and doused our house to make it spread.

I opened my window and leaned out. "What the hell are you doing?"

Jim's head shot up. "I told you you'd regret rejecting me, bitch. You brought this on yourself!"

I watched as the fire spread fast, creeping up the lattice underneath my window. Jim must've followed me home at some point—all so he could return to set it on fire. In all honesty, I hadn't thought about him much these days.

How could someone do such an evil thing? And all over a romantic rejection?

There was no time to think. Jim took off, running down the street as I rushed into the hallway. All I was concerned about was getting Mom, Dad, Grandma, and Nutmeg out of the house. We could deal with Jim when we were safe.

I heard an explosion downstairs, then a blast of heat. It sounded like the kitchen window had exploded. When smoke wafted through the house, billowing upstairs, I ran into Grandma's room. She was still snoring as if nothing had happened. Even Nutmeg was sleeping soundly by her feet.

I lunged onto her bed, shaking her. "Grandma? Grandma! You need to wake up!"

She rubbed her groggy eyes before they landed on me. "Angie, is that you? What's wrong, dear?"

"The house is on fire. Hurry!" I cried, pulling her arm. "We don't have much time!"

Her eyes widened as I tugged her to her feet, then she grabbed Nutmeg. The cat didn't struggle as we ran into the hallway. The smoke was thicker now, spreading fast as we both began to cough.

"Go outside—now!" I told her, running down the hall to Mom's room. "I'll get Mom and Dad!"

Grandma nodded. "Okay, sweetie. Be careful!"

Grandma rushed down the stairs in her bare feet and nightgown, opening the door and running outside. When I opened the door to the guest room, Mom was on the floor, coughing and wheezing.

"Damn smoke," she muttered. "Can't…catch my breath…"

"Mom!" I cried, falling beside her. "Here, I'll help you. We need to get out of here!"

Mom didn't resist as I pulled her to her feet, leading her into the hallway. I nearly pulled her down the stairs and out the door toward Grandma. She took Mom from me, holding Nutmeg in her other arm as they stood on the lawn in the darkness.

"Call 9-1-1," I instructed, as I gave Grandma my smartphone, gesturing at the house. "I still need to get Dad. Be right back!"

I heard Grandma dialing my phone, calling the fire department while still holding onto Nutmeg. Mom, in her pajamas, was looking at the fire with wide eyes. I still couldn't believe this was happening—couldn't believe Jim had done this.

I wasn't just unlucky in love. Now it had tried to kill me.

I rushed back inside, coughing as the smoke grew thicker. I flung open the basement door, gasping at the hot doorknob, then ran downstairs. Dad was sleeping on the pull-out couch, drooling as he slept. How could they sleep through this?

I shook Dad awake. "Dad, come on! There's a fire. We need to get out!"

"What—huh?" Dad asked, startling awake. "A fire?"

"Yes! Hurry, we can talk about it outside."

Dad rose to his feet, then I led him toward the stairs. "I

smelled the smoke when I woke up a few minutes ago. Just thought it was the chimney or something..."

As I led him up the stairs, we heard another explosion, then a blast of fire lashed toward us, blocking our path out of the basement. We were trapped.

"Shit," Dad cursed. "What now?"

"The basement window," I said, gesturing down the stairs. "Go back down. Hurry!"

Dad nodded, heading back toward the couch. An egress window was on the wall behind it for emergencies. Dad insisted I go through first so I crawled out onto the grass, then pulled Dad out. A minute later, the fire spread through the basement as we doubled over and tried to catch our breath.

"God, that was insane!" Dad cried. "What about your mom and grandmother? Are they all right?"

"Yeah, I got them out first. Nutmeg too. Come on, they're waiting on the front lawn."

Dad followed me around the side of the house, meeting back up with Mom, Grandma, and Nutmeg. They were all watching the house go down in flames.

"There you two are. I'm so glad you're safe," Grandma said, hugging me. "How did this happen? Did we accidentally leave the oven on?"

I shook my head. "No, this was arson. You remember Jim, that angry bodybuilder guy from the speed dating thing? I saw him setting the fire from my window. I yelled at him, and he said it was punishment for rejecting him."

Grandma gasped, letting out a string of profanities I had never heard from her. Then she went straight to blaming herself. "This is all my fault, Angie. I brought him into our life. I'm sorry. I'm so sorry, dear."

"No, Grandma," I said firmly. "This is Jim's fault alone.

And once the police get here, we'll tell them and they can hunt him down."

"Good," Dad said with a nod. "He shouldn't get away with this."

"And over a rejection," Mom sneered. "You see how dangerous love is? Best to stay away from it entirely, hun. Trust me."

Grandma just shook her head, petting Nutmeg to keep the kitty calm. Then her eyes went wide. "The recipe book —and your grandfather's photo album. They're under my bed. I forgot to grab them when I ran out!"

"I'm sorry, Mother," Mom said, softly. She patted Grandma's shoulder.

Grandma started to cry. "All those pictures of Lou, gone forever..."

I rolled up my sleeves. "I think I can do it. Stay here— I'll get them both back."

"Are you crazy?" Dad asked. "You can't go back inside. It's too dangerous!"

"Yes, I agree with Greg," Grandma said. "You're kind to offer, dear, but your life matters more to me than photos. *Please*, don't go in."

When I saw how upset Grandma was, I knew I had to. Everything I'd done had been for her—from helping her run the bakery to winning the bake-off against Lucy. What kind of granddaughter would I be if I didn't get the last photos she had of Grandpa?

I took off running, heading to the front door anyway. I heard Grandma, Mom, and Dad screaming my name as I dove inside. I ran through the fire, burning my arm. When I tripped over a fallen beam, I cried out, then heard Grandpa's voice in my mind.

Get up, Angie. Your story isn't over yet.

And who was I to go against Grandpa?

With a groan, I pulled myself to my feet, then headed up to Grandma's room. The recipe book and photo album were under her bed as she promised.

"Got you!" I cried, holding them in my arms. My eyes burned from the smoke, and I let out a few coughs.

But as I turned to leave the bedroom, another wooden beam fell from the ceiling and blocked my path. Smoke began to spread inside her room as I coughed and gagged. I glanced toward the window, knowing it was my only hope. I'd have to jump to safety below.

But as I moved toward the window, my vision became hazy. The smoke felt like it was stabbing my lungs. I fell to my knees, dropping the recipe book and photo album as my world faded to black.

When I woke again, I was lying in the hospital, wearing a gown. The machine beside my bed was making a gentle beeping sound. Grandma, Mom, Dad, and Sonya were there, quietly talking around me. Grandma was the first to notice my eyes opening.

"She's awake!" Grandma cried, reaching for my hand. Mom, Dad, and Sonya rushed to my bedside with her. "Oh, darling, I'm so relieved. I was scared we'd lost you!"

"Good thing I'm a lot tougher than I look," I joked, though it hurt to laugh. Heck, it hurt to talk. "Oh, I feel terrible. What happened? How did I get out of there?"

"Henry, dear," Grandma explained. "He and the firefighters arrived. When he heard you were in that house, he charged in without a second thought. He rescued you—and the recipe book with the photo album."

I sighed in relief. "I'm glad. Where's Nutmeg? And how's the house?"

"Nutmeg is fine—we left her at Sonya's along with the

photo album and recipe book. Sonya and James graciously offered their home to us," Grandma said. Sonya nodded. "The house is mostly destroyed. It'll take a lot of work to fix. There goes all the money we made at the festival..."

"At least we have that money. Insurance will help, then your father and I will pitch in too," Mom said, rubbing my hand. "We're all glad you survived."

"But disappointed you ran back inside that house," Dad scolded. "What were you thinking?"

I looked at Grandma. "I just...I had to do it. For you, Grandma. I couldn't bear to see you sad."

Grandma smiled, trying not to cry. "Oh, Angie. You're too good to me. I love you so much."

"I love you too, Grandma. But what about Jim? Did anyone catch him?"

Dad nodded. "Yep, the police caught the bastard trying to leave town. He still had the gasoline can on him. The idiot didn't even have the common sense to get rid of the evidence. He's in a jail cell right now, awaiting trial."

"Good. He's too dangerous to be walking the streets."

A knock sounded at the door, then the doctor entered. He checked my vital signs, listened to my lungs, and said I'd be okay. I had some smoke inhalation, but I was set to make a full recovery. Everyone was relieved to hear that.

"Well, it's been a wild week," I grumbled. "Where's Henry?"

"Out in the hall," Sonya said. "He's been pacing for a while, worried about you. He kept asking the doctor for updates every two minutes. You were out for a good hour, hour and a half."

"Really?" I asked. "Can you send him in? I want to thank him."

"Of course, dear," Grandma said. "We'll give you some privacy."

Grandma, Mom, Dad, and Sonya left the room. I heard voices in the hall, then Henry walked in a short while later, still wearing his firefighter uniform. He shut the door behind him and looked at me with concerned eyes.

"Angie, it's so good to see you awake," he began. "How are you feeling?"

"Much better. I wanted to thank you for saving my life. If you hadn't gotten there in time...I don't even want to think about it."

Henry nodded. "Yeah, you were unconscious when I found you. I grabbed you and the books you were carrying and got the hell out of there. I'm just...so glad you're alive. It would've broken me if you died. I'm going to tear that bastard Jim apart!"

"Don't worry—he's been caught. I'm just eager to move on. After fixing our house, of course."

Henry crept closer, moving to the edge of my bed. "I'd like to pitch in too. And maybe you can arrange a GoFundMe to help rebuild. The town loves you, I'm sure they would donate. And you're welcome to stay at my house in the meantime."

I smiled. "That's sweet of you, but my best friend already offered. You've done more than enough, really—from saving my cat to my life. Henry Brant is a damn legend in my books."

He laughed, grabbing my hand. "Glad to hear it. Angie, seeing you lying there, with your eyes closed...well, it made me realize how much of an idiot I've been. I saw all the possibilities for a future between us fade. Now that you're here, awake and all right...I don't want to let another moment pass without telling you how I feel."

I sat up straighter. "What are you talking about, Henry?"

"I love you, Angie," he said, looking right into my eyes. "I have from the moment I saw you, the moment you gave me that free cupcake and told me all about your adorable specials. I could just feel it."

I smiled. I felt it too, and it was why I had worked so hard to get us together. Despite the many obstacles in our way.

"But then my fear got in the way and kept me from you. I'm so, so sorry," Henry continued, nervously playing with his hands. "If you could forgive me, I'd like to start over. With a clean slate. No past baggage, nothing standing in our way. I'm just sorry it took me this long to realize it, that you had to nearly die for my revelation. So...what do you think? Could you forgive me?"

There it was—the opportunity I had been waiting for. But could I forgive him for standing me up? I found myself deciding in no time.

I held out my hand. "Nice to meet you, Henry Brant. I'm Angie Linden. Want to go out for dinner sometime?"

He laughed, then pulled me in for a kiss. It was tender and sweet. He tasted like peppermint—and hope. While lying in a hospital bed wasn't the first kiss between me and Henry I had been dreaming about, it was still perfect. I'd finally found what I had been looking for all this time.

My luck had changed for the better.

Chapter Thirty

A month later, Henry and I attended Sonya and James' wedding, hand-in-hand. We had gone on so many dates and had already started living together. Some people in town said it was too soon—always gossiping—but when you knew, you knew. Grandma and our friends and families supported it unconditionally.

Jim had gone to jail, we didn't even need to wait for a trial, as he had pleaded guilty to arson and stalking. We were relieved when we saw him get taken away in handcuffs. I felt safe living with Henry, his strong arms around me every night. Chief Teller eventually offered the job of fire chief to Henry. After thinking it over, he finally accepted, deciding to stay in New Harbor permanently. Something I was very happy about.

With the help of the community, Grandma raised enough money to fix the house and make a few renovations. She tucked both the recipe book and photo album in a fireproof safe. The bakery was thriving—we had garnered a lot of attention from Jim's trial and my feud with Lucy. I knew Grandpa would've been proud. Mom and Dad returned home shortly after I left the hospital, finally on speaking terms again. I was glad they had *finally* decided to be mature adults about their divorce.

Lucy and Jack never returned to their restaurant, putting the space up for sale. Sonya bought it and turned it into another wedding store. Her business was doing well too. And I heard Lucy was in financial trouble since her divorce, something I wasn't too sad about.

As Henry and I danced at Sonya's wedding, I glanced around. Grandma had gotten more serious with Mitch, and it seemed like they were heading for marriage soon. Although she still missed and loved Grandpa, she cared deeply for Mitch. And I knew Grandpa would've wanted her to be happy.

From what I'd heard, Mackenzie and Melissa had gotten more serious, then also Ty and his principal. Ty's family gradually began accepting them. The school board was fine with them dating—as long as they kept things professional at work—and I was glad to see my new friend so happy–and living a life of authenticity after hiding who he was for so long.

As for Henry and me, I definitely saw wedding bells in our future, though I didn't want to jinx it or rush things. I was just happy to be along for the ride—happy that Henry had given us a chance. And it was working out beautifully. He never spoke to his ex-wife or his father again, and I thought that was for the best. His mother was over the moon when he told her we were dating. She still had no idea what Henry's father had done to him, and maybe that was *also* for the best.

"You look gorgeous, you know," Henry whispered in my ear, as we slow danced on the floor of the wedding venue.

Sonya and James were dancing a few feet away. "You're going to make the bride jealous."

I smiled. "You're too sweet, Henry. I'm so happy to be here with you."

"I am too," he said, leaning back to look into my eyes. "I love you."

"I love you more."

As we kissed, the music the jazz band was playing stopped. Then Sonya grabbed a microphone and turned toward the crowd. "All right, everyone—I thought we could do the bouquet toss now. If all the men could clear the dance floor, that would be great. This is for the ladies only!"

Henry kissed my cheek, following the men off to the side. They sat at their tables as Sonya turned around with her bouquet of roses. She tossed it into the air behind her, then I closed my eyes and held out my arm.

The bouquet landed in my hands. To my shock, I opened my eyes, seeing the roses sitting there. Everyone began clapping.

"And my best friend caught the bouquet!" Sonya said with a smile. "I can already hear wedding bells in her future. Okay, back to dancing, everyone. Then dinner!"

As everyone returned to dancing, I sniffed the bouquet. They were incredible. Henry walked back over in his suit and tie, grabbing my waist.

"Congratulations," he said. "You caught the bouquet."

I shrugged. "Thanks, but it's a silly tradition. Doesn't mean anything."

"Oh, no?" Henry asked, pulling me closer. "Because I think it's pretty accurate. You'd make an excellent Mrs. Brant one day…don't you think?"

As I smiled and nodded, Henry leaned in to kiss me, swaying together on the dance floor. I realized that if Jim hadn't set fire to our house, Henry never would've realized we belonged together. I almost felt like I should've thanked Jim while he rotted in his cell.

As Henry and I continued dancing, I felt more than lucky. I was blessed. Henry and I had the rest of our lives to spend together—free from drama and heartbreak.

And just like that, I started believing in happily ever afters again.

THE END

THANK YOU FOR READING

Did you enjoy this book?

We invite you to leave a review at your favorite book site, such as Goodreads, Amazon, Barnes & Noble, etc.

DID YOU KNOW THAT LEAVING A REVIEW...

- Helps other readers find books they may enjoy.
- Gives you a chance to let your voice be heard.
- Gives authors recognition for their hard work.
- Doesn't have to be long. A sentence or two about why you liked the book will do.

About the Author

Dana Gricken is a multi-genre author from Ottawa, Canada, writing stories since she was old enough to hold a pencil. She has been published in fantasy before with *The Dragonwitch Chronicles* and *The Soulless War Trilogy* and has more books coming out in 2024 and beyond like the *Jessica Prince Mysteries* series.

In her spare time, she enjoys reading, playing video games, mailing letters to friends, spreading kindness, educating about mental health struggles, and watching *Star Trek* with her cats. She hopes her books bring joy and make people feel less alone. She wants to write over a hundred novels in her lifetime.

You can connect with her @DanaGricken on all social media or her website:

danagricken.com

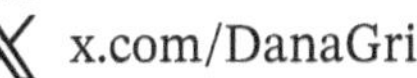

facebook.com/dana.gricken.7

x.com/DanaGricken

instagram.com/danagricken

Also by Dana Gricken With Satin Romance

Riches to Rags

Unlucky in Love

Also by Dana Gricken With Fire & Ice Young Adult Books

Jessica Prince Mysteries

Jessica Prince and the Crimson Caper

Kingdom of V Trilogy

Kingdom of V

The Astrid Legacy

Coming of Age

The Soulless Trilogy

The Dark Queen

The Dark Evolution

Dark Cage

Novels

Chatter

www.ingramcontent.com/pod-product-compliance
Lightning Source LLC
LaVergne TN
LVHW090554110826
845146LV00001B/115
* 9 7 9 8 8 8 6 5 3 4 7 5 7 *